THE TIGER

THE TIGER

Chronicles of An Imperial Legionary Officer

Book 2

MARC ALAN EDELHEIT

This book is a work of fiction. Names, characters, places and incidents are either the product of the author's imagination or are used fictitiously. Any resemblance to actual persons, living or dead, or to actual events or locales is entirely coincidental.

Chronicles of an Imperial Legionary Officer BOOK TWO: THE TIGER

First Edition

I wish to thank my agent, Andrea Hurst for her and her team's invaluable assistance. I would also like to thank my Beta Readers who suffered through several early drafts and provided some very interesting feedback, including a lesson on what old leather should smell like. My Betas: Barrett McKinney, Jon Cockes, Norman Stiteler, Nicolas Weiss, Stephan Kobert, Matthew Ashley, Melinda Vallem, Brett Stewart and Brett Smith. I would also like to take a moment to thank my loving wife who sacrificed many an evening to allow me to work on my writing.

Editing Assistance by: Winslow Eliot, Echo Yupan Lu, Hannah Streetman, Audrey Mackaman

Cover Art by Piero Mng (Gianpiero Mangialardi)

Cover Formatting by Telemachus Press

ISBN-13: 9781519210944

Dedication

To Robert Edelheit, Father and the Best Man I know, who taught me that with hard work comes success.

CHAPTER ONE

MARCUS THOUGHT IT a pleasant spot. The air was crisp, cool, and the scent of the forest was strong. Wind rustled through the tree canopy above, setting off a shower of brightly colored late autumn leaves.

The scout, Marcus, remained still, kneeling on the forest floor, watching silently as the leaves slowly settled. The display that nature put on was simply magnificent. He felt blessed to be here, in the Sentinel forest, to witness it, and his heart swelled at the beauty surrounding him. Silently he offered a brief prayer of thanks to the High Father.

A bird called in the distance. He listened to its beautiful song. For a moment he felt that the bird was singing exclusively for his entertainment. The bird started and stopped, only to begin once again. In search of insects for a morning meal, a woodpecker abruptly began hammering away somewhere off in the distance. Such were the sounds and ways of the forest.

Lieutenant Eli'Far, an elven ranger, had opened his eyes to the ways of the forest and taught him to watch, listen, smell…to feel the forest as if it were a living being. The process involved calming the mind and letting go. It was almost like a form of meditation. Marcus found it difficult to put the experience into words, but he was beginning to understand and sense what the lieutenant was teaching him.

He had spent two years in the company before Captain Stiger had assumed command of the 85th. At the time Marcus had thought himself to be quite good as a scout. With hindsight, he now recognized he had been a bumbling amateur. The captain and Eli had brought change to the company and for that he was grateful.

Eli had taught him that life in the forest, at its base level, followed a pattern. Someone properly attuned to the forest could spot the moment when something disturbed the pattern. It was this disturbance that he had been trained to watch for and one among many other important things that Eli had imparted. Incredibly honored to receive instruction from one of the High Born, Marcus had done his best to be a good student. He had always been a quick learner. He paid as close attention to the elf as humanly possible. Marcus did everything he could to put to practice what Eli had taught him. What at first had seemed inhumanly possible soon became second nature for Marcus as he became more proficient in the ways of the ranger. He was a better scout for it and without question the best in the company. He felt sure it was one of the reasons he had been promoted to scout corporal.

He loved being a company scout and the freedom that came with the job. While scouting and on detached duty, he was not required to wear his armor. Instead, he and the others were permitted to wear their service tunics with light leathers that provided limited protection but were infinitely more comfortable. Unlike the majority of the company, they had also been issued boots, a serious improvement over standard issue sandals, particularly in the winter.

A strong gust of wind blew through the canopy, setting off another shower of leaves. Marcus breathed in deeply through his nose and slowly exhaled. It had rained the night before. He could smell the moist earth, moss and the occasional pine amongst the great old trees. A moose could be heard braying distantly. Marcus had never seen one before coming to the South. They were impressive animals, weighing as much as two thousand pounds. Like the man-eating cats that also lived in this forest, he had learned they were to be respected.

Marcus considered for a moment that he had come a long way from the slums of Mal'Zeel. He had been a criminal and had been sentenced to a term with the legions. That now seemed a lifetime ago. The magistrate had given him a choice, two years forced labor in a lead mine or a twenty-five year term with the legions. In essence, the magistrate was doing his best to give Marcus a fresh start, a chance to make something of himself, though at the time he had not seen it that way.

Marcus had never seriously contemplated joining the legions. Who wanted to voluntarily sign up for a twenty-five year term of service? Life with the legions was hard, with the potential to be carved up by some distant battle-crazed barbarian. The slums of Mal'Zeel were awash with legionary cripples, who were missing limbs or suffering from some debilitating injury. Such men, deemed unable to march, were discharged with a small monthly disability benefit and whatever pension funds they had accrued during their service. Having not completed their signed twenty-five year term, they were not entitled to any lands. Unable to work, even if they could find a job, they survived on the grain dole and simply drank or diced their meager monies away. Such wretches were shadows of their former selves. He had pitied them. Still, Marcus had not hesitated to accept the offer of a term with the legions. Forced labor in a mine was the same as a death sentence.

I am a very different person now.

He had already resolved, should the opportunity ever permit it, to find the magistrate and thank him.

A fresh gust of wind rustled through the forest. He closed his eyes to listen as the wind made its way through the trees. He breathed in deeply through his nose and slowly exhaled, enjoying the smells, the sounds. He could hear the leaves rushing together and the branches swaying. The trees creaked and groaned with the wind.

The gust eventually abated and, with it, Marcus became aware of a disturbance. He felt it, a subtle change in the pattern of the forest. It was not unexpected. He had been waiting for it. Marcus sighed deeply. His moment of serenity and peace was gone.

He opened his eyes. His small bow lay on the ground before him. He slowly reached forward and picked it up. Three arrows were stuck loosely in the forest floor to his right and within easy reach. He quietly took one, nocked it and then looked up.

The Vrell Road lay twenty-five yards away. Marcus could not recall the road's actual name. People simply called it the Vrell Road, as that was the only place it went.

He shifted, leaning forward to put his weight squarely on his knees. Concealed behind a stand of bushes, he was right at a spot where the road bent at a sharp angle. Around the bend came a heavily loaded supply wagon pulled by a pair of oxen and driven by a bored-looking teamster. Marcus allowed the wagon to continue past and out of view.

Undetected, he just sat and watched. A second wagon slowly followed the first. Both teamsters carefully negotiated the bend and continued on out of view. A third wagon followed and then a fourth and fifth. Marcus continued to count. When the twentieth wagon turned the bend, he calmly and coolly raised his bow and drew back, increasing the tension as he pulled.

He carefully aimed, and then released. The bow twanged. In a practiced fluid-like motion, he nocked a second arrow, rapidly aimed and released.

The wagon came to an abrupt halt and the teamster stared dumbly in shock at the two oxen. One had collapsed without uttering a sound. The other brayed and kicked about in pain. It seemed to take the teamster a moment to realize that an arrow protruded from the neck of the beast. Eyes wide, he was just starting to look into the forest when Marcus released his third arrow. Its flight was true and took the teamster fully in the neck. Desperate, the man grasped at the arrow, which had punched completely through the soft tissue and exploded out the other side of his neck. The teamster stood up in what appeared to be shocked panic. He teetered a moment before his legs gave out and then toppled from the wagon, landing heavily, blood spurting in jets from the wound.

Marcus grabbed his quiver, stood, and made his way deeper into the forest. Shouts of alarm from the rebel supply column rang out behind him. Marcus assumed a similar thing was happening to the next two wagons, which Todd and Davis were charged with handling. The shouts faded the farther he got from the road.

The pace he set could not quite be described as a run, but was swift enough that it was a near jog. Eli had taught him well and he was mindful to leave little evidence of his passage lest someone track him down.

It was a mile before he came to a stop in a small clearing, the rendezvous point. A few seconds after his arrival, Davis and Todd appeared. They nodded at each other in greeting. Satisfied that everyone had arrived without incident or injury, Marcus said nothing but turned and immediately set out, with the others following along as they made their way to the next ambush point.

Today was the day the rebels would learn that their march on Vrell would be contested. The scouts, operating in small units, had been positioned along the road to harass, confuse and slow the enemy. Priority targets were draft animals and teamsters, followed by officers and sergeants. Orders were to strike rapidly and disappear, shortly attacking elsewhere, making it appear that the road and advance was contested by a major force. Though the enemy would think otherwise, there were no more than thirty-five men operating under Eli's direct command, most coming from the garrison companies.

Farther up the road and much closer to Vrell, well in advance of the enemy, Captain Stiger with the 85th and the bulk of the Vrell garrison were preparing for the enemy's arrival. Marcus was not sure what was being planned, but he was confident the captain would be making a stand. Captain Stiger simply needed time to prepare for that stand and Marcus was going to work hard to give it to him.

Marcus smiled as they arrived in a small clearing that they had selected earlier. He stopped and took a quick drink from his water skin, thankful once again that he did not have to wear the heavy armor of a common legionary. He wiped the sweat from his brow and took one more pull on the skin.

"Remember, three shots only and then hoof it back here," Marcus looked at the other two scouts. "No risks and no foot-dragging to watch."

The others nodded in grim understanding. They were playing a dangerous game. Taking more shots or hesitating a few seconds to watch the aftermath might be tempting, but it could also prove risky should the enemy be given time to gather their wits and respond. The orders were to strike from hidden positions and, if possible, remain unseen as they melted back into the forest.

Satisfied that they were in mutual understanding, Marcus sent them on their way. Each headed off in the same general direction toward positions that had been carefully selected with an eye toward concealment. So quick had they moved from the previous ambush that Marcus judged it unlikely the enemy column they were approaching was even aware of the attack on the supply column just a few miles back.

Marcus took care to move as silently as possible. He picked his way through the forest toward the road, barely a mile away. The enemy had scouts and skirmishers of their own, of which they had seen little. The rebels appeared to not expect any resistance and, as such, had not pushed skirmishers and scouts out to screen the flanks of their march. Marcus grinned. He was about to punish them for that lapse.

As he neared his selected spot, Marcus could begin to hear the steady tromp of many feet ahead of him through the brush. He and his men were about to attack an infantry column, which would be a much more dangerous undertaking. Marcus eased behind thick brush and knelt down.

Through the brush, he could see the rebel infantry marching by, a little under twenty-five yards away. He took his bow from his back, leaving the quiver in place and stuck three arrows tip-first into the soft forest floor, just deep enough that they would stand up on their own.

The rebel soldiers looked far from impressive. Dressed in near rags, many were barefoot. Very few wore any real type of armor, with only a handful here and there wearing the odd helmet. They were armed with long wooden spears, topped by iron tips, but more curiously, they did not carry shields. Spearmen usually carried shields. The rebel infantry kit included bags that were either slung over shoulders or hung on backs from ties around their necks. Marcus assumed these contained personal possessions and rations.

The rebels did not march in step or ordered rows as a legionary company might, but simply walked in clumps. From a professional soldier's view, they looked very much like the rabble that they were. Still, that did not stop Marcus from respecting them and what they were capable of doing. After all, it was men like these who had forced four imperial legions to retreat northward, stranding both his company, the 85th Imperial Foot and the garrison of Vrell behind enemy lines.

Marcus studied the column for a few seconds before he saw what he took to be a sergeant. The man carried himself with an air of importance and authority. He was well dressed and, unlike his men, he wore boots. He was also better armed than the others, having a shield and a short sword, worn on his right side.

In one smooth motion Marcus took an arrow, nocked it, aimed and fired. The arrow landed with a meaty thwack and heavy grunt, taking the man full in the chest. He staggered before falling to his knees. Marcus grabbed another arrow, aimed and released, hitting the man who had been marching next to the sergeant. So fast did it happen that the second man was hit before those around him seemed to realize they were under attack. The second man cried out as he collapsed onto the road, where he rolled in the dirt, tripping the man directly behind him.

Captain Stiger's orders were not only to strike at the enemy's supply, but also to prune the enemy ranks of their leadership. Eli had added to those orders and had made it clear that they were also to strike down those who were near the officers and sergeants, so it would rapidly become apparent that being around leadership was an unhealthy proposition. This would also have the future side-effect of making it easier to spot any rebel officers and sergeants.

Marcus took his third shot as cries of alarm and screams of rage and pain began to sound up and down the column. Davis and Todd, having taken his cue, also struck. A horse somewhere up the road screamed in pain. With a deep sense of satisfaction, Marcus melted back into the forest. One of his men had found an officer.

CHAPTER TWO

HOLDING THE REINS in his right hand, Stiger pulled Nomad up to a halt. The sound of many axes, chopping away, came from the trees along this portion of the road. He leaned back in the saddle and stretched out his sore back. He had been in the saddle nearly every waking minute for the past five days, riding up and down a forty-mile stretch of the Vrell Road. He intended this to be his defensive corridor. When the enemy encountered it, their advance would come to a near crawl. Stiger's defenses began with the near complete destruction of the road. His plan included four fortified defensive lines for the enemy to overcome. Accordingly, he was spending all of his time overseeing the work, providing advice and giving direction where he felt it was needed.

Stiger took a long pull from his canteen and then wiped his mouth with the back of his forearm. He was dusty, grimy, tired and extremely saddle-weary. He had not bathed or shaved in several days and felt thoroughly dirty. Being dirty made one itch. Stiger hated the feeling.

What I would not give for a proper bathhouse, Stiger thought with longing, scratching at his stubble. *A bathhouse and a shave.*

If he had to guess, Nomad was just as tired of the saddle and road. The horse was becoming somewhat temperamental. Like his master, he needed a break. *Soon, old friend,* he thought as he patted the neck of his horse affectionately. *You will get a rest.*

Sergeant Blake, who had been following behind, pulled up his mount next to the captain. The sergeant looked less ill at ease on horseback than he had when they had first begun their journey. Stiger had discovered, to his amusement that Blake was a terrible rider. The sergeant had been terrified of his mount, but that had not stopped the tough old veteran from tagging along. He was there to make sure that no harm came to Stiger. Accompanying the sergeant was an escort of five troopers from Lieutenant Lan's command, which fanned out protectively around the captain. Stiger handed his canteen over to Blake, who took it gratefully.

"And here I thought marching built up the thirst, sir," Blake said, taking a long pull before handing it back. Stiger nodded absently.

Corporal Beni hurried over from a nearby work detail. He, like all of the legionaries, wore his segmented armor while he worked. There was no excuse for removing it. The only relief the men were permitted was to stack their shields and helmets. They were legionaries and an enemy army was approaching. His men had to be prepared at a moment's notice to fight. Such was the way of the legions, whether in peace or in war.

"Good afternoon, sir," the corporal saluted.

"The work seems to be progressing well," Stiger said with a nod in reply to the salute. The corporal had been assigned several files of men from the garrison, along with his own file, to work this stretch of road. They had accomplished a great deal in the short amount of time they had been at work. The road was almost completely blocked with piles of felled trees. "Any problems?"

"No, sir." Beni struggled not to grin. "Not at all. Them garrison boys are a bit rusty, but as they say, 'It's not the toil that's hard, but the legion's discipline.'"

Stiger was amused by the corporal's comment. Beni was taking well to his responsibilities. He was showing real promise. Once again, Stiger was thankful for Blake and Ranl. The two veteran sergeants had recommended good men for promotion and it was paying off handsomely. Should Beni survive the coming storm, Stiger had no doubt the corporal, given more seasoning and time, might one day be promoted to sergeant.

"We are making good progress, sir," Beni continued in a more serious manner, clearly proud of all they had accomplished, "and should finish with this here stretch of road today. Tomorrow we will move on."

"Very good, corporal," Stiger said with a satisfied nod. "Don't let me keep you further. Excellent work, by the way."

"Yes, sir," Beni replied, puffing up at the rare compliment. The corporal saluted again before returning to his work detail. Some of the men had stopped to watch and listen.

"You lazy lot! The empire doesn't pay you to stand around all day!" Beni shouted at his men, who jumped back to work. "Stop to bloody gawk again and you will find yourselves on report!"

Stiger watched the detail work for a few minutes. He had never commanded such a large body of men and the responsibility alone was keeping him up at nights. He was essentially responsible for the equivalent of a regiment, or in the old cohort system around two cohorts. By rights he should have more officers to assist him. Two or three more to take on some of the burden would have been more than welcome.

Unfortunately, thanks to Captain Aveeno and Castor, that was not to be. The garrison had been purged of her senior officers and Stiger had to work with the cards he had been dealt.

The enemy was coming and he had to focus on that. Stiger and the garrison had been abandoned, without the courtesy of a heads-up. The legions had simply left and the more he thought on it, the more he became convinced it had been intentional. Stiger's anger burned hot at the thought. Unknowingly, he had been sent on a suicide mission.

They wanted the rebels to do their dirty work for them, he thought. *I will show them I am not so easy to kill, no matter how outnumbered.*

Stiger had taken that anger and directed it at the rebels. They were coming and he intended to make them pay a steep price for every foot, yard and mile because that was his duty, his trust and responsibility. It was simply who he was. He would deal with the rebels first and then with those who had sent him to die.

A large tree a hundred feet away cracked loudly and crashed into the road. Along this stretch of road, at least two hundred yards from bend to bend, there were already hundreds of trees down, blocking the way. When the trees adjacent to the road had been dropped, additional ones further in were set upon by axe parties. These then were dragged into the road and piled atop those already down. Stiger had explained in detail what and how he wanted done, in such a way that it was designed to make passage by wagon impossible and by foot difficult.

To complicate matters for the enemy, every three hundred yards, men were hard at work with shovels and pickaxes digging trenches ten feet deep and ten feet wide. These trenches cut right across the roadway. The enemy infantry would be able to avoid the trenches and felled trees by simply walking around them, but their supply and artillery train would be forced to clear the road and bridge each gap.

Along the road and off to the sides, the men were digging small pits. These were just large enough for a foot. Sharpened stakes were placed inside and then covered over with leaves. The Rivan had used similar pits and Stiger did not see why he could not borrow the practice. With the forest rapidly shedding its canopy, these pits would become extremely difficult to spot. It was a cruel tactic that would almost certainly cripple.

In war, there are no rules.

The Rivan had taught Stiger many things, but most important, through the months of hard fighting in forests of Abath, they had shown him how to effectively slow an advancing army. Accordingly, Stiger was using everything he could think of to delay the enemy.

Stiger's eye was drawn to a man off to the side of the road, in the trees. He had a large bag and every few feet, he stopped to toss something metallic. He was one among many seeding this stretch of forest alongside the ruined road with caltrops. A supply of these weapons had been found in the castle storerooms. Caltrops were an ingenious yet simple weapon that had four small sharpened spikes and were arranged in such a way that, when tossed, one spike always pointed upward, while the others provided a stable base. Caltrops were small and, when scattered amongst the leaves in the forest, difficult to spot. *A crippled enemy is one who cannot take his place in a line of battle.*

"The boys are working mighty hard," Blake said gruffly, shifting uncomfortably in his saddle.

"They are," Stiger agreed, watching a detail drag a large tree into the road. Just beyond them, another tree creaked loudly before cracking with a powerful snap. It fell with an impressive crash into the road, kicking up a storm of dust and leaves. "I just hope the scouts can buy us enough time."

Eli's command was a paltry force and Stiger suspected that their casualties would be rather heavy. He hoped Eli did not lose too many of his scouts, for when the enemy entered his defensive corridor, he would need them to be his eyes and ears. Without a sufficient number of scouts, Stiger could find himself at a real disadvantage. But there was no helping it. The enemy had to be slowed long enough for him to prepare a proper welcome.

"They will, sir," Blake said, firmly. "They have not let us down yet."

Stiger nodded absently as he watched the work party struggle with the tree. His mouth tasted dry and dusty. He leaned over and spat on the leaf-covered ground. It did not help. He took another pull from his canteen and then spat it out, feeling much better.

What is so important about Vrell? Stiger asked himself, resting his hand on the saddle pommel and sitting back up straight, stretching again. It was a question that had been bothering him. There was not much of value in the valley itself, other than agricultural products. The rebels must have thought otherwise, though, for sending a force of over twenty thousand strong indicated that Vrell held some strategic importance. Stiger could not see it. There was absolutely no reason why the enemy should want the valley so badly.

Interestingly, Stiger reflected, Castor had wanted it too and would have gotten it had he and Father Thomas failed in defeating the minion of the twisted god. The vision the sword had shown him had led him to believe he had witnessed General Delvaris's last moments as he too had fought a minion of Castor. So if Stiger's thinking was correct, Castor had coveted the valley for a very long time.

Why? He asked himself. Castor and now the rebels... Surely those twenty thousand men were needed at the front, where they would be facing the full might of the legions. Like a puzzle lacking the final piece, he felt, he was missing something. *Why is Vrell so special?*

A cold, bitter wind blew through the forest, setting off a near storm of leaves. Winter was only a few weeks off and once it arrived, fighting in the mountains around Vrell would become nearly impossible, let alone making any attempt at storming Castle Vrell's impressive walls. The castle itself, with its massive walls, seemed nearly impregnable. However, Stiger knew from experience that there was no such thing. Where there was a will, there was always a way. Given enough men and time, Castle Vrell's walls could be overcome.

Stiger had just around a thousand men to defend and most of these were of questionable quality. As such, delaying the enemy's advance had become a critical part of his plans. If he delayed the enemy long enough, at least for the first real snows to block the pass into Vrell, he would have the winter to retrain the garrison and be much better prepared for fighting come spring. If the rebels arrived before the snows, then they might just be able to take the castle from him. No matter how formidable the walls, overwhelming him through numbers alone was a distinct possibility. This was the main reason he felt he could not just wait, secure behind the walls, for the enemy to arrive. No, waiting was not an option. The rebels must be slowed and delayed as much as possible and the longer Stiger held out, the better the chance for the legions to return. There was no doubt in the captain's mind. The legions would be back, most likely commanded by someone other than Generals Mammot and Kromen.

As he watched his men work, Stiger understood he would have to do more than fell trees, lay traps and harass the enemy's march. He would eventually have to give battle, perhaps several times, before retiring behind the safety of Castle Vrell's walls to ride out the winter. If he had to fight, Stiger would do it on his own terms and not the enemy's.

Thankfully, the rebels were confined to one road, deep in a very dense forest. Stiger was lucky in that respect. There would be no option for multiple lines of advance, or even room for the enemy to maneuver and rapidly bring the entire power and weight of their army to bear upon him, at least until they got to Vrell.

The captain rubbed at his tired eyes. Today he intended to visit with Lieutenant Banister. The lieutenant, along with half of the man's company, was working to construct Stiger's defensive lines. When ambushes were no longer possible, Stiger would stick his men behind those fortified lines and force the enemy to deploy and assault him, costing additional time and bleeding them further.

Much of the work that was being done on these lines required trained engineers. A legion would have an engineering company attached to it to help provide skilled direction for such tasks. This was another complication he was being forced to overcome. The garrison had had only a single file of engineers under the command of a junior lieutenant. That lieutenant had been eliminated in Captain Aveeno's purge. Luckily, the engineers themselves had been pretty much left well alone. Stiger had them busy directing and laying out his defensive lines.

"I wouldn't want to be the rebels," Blake commented as he and Stiger watched another tree fall into the road with a crash and flurry of leaves mixed with dust.

"Neither would I," Stiger said with a solemn look directed at the sergeant.

"Sir," Blake said hesitantly. "I've been wondering something."

"Yes?" Stiger looked over at his sergeant. Blake was rarely hesitant about speaking his mind.

"I've heard it said that paladins can heal the injured," Blake said. "Do you believe that to be true?"

"It is true," Stiger affirmed. "I've seen it done."

"You have?"

"During the campaign in the forests of Abath," Stiger explained, staring off into the distance. "A paladin joined us, Father Griggs. I witnessed him heal a mortally-wounded man."

"Really?" Blake asked, eyebrows raised.

Stiger nodded, but said no more. Thoughts of that campaign and what he had faced at Father Griggs's side yet haunted him still.

"In the fighting to come, can Father Thomas heal those who are wounded?"

Stiger stared hard at the sergeant for a moment before looking away. He was silent for a time, watching the details toil away. He placed his hand on the hilt of his sword and felt the familiar electric tingle. Several minutes passed by before he replied.

"I have asked him that very question," Stiger breathed quietly so that only Blake could hear and none of the escort. "He said he would do all he was permitted, at least until High Father's call changes."

"I see," Blake said.

Stiger looked over at his sergeant with a grave look. "Father Thomas's call did not end with the defeat of the minion of Castor. He feels a need to remain and that means there must be more evil about."

"Oh shit," Blake cursed and then caught himself. "Sorry, sir."

Stiger agreed with his sergeant's sentiments. "Oh shit indeed."

Blake abruptly turned to look in the direction of Vrell and squinted. Something had caught his attention. Stiger looked as well and saw one of Lieutenant Lan's troopers picking his way on horseback through the work details and felled trees.

"Sir," the trooper saluted, fist to chest, before pulling a dispatch from a saddle bag. "From Lieutenant Lan, sir."

Stiger took the dispatch and opened it. He had left the lieutenant in command of Castle Vrell. Both cavalry commands had been charged with holding the castle should the citizens of the valley rise up. It was not much of a force, but having pulled the other companies out of the valley and put them to work on the road, it was all he had left. Besides, the imperial cavalry was made up of the minor nobility and they were notorious for their disdain of manual labor. Stiger doubted they would be of much help, other than holding onto the castle.

Stretching in his saddle, he rapidly read through the dispatch. The lieutenant reported he had worked out a date for a meeting with the council to be held in the valley at a local tavern. Though the people of the valley were not imperial citizens, the council were the elected local representatives that governed some of the day-to-day affairs of the people. Stiger hoped to enlist their support in defending the valley and their homes. He had desired to attend and work to smooth out relations between the empire and people of the valley, but with the enemy marching on Vrell, he could not risk it. With luck, Lan would be able to win them over.

The lieutenant also reported that the return of the seized food stores had begun. It had been received enthusiastically by the locals. After scanning through the remainder, Stiger took out his dispatch pad and charcoal pencil. He wrote out an acknowledgment of receipt, sealed it and handed it over to the trooper.

The trooper saluted and started back toward Vrell, carefully picking his way back. With mixed feelings, Stiger watched him go. The more immediate threat was the approaching rebel army. The council could wait. Besides, Stiger had instructed Lan to deliberately slow the return of the food stores. The people of the valley were desperate to make it through the coming winter. As long as the food was coming, no matter how slowly, they would be less likely to start trouble. If everything worked out, Stiger would not only be able to sufficiently delay the enemy, but he would have time to get a handle on the valley during the coming winter months.

The captain took one more look around. The nearest work detail was from one of the garrison companies. It had only been a few weeks since he had freed them from Captain Aveeno's clutches. Though freshly shaved and looking like proper legionaries, they were sorely in need of retraining. He had already been forced to start rotating them through a hasty refresher program, one day of labor and one of training. The schedule was impacting his defensive preparations, but Stiger knew there was no helping it. The garrison companies, his men now, would shortly be coming up against the rebels and they needed to be ready, which meant training and more training. With each passing day Stiger was feeling the sands of time running out. What he was not running out of were headaches and problems to overcome.

"Let's go," he ordered and kicked his horse forward. It was time to check the next section of road where Lieutenant Brent and his company were hard at work. After that, they would call on Banister to see how the first defensive line was coming. As he went by, Stiger looked over at Corporal Beni. Their eyes met. Stiger offered a nod of encouragement and then continued on.

CHAPTER THREE

BRADDOCK HESITATED BEFORE stepping into the council chambers. He could hear raised, angry voices out in the hallway, bickering back and forth from within. There were a number of heated discussions going on and the Thane of the Dvergr mentally winced at the thought of stepping into the room. Bickering and self-righteous anger seemed to be a failing of his race. When other peoples worked together, his frequently stood apart, just for spite.

They act like children, he thought. *They make me the adult.*

Looking dangerous, with fierce expressions and bristling with weapons, four of Braddock's household guard stood aside for their thane. They snapped to attention, standing stiffly and eyes to the front. Two would enter after the thane and two would remain outside. While the Large Council met, upon their lives no one would be permitted to interrupt.

"Your preposterous claim to our mine is what it is," a voice louder than the others thundered with ill-concealed rage.

Braddock recognized the voice as belonging to Hrove, chief of the Hammer Fisted clan. Hrove, in his prime, was more renowned for his cut-throat business dealings than his prowess on the field of battle. Braddock found him to be difficult and prickly, though surprisingly, Hrove regularly offered good policy advice. Braddock could easily guess to whom Hrove spoke.

"And what is that?" Tyga, chief of the Rock Breakers, asked, anger lacing his tone.

The silver mine in question had been the heart of a long-running disagreement between the two, one that bordered both of their clan territories. For years the dispute had regularly threatened to erupt into something more. If Braddock was not careful and did not manage it correctly, the disagreement could end up resulting in a blood feud between the two clans. The last thing he needed was to have two of his most powerful clans at each other's throats.

Tyga was the complete opposite of Hrove. He was strong and powerfully built, even for a dvergr. The chief of the Rock Breakers was well-known for his coolness on the battlefield and skill as a warrior. He lived strictly according to the Way, the code of honor passed down in scripture that all dvergr were required to follow. Tyga had purportedly never lost an honor duel. Such duels were frequently to the death and few held sufficient courage to challenge him.

"Hot air," Hrove said clearly, with the intention of provoking Tyga further. "It is just hot air."

"Hot air!" the raised voice of Tyga shot back incredulously with a laugh. "Hot air! You honorless dog!"

Braddock shot a look to Garrack, who shrugged sympathetically. This was one battle that only the thane could fight. The argument between the two chiefs was just one of many that could be heard coming from inside the council chambers. Braddock rubbed the back of his neck in irritation.

"Did you just call me a dog?" Hrove said. "You should speak! You smell worse than my hounds after they chase rats in the sewers!"

"I should strike you down where you stand," Tyga hissed and Braddock could hear chairs scrape back. If Hrove wasn't careful, Tyga might issue a challenge, despite Braddock's recent edict prohibiting such activities.

The thane had heard enough. The two would likely resort to fists, and he could not allow it to come to that. This meeting was too important. He needed their attention, not a brawl. Braddock nodded to Garrack, who grinned at him, before stepping forward through the open double doors of the council chamber.

"Braddock Uth'Kal'Thol," Garrack called in a powerfully deep voice that instantly silenced the uproar. "Thane of the Mountains, Ruler of the Dvergr Nations, Blessed of the Gods and your liege lord!"

Sighing heavily, Braddock drew back his shoulders and stepped through into the chamber. Both Braddock and Garrack had arrived dressed in their finest tunics, as had all the chiefs who were waiting for him. For a moment Braddock wished he had chosen to wear his ceremonial armor, as it would afford some basic protection.

This council was being held in the Old City and like everything here, the chambers, located in the governmental complex, had long been abandoned. The once proud city, now little more than a crumbling ruin, dated back to a time before the clans had made the decision to withdraw from the wider world. Like so many others, the clans had quit this city in favor of sanctuary deeper into the mountains and away from the other races.

Having been cut straight out of the heart of the mountain, the room itself was simple and rectangular-shaped. The dvergr preferred their governmental meeting places to be functional and utilitarian to better focus those charged with handling the people's business. Public service was a sacred trust and governmental spaces were designed with an eye to remind public servants of that.

Servants had thoroughly cleaned the room, though Braddock still detected a hint of mold and age. Three large, stout tables had been arranged in a U shape. The head table was placed so that Braddock held the commanding position at the bottom of the U and opposite the doors. Oil lamps in mirrored recesses set along the walls filled the room with an adequate supply of light.

Chairs scraped as the nine clan chiefs and one gnome respectfully stood for their thane. The top of the gnome's head barely made it to the tabletop and he had to rise up on his toes to get a better view.

Large Councils were rarely, if ever, held. They were called only during times of crisis. Most day-to-day governmental issues were solved by the Small Council, which consisted of three chiefs and the thane. The chiefs served on a rotating basis, changing seats every four years to provide their guidance and support to the thane. This was the first time in three hundred years that the entire Large Council had been gathered and convened. Braddock could almost feel their excitement at being present for such a historic event. The last time had seen Braddock's father preside over the noble body.

Braddock stomped to his rightful place at the head of the table, all eyes critically studying him. Garrack followed closely behind his liege, eyes forward, with his hand resting casually on the hilt of his sword.

Braddock had been thane for the last fifty-five years and under his rule his people had prospered. But that prosperity had not stopped several of those attending from actively working to undermine his authority. Given the right opportunity, one or two might even seek to replace him. Coldly looking over his vassals, Braddock resolved not to give them that chance.

He took a moment to glance around at his chiefs, each representing their clans. Braddock represented the Ironbound. Besides Hrove and Tyga, there was Agax of the Steelhands, Krieg of Stouthearts, Haggid of the Stone Anvil, Dagga of the Dotga, Vox of the Stone Breakers, Mahgdo of the Forge, and Kiello of the Bloody Axe.

The chief of the Bloody Axe, strong and dignified in bearing, nodded in greeting to Braddock. The thane gave a curt nod in reply. Kiello's clan had won its name during the most desperate of times in the last battles of the Gate War. Though he did not often speak unless he had to, Kiello was one of Braddock's most ardent supporters. Unlike some of the others, he could be counted on to put the needs of the people ahead of his own.

Several of the chiefs were blood enemies or their clans were involved in ongoing feuds. Much of this drama was brought to the thane's attention, leading him to impose his will in an attempt to stop the bloodshed. Braddock felt that the constant infighting, honor duels and stubbornness were failings of his people. It held them back from achieving greater things. Unfortunately, whenever Braddock had been forced to intervene, no one ended up happy, least of all the thane.

Braddock rested a calloused hand upon the hilt of his sword as he considered his chiefs. The heart of the problem was a prickly sense of self-honor or, as his people liked to call it, personal legend. Someone was always stepping on someone else's honor, which led to bad feelings, hasty words, a brawl and, ultimately, an honor duel. Braddock almost spat in frustration, but managed to restrain himself. It would not do for his vassals to witness his disgust. His people needed a focus, some noble goal that through forced cooperation would keep them from bumping heads and working toward the common good, which in turn would lead to much greater personal legend.

Though Tyga's eyes were on his thane, for a moment they flicked over to Hrove. Tyga's body language radiated with malevolent intent. Braddock caught it all and saw Hrove's return look at Tyga. The wily chief actually winked at Tyga, which caused the other to go red in the face. The only thing that held Tyga back was the thane's entrance.

Why can they not see? Braddock asked himself. Where once there had been many clans, now there were just twelve. One resided across the Narrow Sea to the south. Another was rumored to be somewhere in the far north, but no one had heard from them in centuries. For all Braddock knew, the ten clans represented in this room might be the last of dvergr.

The Gate War had decimated his people, leaving in its wake only a few thousand haggard survivors. The dvergr had barely managed to get through the tough times that had followed. Shattered, the remaining clans dispersed and abandoned the ruins of their once proud cities, instead choosing to burrow beneath the mountains and beyond the reach of their enemies. For the most part, the dvergran nations had simply turned their backs upon the wider world and disappeared.

Not one who lives today lived back then, Braddock thought, saddened. *That is the real problem. To all dvergr the Gate War has become history, no longer even a living memory in the minds of the elderly.*

Since that forlorn time, the people had once again grown numerous and built proud cities. No longer did dvergran cities feel the touch of the sun. These were hidden deep within some of the most formidable of mountain ranges, locked away and isolated.

What I do today I do for my children and their children yet to come.

Braddock placed his fists upon the table and leaned forward, looking upon his vassals. His word was law and his call had gathered them here, some like Kiello having traveled over a thousand miles to attend. He had ordered a suspension of all such feuding, honor duels, and other nonsense, but that had not stopped them from bickering like old women. Their personal and clan honor was such that Braddock's word kept their respective clans in peace, at least for the moment.

"Winds of change are blowing," the High Priest of Thulla, the god of the dvergr, had told Braddock prior to reading the auguries, which foretold of dire comings. Thinking on what had been revealed to him, Braddock alone understood this was no time for blood feuds, for a black cloud was upon his people and time was running out. His hand had been forced.

Damn the Oracle and the strange prophecy she made when the Gate War ended.

Braddock forced himself to relax and took a moment to look around the table, intentionally keeping his vassals standing expectantly. There was one empty place, next to the gnome. That was reserved for The Master. Braddock knew he should be offended the elderly wizard had not shown, but the distance was great and Thoggle's health was slowly failing. It mattered little to Braddock that Thoggle had elected not to attend the Large Council. As long as the wizard showed up when he was needed was what counted. Some of those here would take Thoggle's absence as a sign of weakness on their thane's part.

That, Braddock thought with heat, *would be a mistake.*

The Thane of the Mountain finally sat. The clan chiefs waited a respectful half-second before taking their own seats, chairs grating on the stone flooring. Garrack, as Braddock's chief aide, took up a position behind his thane and to the right. Some would say that Garrack was his chief advisor, the thane's right hand. Such an assumption would have only been partly correct. No one other than Braddock and Thoggle knew of Garrack's great responsibility and purpose, which had been passed down from father to son.

Two members of Braddock's household guard stepped into the room and closed the two ancient oak doors with a solid thud. The hinges, freshly oiled, did not make a sound. One of the guards locked the door with a key, which he then tucked into a pocket. The two guards took up positions on either side of the door, hands resting casually upon their sword hilts, ready to act if called upon to protect their thane. Their presence reinforced his strength but also his weakness.

"We appreciate your willing attendance," Braddock began. "It is my—"

"You commanded our attendance," the gnome spat in a high pitched voice that dripped with malice. The gnome was half the size of a fully grown dvergr and half as wide, with mean black eyes, straight black hair and small, nimble fingers that never seemed idle.

Though no one was particularly surprised, several of those present looked amused at the interruption, while others were appalled at the gnome's behavior. One of Braddock's guards took a menacing step forward, before Braddock waved him back. Had he not stopped him, the guard would have separated the gnome's head from its shoulders, without a second thought.

"Nevertheless, Cragg, your presence *here* is appreciated," Braddock said evenly, keeping a tight leash on his temper. He had long years of experience working with gnomes and yet the mean little shits still managed to test his patience.

"Is it?" Cragg asked in a mocking tone, small eyes fixed on Braddock in challenge.

"It is," Braddock said with steel, shooting the nasty-natured creature a scathing look that dared it to speak further. The guard took another step forward and started to draw his sword. This time, Braddock did nothing to intervene.

Cragg, who seemed to have abruptly realized his peril, gave a respectful nod. Though caustic, Cragg, the leader for his people, had more common sense than most of his kind.

"I am pleased to attend," Cragg said, eyeing the guard carefully.

Braddock felt relieved and waved his guard back. The thane loathed his gnomes, but at the same time respected them. As the gods had commanded, gnomes had long served the dvergran nations. They were an intelligent, industrious and, like his own, a very determined people. But by nature they were an ill-tempered lot.

Killing one of the insolent bastards might feel good, but it never ever did any good. Once you dealt with one, another just as nasty would soon take the deceased's place. Besides, Braddock had called the vile little creatures forth from their depths because he needed their help. If the dvergr were going to war, he was determined that the gnomes would be at his side, as was their rightful place.

Braddock's bodyguard gave the gnome an intense look before returning to his original position by the door. Gnomes were impossible to read. They only understood strength. Cragg watched the guard for a moment and then returned his attention to the thane.

Braddock leaned forward, about to say more, when the lock clicked loudly and the ancient oak doors unexpectedly opened, swinging inward. Impossibly, someone had unlocked the doors from the other side. The guards whirled and reached for their swords in surprise, for no one was allowed admittance under pain of death.

A small, scrawny, beardless, middle-aged dvergr stood before them, looking curiously into the council chamber. Dressed in the blackest of robes, he carried a thick wooden staff with a large chunk of oddly-formed purple crystal set atop. The guards, in spite of being hard-bitten veterans, fell back in disgust mixed with horror.

Several of the chiefs sucked in their breath. Braddock shook his head with disgust at the sight of a beardless one. Voluntarily shaving one's beard was considered one of the greatest sins a dvergr could ever commit. A long, uncut, neatly braided beard was a sign that one honored the gods, for it was commanded in the scriptures. Only criminals and cowards were ever forcefully shaved, announcing to all and the gods their eternal shame.

Ogg, Thoggle's apprentice, on the other hand, shaved of his own volition and he was neither a criminal nor a coward. Braddock knew this from personal experience. Though considered only an apprentice, he was a powerful wizard and thankfully one of only two amongst the dvergr nations. He was also extremely dangerous and unpredictable.

"Ogg," Garrack roared with displeasure, sparing his thane the indignity of having to address a beardless one. "I expect you to have a solid reason for this intrusion."

Ogg had stopped in the doorway. He had been sizing up Braddock's guards. The wizard slowly tore his gaze from the guards to lock eyes with Garrack, a thin bitter smile playing across his beardless face, before shifting his look to

Braddock. The Thane of the Mountains could almost read the madness in the wizard's eyes, which seemed to be a curse that afflicted all of their kind who transgressed with magic and strange gods. Despite that, Braddock knew there could only be one reason Ogg was here.

If it was as he suspected, Braddock feared that Thoggle had passed to the shades. If he had, as the only other wizard remaining among the dvergran nations, then the title of The Master had rightfully passed to Ogg.

While Thoggle lived, there was a check upon his apprentice. If The Master were dead and gone, things would become unpredictable. Braddock knew not what to expect from Ogg. This was not a good omen with which to begin his campaign.

"I believe…" Ogg said in what sounded like an amused tone, as he offered a respectful bow to his thane. This was followed almost immediately by a soft maniacal giggle, which bubbled up and faded away just as rapidly. "…I believe I have a rightful place on this—ah—venerated council."

"The Master has a place here," Hrove stated scornfully. The chief turned his head and spat upon the stone floor in disgust. "Remove yourself! Your very presence dishonors us!"

"Thank you so much for such a warm welcome," Ogg replied, becoming serious. The amused look slipped from his face as he turned his gaze upon Hrove. Braddock could not help feeling that there was a dangerous menace in the wizard's eyes. Knowing Ogg as he did, Braddock wondered if the Hammer Fisted clan would soon be in need of a new chief.

"I thank you for the clarification," Ogg continued. "As it is clear I do indeed have a place here, *with* this noble body."

"You what?" Agax demanded angrily, shooting Braddock a concerned look before turning back to the wizard. "What game are you playing at?"

"I play no games! Hrove here just explained The Master has a place here," Ogg said patiently, as if speaking to a child. He had yet to take his eyes off of Hrove, even as he spoke to Agax. Hrove returned Ogg's gaze without a hint of fear. "Therefore, I have a place here."

"You?" Hrove breathed.

"What happened to Thoggle?" Braddock demanded, impropriety be damned. Though he loathed Thoggle and Ogg's kind, as did nearly every other respectable dvergr, he had personally valued the ancient wizard's counsel. Turning from the dvergr gods to worship another was an unforgivable offense amongst his people. The only reason both Thoggle and Ogg had their heads was that the priests long ago had permitted the practice of magic, under certain conditions. Those conditions came with responsibilities to the people.

Instead of answering, Ogg walked slowly around to the seat reserved for The Master. His staff's metal tip made a clicking sound as he walked, passing by several of the chiefs, who turned nervously to keep an eye upon him. Ogg made a show of considering the chair for a moment, before finally pulling it back and sitting down. He carefully leaned his staff against the table. Cragg, sitting beside Ogg, squirmed to the far side of his chair and looked ready to bolt at a moment's notice. Ogg winked at the gnome, who then began to tremble with fear, something Braddock had never seen before.

"Good to see you again, Cragg," Ogg said as he repositioned himself. Cragg shrank back farther away from the wizard, if that was possible. Ogg looked up and around at the assembled chiefs with a broad, beardless smile. He leaned his forearms on the tabletop, his hands clasped together.

"Well?" Braddock demanded, not the least bit surprised at the wizard's behavior. Ogg always enjoyed making a grand entrance, though this time it was reckless and should it continue, he might have to take steps to put the wizard in his place.

"My Thane?" Ogg asked, an exaggerated look of profound confusion passing across his face. "What were we discussing?"

"What happened to Thoggle?" Braddock demanded, going along with Ogg's charade.

"Oh, that!" Ogg exclaimed, eyes lighting up, with a snap of his fingers. "Right, Thoggle. He moved on."

"Moved on?" Garrack demanded. "What do you mean moved on? Explain yourself!"

"Yes." Ogg shrugged, his eyes teary. It was a shameful display of weakness that no dvergr with honor would have permitted. Braddock realized that Ogg was playing with the council. He was enjoying his moment of triumph.

Play your games, Braddock thought. *Enjoy your moment, but by the gods, I will watch you.*

"It was time," Ogg continued with a sad snuffle. "Thoggle moved on and now the apprentice is The Master."

A chill went through the room at this statement of confirmation of what they all had feared. Several of the chiefs exchanged worried looks.

Braddock took a deep breath to calm himself. He leaned back in his chair, which creaked alarmingly, and considered the disturbed wizard, who gazed right back at him. Had Thoggle lived, the thane had no doubt that Ogg would not be here in attendance. Still, as The Master, Braddock needed his services and Ogg was bound by his gods to provide them. The thane shot a look at Garrack. Though his face looked stern, Braddock thought he could detect deep sadness through the facade. Garrack nodded ever so slightly.

"Very well, Ogg," Braddock said slowly, as his bodyguards once again closed the door with a heavy thud and locked it. "I recognize you as The Master."

"So very kind of you, my Thane," Ogg responded with an odd lopsided smile, made more so by his beardless face. Braddock felt a shiver run down his back, as if a draft as cold as death had entered the room. "I stand to serve the clans."

Braddock nodded, thinking on ways he could capitalize on this turn of events. He was now stuck with Ogg. There were some things that only The Master was capable of dealing with, like the filth squatting in Grata'Kor. A thought occurred to Braddock.

"Ogg, have you taken an apprentice?" he asked, keenly looking back at the wizard, who looked genuinely surprised by the question.

"Currently...at this time, no," Ogg responded, brow furrowed and blinking. "Though, I must say, what a terribly intriguing and fascinating thought..."

Braddock considered Ogg for another moment, before turning back to his vassals. The wizard was a dangerous and unpredictable person, but the more immediate threat to the thane's position were some of those seated around the table. He would not allow Ogg to make him look weak.

Braddock had prepared a welcome speech, but Ogg's arrival had disrupted that and it now seemed trivial. It was time to take back control of the meeting.

"You must be ready to march in four weeks," Braddock stated bluntly, knowing this news would shock and surprise.

"Four weeks?" Hrove hammered a powerful fist down upon the table, which shuddered under the impact. "The call you put out said twelve weeks. By rights we should have six remaining. More than half of my lads are still on their way!"

"Aye," the extremely elderly Krieg, showing a modicum of life, spoke up in support. "My men have almost the farthest to travel. Only a handful have arrived thus far."

Protests and conversations broke out around the table. Braddock held up a hand calling for silence and when that failed to work, he stood, commanding their attention.

"I understand your concerns," Braddock said after a moment of silence. "However, events have transpired that make an earlier move necessary and more practical."

"What events do you speak of?" Krieg asked in a wheezy and labored voice as the energy he exhibited a moment ago drained from him. He seemed to sag back into his chair, growing frailer by the second. Krieg had lived a long life and had reached the unheard-of age of seven hundred and two years. Braddock could see the time rapidly coming when Krieg would be succeeded by his eldest son. Age might just be the old warrior's final battle.

"The tainted humans have abandoned their forts in the valley," Braddock answered directly. "The majority have marched out of the valley. The only substantial force remaining is that holding the citadel at Grata'Kor."

"What?" Hrove exclaimed in astonishment. "When did this happen?"

"Two weeks ago," Braddock answered.

"Why were we not told?" Hrove demanded.

"We just learned of it ourselves from the emissary," Garrack countered.

"Do we know why?" Krieg pressed, making an effort to be heard as several side conversations broke out among the chiefs.

"No," Garrack said loudly over the hum of side conversations, cutting into them so all eyes turned back as Braddock once again took his seat. "We do not and the emissary did not know why either. I have dispatched scouts to uncover the reason behind their leaving. Perhaps the empire has recalled them to fight against this rebellion we have heard about.

"Regardless, we need to strike sooner rather than later," Garrack rumbled on, stepping up to the table. Garrack was tall for a dvergr. He was also a renowned warrior of exceptional skill. His frank manner might not have earned him many friends on the council, but he was respected. "They know nothing of us. We must act before the bulk of their force returns…if they return, that is."

"It will make our job easier," Hrove nodded thoughtfully, stroking his long brown beard, which had been braided into several neat strands. "Are the tunnels into Grata'Kor still intact? I can't begin to imagine the condition they are in after all these years."

"Most remain passable," Garrack responded with a heavy nod. "There should be no problem getting a sufficient force into the citadel and achieving surprise."

"In short," Braddock said, slamming the table with a powerful fist, "we take Grata'Kor back and restore the Compact."

There was a moment of stunned silence as the chiefs digested this. Braddock might not personally enjoy the company of many of them; however, all were intelligent. They would not have risen to their current positions and remained long in them had they not commanded the respect of their people.

"The emissary reported there was great evil in Grata'Kor," Krieg wheezed as he spoke. "I don't like going in with only a handful of my men. It is like stepping into the mine with only one boot on."

"I don't like it either," Haggid agreed forcefully. "We should delay and hit them with our full and combined force."

"If we wait," Braddock said firmly, "it could cost us additional lives."

"Going in with our partial strength could see the same," Krieg stated just as firmly, once again exhibiting life. "How do you intend to deal with Castor's filth?"

"We will have surprise on our side," Braddock insisted and then gestured over at the wizard, "and we have The Master."

All eyes turned to Ogg, who looked back at Braddock with a cold, thin-lipped smile. Before Ogg could manage to say anything that might inflame the chiefs or cast doubt upon his decision, Braddock decided to change tracks.

"How many here have their full complement on hand?" the thane asked.

Three hands went up.

"Including mine," Braddock said. He had hoped for more. "Four full war bands then, with six other partials."

"With four war bands, we outnumber the entire imperial force, even before they abandoned the valley, at least two times over," Garrack said with conviction. "We can crush these vermin."

Braddock nodded in agreement and then decided to end debate on the subject. "We will launch the attack in four weeks. That is my final word on the matter."

There was silence at this, which lasted only a moment before Krieg stirred.

"Once we take Grata'Kor," the old dvergr wheezed, "what then, my Thane?"

"We restore and fulfill the requirements of the Compact," Braddock said simply, knowing what Krieg really sought.

"Then what?" Krieg continued probing, eying his thane critically with eyes made watery from age. Braddock knew Krieg wanted to hear more, and craved to hear more. It was something all dvergr had waited many years to hear their thane say.

"Too long have we remained hidden, apart and isolated from the world," Krieg pushed onward. "We have shrouded our existence like cowards. It was once necessary but no longer. We are a proud people, my Thane. Don't you feel what I feel? Is it not time? Before I pass to the shadows and shades, I want to hear the words. I wish to pass on from this world proud and happy."

Silence settled upon the chamber, as Krieg collapsed back into his chair, gasping from the effort of his speech, which had touched the thane's heart as it had every other dvergr in the room. Braddock looked around the table at the faces of his vassals, some of whom he trusted and others he most certainly did not, would not and could not.

Is it time to return? Braddock asked himself as he leaned an elbow on the table. Absently he ran a hand through his neatly braided beard, feeling the tight prayer braids with his rough and calloused fingers. *Have my people recovered? Are they strong enough to face the world once again?*

All looked expectantly for his response....all except Ogg, who was engrossed in reading from a tome he had pulled forth from the depths of his black robes.

"We return," Braddock spoke quietly. "We take back what is rightfully ours!"

This was followed by silence, all eyes upon the thane, almost as if they could not believe what they had just heard. Several chairs creaked, shattering the moment. Then the chiefs leapt to their feet and roared their approval at this declaration, with many pounding on the table. Krieg sat where he had collapsed. He looked triumphant, but was too tired to do more than grin. Braddock noticed only Ogg seemed unmoved. The beardless dwarf looked up at his thane with a curious expression. The wizard flashed him another odd smile, before offering a wink from those mad and disturbed eyes.

CHAPTER FOUR

M ARCUS FELT A FRIENDLY hand come to rest gently on his shoulder. He had been sitting with his back resting against an ancient oak. He glanced over at Eli, who, in the dim gloomy predawn light, offered the scout corporal a closed-mouth smile. The air was chilly and in the trees above, the birds were just beginning to stir in their roosts.

Marcus had been waiting patiently for Eli to complete his scout of the enemy camp. Had the elf not been with him, Marcus would have done the job himself. As good as he was, the lieutenant was better at this kind of work. There was no one more skilled at stealing about than an elven ranger.

Enemy sentry in sight...over there, Eli signed, using the sign language he had taught the scouts. *I will handle. You stay here.*

Marcus nodded his understanding. Eli pulled out a slightly-curved, wicked-looking knife around eight inches long, and silently moved forward through the brush. In moments he disappeared without a sound into the gloom.

Marcus closed his eyes, controlled his breathing and focused, listening to the living forest around him. The experience was almost trancelike. Whenever at rest, he found himself slipping into this state more and more often. It felt natural and relaxing. The deeper he went, the more it seemed he could actually feel the forest, as if it were a single living being. Marcus struggled to explain it to himself, let alone others, yet it felt more real to him than... He abruptly sensed a disturbance off to his left. The pattern had been interrupted and it almost felt as if something was warning him that someone was approaching, moving stealthily towards him. He opened his eyes and turned his head left to look just as the lieutenant silently emerged through the brush.

The elven ranger stopped, eyeing Marcus with what the scout corporal thought was a particularly odd expression. Eli hesitated a moment before coming closer. It seemed as if the elf was studying him as a child studies a strange bug.

All clear, Eli signed with his fingers, that odd look still in his eyes. *Let's go.*

Marcus stood, grabbing his bow and followed Eli. Though the forest was still dark and heavily shadowed, the sun was just beginning to peek over the horizon. The sky had become considerably brighter. Many of the trees had shed the majority of their leaves over the previous days, which permitted the light to penetrate the forest more easily. They approached slowly, carefully, gliding through the leaf-strewn forest floor, barely making a sound as they went. He could hear the enemy camp beginning to stir the closer they got.

The objective had been to slow the enemy advance, sowing fear and causing confusion. So far the raids had been an outstanding success. Each time the scouts struck randomly along the rebel column, the enemy was forced to halt their march and deploy skirmishers in an attempt to force them back. More often than not, the enemy skirmishers found nothing, as the scouts were long gone.

The targeting of officers and sergeants had also had a dramatic effect. Without leadership, some of the rebel companies simply refused to march, which brought the

entire enemy column to a halt or saw other rebel companies attempting to struggle by the halted unit along the
narrow road. Whenever an officer was struck down, replace-
ments had to be sent forward and this took time. The rebel
advance had become painfully slow.

Marcus had lost track of the number of men he had
killed, maimed or wounded. Initially, he had kept score, but
with the pace of their operations and bone tiredness that was
on him, he had simply given up. All he knew was there had
been many. He did not care why or even question whether
the rebel cause was just. They had rebelled against the rule of
the empire and his job was to kill them. Like all legionaries,
he left politics to the politicians. All that mattered was that he
well understood that if given the chance the rebels would as
willingly take his life as he was intent upon taking theirs.

In the last few days, rebel scouts and skirmishers had doubled and then tripled in number, as the enemy attempted
to push the imperial scouts back from the main column.
In the forest, this was extremely difficult to do. Conversely,
for Marcus and the other scouts, once they struck, escaping
into the depths of the forest was quickly becoming much
more hazardous and difficult.

To make matters worse, many of the enemy scouts and
skirmishers appeared quite skilled. There had been several
unexpected encounters that had been extremely violent.
Two of the scouts from the garrison had lost their lives to
such unanticipated encounters. The garrison scouts were
not quite as skilled as those from the 85th, but they were
learning rapidly as Eli and Marcus worked with them at
every available opportunity.

Marcus was tired. The pace was beginning to take its toll
and he was looking forward to returning to the scout camp
for some well-earned rest.

The lieutenant suddenly stopped, crouched down and pointed ahead. Marcus moved forward and crouched down next to the elven ranger. With the prospect of action, he found he was wide-awake and alert. They were at the edge of the enemy camp, which was slowly beginning to stir as the sergeants, corporals and cooks began to prepare for the day. The bulk of the men from this infantry regiment were still asleep. The smell of wood smoke from many smoldering fires hung heavily in the air, as did the stench of human and animal excrement.

So far they had avoided striking at any of the enemy marching camps. This had been intentional, as they had only raided the rebels while they were on the move. Eli had explained he wanted to create a sense of safety and security, in that it would appear to the rebels that the imperials were afraid of hitting well-guarded camps. Marcus knew that this morning, across the rebel line of advance, the enemy would have their only sense of safety shattered. Six of the enemy camps would be hit by lightning raids.

Like the others Marcus had seen, the rebel camp was shabby and had a look of extreme disorder. These men were not professional soldiers and it showed. Before bedding down for the night, the rebels had not even bothered to clear the brush from their camp. As near as he could tell, there were around five hundred men sleeping on their arms amidst the brush or, if they were lucky, sleeping in a handful of tents. There had been no attempt to fortify the encampment as the legions would have done when the enemy was about. The rebels had simply created their own clearing by chopping down the trees, which they then used to fuel fires. They had posted sentries, but not enough to hinder Eli and Marcus.

There was a large ornate tent just feet away, in the direction Eli was indicating. This was their target, what Eli and Marcus suspected to be the equivalent of a regimental commander. Marcus had spotted him two days ago, but had been unable to get close enough for a kill shot. On the road, he had been heavily protected with a strong bodyguard and large screen of skirmishers moving skillfully through the forest, parallel to the road.

Surprisingly, the regimental commander's tent was on the outer edge of the camp and not at the camp's center, where he would have been better protected. Marcus marveled at this arrogance. *Or is it simple stupidity?* he asked himself.

He assumed that perhaps the regimental commander had wanted to separate himself from the rank and file, or perhaps it was just the smell. Sanitation did not appear to be too high on the rebel list of camp priorities. Marcus wrinkled his nose at the rank smell in the air.

There were two bored-looking guards standing post out in front of the tent. The nearest tents and sleeping men were only around ten feet away. As they waited and watched, one of those nearby men who had been sleeping on the ground stood stiffly, stretched and stumbled off in the direction of the cook wagons, which had been placed in the center of the camp.

The food wagons, Marcus thought with amusement, *are better protected than their regimental commander.*

Marcus and Eli had considered waiting for the regimental commander to wake and leave his tent, but that likely would not occur until the sun was well up, increasing their chance of discovery. So instead, they had settled upon a more direct approach.

On the other side of the enemy camp, there was a sudden shout, followed by cries of alarm as Bryant and Davis struck, raining arrows into the mass of sleeping men. The camp exploded into activity. Some rushed toward the action, while others remained where they were, looking in the direction of the commotion and talking excitedly amongst themselves.

Eli and Marcus waited, ready, bows nocked. Within seconds, an older man, half-dressed, pushed the tent flap aside, a stormy expression on his face. Eli loosed. Before the regimental commander had taken more than half a step, the arrow hammered into his chest. With a strangled cry, he fell backward into his tent and out of sight. The two guards who had been looking toward the commotion on the other side of the camp turned around in surprise. Marcus let fly. His first arrow flew true, taking the guard on the left in the neck. The scout corporal had a second arrow nocked as his first target began to fall, gurgling his death rattle. Marcus let loose his second arrow, taking the other guard in the back as he was turning to look at his companion in shock. The man fell forward to his knees, grunting in pain as the wind was knocked from his lungs by the impact.

Eli rushed forward, short sword drawn, carrying his bow lightly in his left hand. Marcus nocked another arrow. With the guards down, his job was to cover the lieutenant. No one seemed to be watching the regimental commander's tent or notice the drama that was playing out. All of the attention was focused on the other side of the encampment, where men were yelling in alarm, pain and panic. Officers were beginning to shout what Marcus took to be orders, in one of the many guttural southern languages that he did not know. It sounded to the scout as if they were calling for their men to fall in.

Marcus watched the lieutenant enter the tent. Within a second or two, the elf emerged and made a dash for the trees. Eli's sword was dark with blood. A new shout of alarm drew Marcus's attention. A rebel officer, likely an aide, had seen Eli emerge. He was hurrying to the tent. Marcus aimed and loosed a fraction of a second later. The arrow hammered the officer squarely in the chest. He stopped, stood dumbly for a moment, clutching the arrow with both hands, before falling to his knees, a bloody froth bubbling up from his mouth. A moment later he toppled over onto his side, where he lay still.

There were additional shouts of alarm, with men pointing in their direction. Marcus calmly reached over his shoulder, drew another arrow, nocked and fired, striking another man. He loosed again and was rewarded with a scream of pain.

"Let's go," Eli shouted as he reached the edge of the woods. Marcus let fly a final arrow as the rebels began work up their courage to charge his position. Without waiting to see the result, he turned and ran, following on Eli's heels into the forest and toward safety.

CHAPTER FIVE

"**Y**OU SERIOUSLY EXPECT us to furnish levies?" Councilman Vargus asked in an incredulous tone, barking out a harsh laugh. Lieutenant Lan thought not only did the man look like a bull, he had the voice of one too. "Furnish levies...after how the empire has treated us?"

Lan had made the long ride down from the castle and into the valley to meet with the councilors. Sergeant Mills and Legionary Sulla had accompanied him as his escort. It was Lan's first opportunity to travel into the valley and he was impressed. The valley was huge, lush and fertile. An assortment of farms occupied the base, most run by single families. Others were large enough to be called plantations. Higher up, neatly ordered vineyards climbed the slopes until the grade became too steep. The party had ridden through several small villages on their way to Riverton for the meeting, which was being held at a tavern called the Pact. No one they had encountered had looked particularly thrilled to see them.

The locals called Riverton a village, but anywhere else in the empire Lan would have considered it to be a moderately sized town. The town was located in the southern end of the valley and despite the size of Riverton, they had easily found the Pact, which was on the outer edge of town. The building itself was two stories high, with the second story looking as if it had been built as an afterthought. An old, weathered sign hung out front. The sign had no words, only the image of two hands shaking before an oversized mug. For those who could not read, the sign was clear enough to convey what waited inside. Like many such establishments, the proprietor and his family lived on the second floor, while the business of serving drinks occurred on the first.

The public side of the tavern consisted of a clean single room that was barely large enough for the seven tables set aside for patrons. As Lan entered, worn, tired and cold from his long ride, a large fireplace, complete with a rough stone mantle, was off to the left, fire crackling with friendly warmth. The bar, lovingly polished, was opposite the entrance and along the back wall. A small kitchen that doubled as a stockroom backed off the bar. From the kitchen, the aroma of freshly cooked meat wafted outward and into the common room, where it mixed with the smell of stale beer.

Several of the tables had been pushed together and a number of people sat around them, including the lieutenant and the councilors. This was no mean place, Lan reflected, as the meeting dragged on. It was the kind of establishment that respectable locals retired to in the evenings after a hard day's work. Here they would have a quiet drink and share news. It was not the kind of place one would go to for serious drinking and a good time. It was cozy and warm. He liked it.

"That was Captain Aveeno's doing," Councilman Bester pointed out in an attempt to placate Vargus. "Not the lieutenant's."

"A servant of Castor?" Vargus asked mockingly, pounding the table with a large fist and rattling the mugs. "You expect me to believe such shit?"

"I was there," Bester said, becoming hot. "I know what I saw."

"We are not asking for levies," Lan interjected, holding up his hands. This back and forth had been going on for some time and he was becoming frustrated at the lack of progress. They seemed to be going round and round. "We do not ask you to put men forward."

Four of the valley's five elected councilors were present. Lan had been briefed by Lieutenant Cannol on all of them. They included Londnom Bester, Darrik Quintus, Aallond Hief and Ash Vargus. The elderly Atticus Ravana was ill and could not attend. He lived clear across the far side of the valley and had sent his regrets, along with his youngest son, Benus Ravana. The boy, still in his teens, had a serious air about him that contradicted his years. Lan felt he looked bookish, like an accountant, more comfortable with ledgers and numbers than people. The boy sat off to the side, silently taking meeting notes in a roughhewn book, presumably for his father.

Vargus, the proprietor of the Pact, was a large, well-muscled man who had a hard look to him. Lan understood from Lieutenant Cannol that Vargus was highly respected. His words carried weight and besides running the tavern and serving on the council, he also acted as the local magistrate. Lan had quickly discovered Vargus was far from cordial, instead blunt to the point of insult and downright hostile toward the empire.

A handful of locals had also turned up, curious as to what would be discussed. They had not been asked to leave, which had surprised the lieutenant. Though he did not much like it, he figured this was probably typical of small communities, where nearly everyone got their say.

"Then what do you want?" Hief asked, a deep scowl upon his face.

"Peace, first and foremost," Lan explained patiently. "Captain Stiger would very much like us to work out an agreement to create a firm basis for future interactions between the garrison and the people of the valley."

"We got that part," Quintus said. Quintus seemed to be the chair of the council, though no such position officially existed. The others on the council simply deferred to him. It was clear the man was held in high esteem. "We can work on an agreement easily enough. What we all want to know is *this* support you speak of…"

"We would appreciate the valley's assistance to help us prepare the castle for defense," Lan explained, trying to not lose his temper. Like impatient children, they kept interrupting him. It was almost as if he were being tested. "We will do the fighting. However, we need substantial help in support roles. Such as—"

"Support roles?" Vargus barked and shot the others on the council a knowing look. Several of those watching from the bar grumbled. "You people never asked, just took and kept taking. Why ask now?"

Though the evening air was chill outside, the tavern was comfortably warm, made so by a well-fed fire. Perspiring slightly, Vargus had rolled the sleeves of his tunic back, revealing scarred forearms. The marks were the kind acquired from years of arms drill and they immediately caught the lieutenant's attention. If Lan had not known better, he would have thought Vargus could have passed for a retired legionary officer or even a sergeant. Everything about the man's demeanor shouted retired military. As the discussions wore on, Lan found himself wondering if Vargus had served at some point in an auxiliary company.

The others had not that much about them physically to remark on. Most seemed fairly average, though all looked to have come from imperial stock. Quintus owned a number of vineyards along the south side of the valley. He was one of the main producers of the wine that Lan was becoming very fond of. Prior to the rebellion, Quintus had supplied much of the nearer cities, like Aeda, with high quality wine.

Hief was a master smith who owned a smithy here in Riverton, where he focused exclusively on the manufacture and repair of farm implements. He was also heavily muscled, though he had the look of going a bit soft with age, as his middle section was beginning to show a slight bulge.

Lan could not remember what Cannol had told him that Bester did for a living, but it hardly mattered, the man seemed genuinely friendly toward the empire and had greeted the lieutenant warmly.

"We need help preparing the defense of the castle," Lan pushed on, ignoring the interruption. "Manufacturing of arrows, hauling rocks, pitch and oil, preparing food and bandages…"

"You want us to supply a labor force?" Quintus narrowed his eyes. "Is that it? Slave labor?"

"Nothing of the sort," Lan said, shocked. Though these people were not imperial citizens, they were freemen, belonging to a province of the empire. They could not be condemned to a life of forced servitude without just cause. "Your people are free. We will, of course, pay."

A drink rested before each of them, either valley-made beer or wine. Lan had elected the wine, which he found exceptionally agreeable, though not quite as fine a vintage as his family produced in Venney.

Well, it is no longer home anymore, he thought bitterly, taking a sip of his wine.

His older brother had inherited everything and as a second son, Lan had been forced into the cavalry to make his own way in the world. Serving in the cavalry was a stepping stone for those of the nobility that could not inherit. After a successful term he would be eligible to enter public service, perhaps even as a local magistrate and begin to build a comfortable life for himself. The more successful his service and honors earned, the better the position he would be able to secure upon leaving the legions.

Cut off from the empire with a rebel army marching on Vrell, the prospects of surviving long enough to complete his term were looking remote and that was one of the reasons this council meeting was so important. Lan had to convince them that it was in their best interest to help defend the valley against the rebels. Without the valley's support, they might not be able to hold Vrell.

One of Vargus's daughters refilled his drink, pouring warmed wine from a heated jar. Beer was refilled from a tapped keg in the corner, behind the bar. She was exceptionally pretty, with a fine figure and Lan found his eyes lingering on her from time to time as she occasionally made the rounds refilling drinks.

"Thank you." The lieutenant smiled in a friendly sort of way at her as she finished. In return, he received a distasteful look, as if she had swallowed a bug, before she moved on, leaving him with a frown.

He let it go and chalked the attitude up to a reflection of the animosity generated by Captain Aveeno's actions. He shrugged, hoping this meeting would improve relations. He was proud of his service in the empire's legions and it bothered him that the people of the valley viewed the legionaries poorly, almost as enemies. Lan wished to prove worthy of the trust the captain had placed in his hands by having the negotiations succeed. However, it was becoming increasingly important to him to win these people over. The legions were here to protect these people and they had failed to do so. He was determined to make up for that failure.

"No doubt you will attempt to pay with imperial coinage," Vargus scoffed, waving a dismissive hand in the lieutenant's direction. "The empire has abandoned you boys and is not coming back. Your coin is worthless."

Lan stifled an angry response and instead reached into a pocket and pulled out an imperial gold talon. He made a show of examining it, before tossing it onto the table. The coin landed heavily on the wooden table top with a solid-sounding clink. "Is gold so worthless here in the valley?"

Bester looked up and actually smiled at the lieutenant, amusement dancing in his eyes. "No, it is not. Gold has value here."

"Then we can pay," Lan insisted firmly, leaving the coin out for all to see. "Though I respectfully suggest that it is in your interest to assist us…to work with us."

"Why is that?" Vargus demanded.

Lan's patience with the confrontational councilman was reaching its limit and he struggled to control a sharp retort. Instead, he took a deep breath, which he followed with a slow a sip of his wine before continuing.

Lan set his mug of wine down on the table. "I don't believe the rebels will view your previous support for the empire in a favorable light. Your people are bottled up in this valley. Without help, the castle may fall. If it comes to that, well… I think you can imagine what will likely happen to your people."

"We should never have supported the empire," Vargus snorted in disgust, glancing over at his fellow councilors.

Hief, a sour look on his face, nodded in agreement. "It was a mistake and now the legions have gone. We will pay for our shortsightedness with the blood of our families."

"The legions always come back," Lan said, eying Vargus and Hief before shifting his gaze to Quintus. "Help us to hold the castle! The legions will be back. Of that you can be sure."

"We are of the empire, or have you forgotten?" Bester asked in an appeal, shooting a look around at his fellow councilors. "We cannot abandon our roots and commitments so easily."

"Where has that gotten us?" Vargus retorted angrily, slamming an empty tankard down on the table, having just drained it. "We invited them into our valley. They have given us nothing but heartache. They don't even remember the Compact, let alone honoring it anymore, as is their responsibility!"

"Captain Stiger asked me to app—"

"Captain Stiger," Quintus interrupted. "I've heard a lot of this Captain Stiger. Why isn't he here? Why send you in his stead?"

Lan took another deep breath. He had never conducted a negotiation like this before. He well understood these men were angry with the empire and as such he was doing his level best to remain calm. He was also not sure what the Compact was. Perhaps it was some agreement the legions signed when the empire had annexed the valley. When he returned to the castle, he intended to ask Cannol.

"The captain offers his regrets...unfortunately he is in the field—"

"Can he stop them?" Bester asked, steering the subject away from rocky ground. "Can he stop the rebels before they get to Vrell?"

Lan thought carefully on his response, as all eyes turned to him and the tavern became deathly still. He briefly considered dissembling, but immediately discarded that thought.

Though it was no fault of the empire, these people felt that they had been betrayed. Trust had to be rebuilt. That was why he had to be straight with them. If he could rebuild that sense of trust, perhaps they would take steps to support the legions. Honesty was in order, no matter how distasteful the truth.

"No," the lieutenant said, after a very pregnant moment. "Captain Stiger cannot stop the rebel army. We simply do not have enough men. The rebels can only be delayed, hopefully long enough for winter to set in and snow to block the pass for the season."

A heavy silence seemed to have settled upon the tavern, broken only by the pop and crackle of the fire. Bester leaned back in his chair, breathing in deeply and exhaling heavily, cheeks puffed out. He exchanged looks with Vargus, whose anger had drained away and now looked weary.

"Then you mean to hold the rebels at the castle," Vargus said, more as a statement than a question, his gaze coming up to meet Lan's.

"That is part of the plan," Lan admitted, not wanting to reveal too much, or even mention the captain's defensive corridor. There was a chance that there were rebel sympathizers present. He could not take the risk of giving out too much information. "Captain Stiger will fall back upon the castle when he judges it practical. To hold beyond this winter and ensure the safety of the valley, we need your help and support."

"Son, just how large is this rebel army?" Quintus asked, running a hand through his hair.

"We believe the enemy's strength to be around twenty thousand strong. Perhaps more, perhaps less. Regardless, it is a substantial force."

"Twenty thousand!" Vargus exploded, sitting up in his chair. Several of those at the bar started talking to each other excitedly. Lan leaned back and took another sip of wine as the council degenerated into several side conversations with people from the bar interjecting their own thoughts and opinions. It seemed that things had finally slipped completely out of control and perhaps he had made a mess of the meeting. Lan finished his drink in one pull, not even bothering to taste the fine wine as he downed it.

"Lieutenant, would you mind excusing us for a few minutes?" Quintus asked after a bit, having called for quiet and received it. "I believe we should like very much to discuss your request amongst ourselves."

"Of course," Lan said graciously, pushing his chair back with his legs as he stood. Leaving the golden talon on the table, he grabbed his cloak from the wall and stepped outside.

After the warmth of the tavern, the cold night air struck him like a slap to the face. The lieutenant pulled his cloak tighter about himself as he stepped into the street and closed the door. Two oil lanterns hung to the sides of the door. The lanterns provided a dim patch of light by which to see a few feet out into the dirt street. Sergeant Mills, along with legionary Sulla, both of whom had been waiting outside, stood to attention and saluted. Lan returned the salute.

"That was quick," Mills commented ironically, relaxing. Lan had been with the councilors for well over two hours. "Time to go?"

"They desired to discuss matters amongst themselves," Lan said tersely as he kicked at a small stone with irritation. The street had once had a layer of crushed gravel, but time had seen the gravel either dispersed or ground down into the dirt.

The sergeant sighed and leaned back against the wall of the tavern, apparently content to wait. Waiting seemed to be a mandatory requirement for serving the empire. If you were not good at waiting uselessly about, sometimes for hours on end, a life in the legions was not for you. Lan chuckled to himself. Usually the reason more often than not for such interminable waits was for someone else to do their job so you could do yours.

Outside of the tavern, it was deathly quiet. With the sun well down and the moon up, the town for the most part had settled in for the night. Though Lan could not make out what they were saying, the muted voices of the councilors, sometimes raised, could be heard from inside. The debate, for that is what it seemed to be, continued for a long time.

Lan bit his lip. Usually such negotiations were handled by more senior officers, men who had much greater experience at this kind of thing. He was afraid he had made a terrible mess of things.

The lieutenant looked over at his horse, Storm, who was tethered to a hitching post a few feet away, along with the other two horses. It had been a long ride down from the castle and he was not looking forward to the journey back, in the dark. Riding at night was a dangerous business. It would be easy to miss a pothole or for his horse to make a misstep in the darkness. Still, he felt he had little choice. He needed to return to the castle as soon as possible. There was too much to do in preparing the castle for assault.

"A few days ago, these people might have ambushed and killed us out of hand," Mills comment idly. "From what I hear, I find it hard to believe they will be kind enough to help us defend them."

"Captain Stiger changed the dynamic," Lan responded wearily, stifling a yawn. He was beginning to feel the effects of the wine. "Besides, as I see it, they really have no other choice. Let us hope the fools can see what is before their eyes."

Mills grunted in reply.

Lan leaned against the wall of the tavern and waited, closing his eyes. He had heard more than enough talk to last him the night. Thankfully, Mills was silent for a time, though Lan thought he heard the sergeant mutter, "Bloody Stigers," under his breath. Time passed and the debate inside continued unabated...then...

"Sir," Mills called his attention, coming off the wall and nodding out into the darkness. A rider could be heard approaching. The sergeant's hand went to the pommel of his cavalry sword as he straightened up. Sulla did the same, until Lan waved both of them back, not wanting to create an incident that could prove the undoing of any hope for improved relations. Both men relaxed but remained watchful.

A young man rode up, emerging from the darkness and into the lantern light. He seemed surprised to see legionaries standing in front of the tavern and gave all three a suspicious look before dismounting. He had a military bearing about him and wore what looked like a gray service tunic under a heavy cloak. He seemed cocksure and though he did not wear armor, he was armed with what appeared to be a legionary short sword.

He tied up his horse at the hitching post and walked past the legionaries with steady purpose and entered the tavern, closing the door behind him. Lan looked over at Mills, who shrugged in reply. The debate that had been raging inside ceased the moment he entered.

A short time later, the young man emerged, tucking a piece of paper into a pocket at his waist. He gave the lieutenant a curt nod, untethered his horse from the post and mounted up with well-practiced ease. Without saying a word or sparing the legionaries a second glance, he wheeled his horse about, kicked her forward and rode off, the darkness swallowing up both rider and animal.

"I don't like that," Mills broke the silence uneasily. "I don't bloody like that at all."

"Neither do I," Lan admitted as the door to the tavern opened. He turned to find Councilor Hief looking out.

"Lieutenant," Hief said, fully opening the door. "We are ready for you."

The tavern seemed much warmer than before. The fire had been fed and crackled loudly. The other councilors were silent, though Vargus seemed angry. The man's face was red with what Lan surmised was sullen resentment and anger. No surprise there, Lan thought.

"Lieutenant," Quintus spoke formally for the group. "We have discussed your request. We are willing to begin discussions for a lasting agreement concerning how the garrison interacts with the valley. Councilman Bester will travel to the castle to the work out the details."

"That will be acceptable," Lan responded, relieved and becoming hopeful. Bester, as a supporter of the empire, seemed an easy man to work with.

"As to the supporting role you have requested," Quintus continued, "you must understand that the garrison has been harsh with our people..." Quintus held up a restraining hand as Lan made to protest. "I know you were not part of the garrison and that it appears evil was the root cause. Regardless, you are now part of the garrison and there are people we must speak with before we can in good conscience make a decision to render you the assistance you have requested...or even, for that matter, withhold it."

"I see," Lan said, grinding his teeth in frustration. Captain Stiger would not be pleased with this result.

"Do you?" Vargus demanded angrily, leaning forward and jabbing a finger at the lieutenant. "Do you know what your precious legionaries did to my daughter?"

"No, sir," Lan said, becoming wary. "I do not."

"Vargus..." Bester pleaded, shooting a nervous look in the lieutenant's direction and then back to the tavern proprietor. "Please. No."

"He needs to know," Vargus stated, barely able to control his rage. He fixed Lan with an intense gaze. "My daughter, the one pouring your wine...she was raped and beaten by three legionaries as she walked home on market day. That was just two months ago! My daughter! Raped by legionnaires...men who the empire supposedly sent here to protect us!"

The lieutenant did not flinch from the enraged father's gaze, but instead returned it, refusing to look away. This was not the work of his men and he saw no reason to apologize for it, though just the same, he was appalled and embarrassed that legionaries had done such a shameful thing. Lan broke the tavern-keeper's gaze as he saw Vargus's daughter, who had just finished refilling a drink, flee behind the bar and duck into the kitchen, her head down, clearly ashamed. The kitchen door banged closed. Lan stared at it for a moment, before turning back to the hurt father, whose look nearly broke his heart.

"Yes," Vargus continued breathing heavily, an anguished look of pain upon his face. "My daughter's name is Jenna and she is but one of many. The garrison took such liberties with our women and...children."

"Such behavior is unacceptable," Lan stated. "If you know the offenders' names, I will personally see that they are dealt with."

"Oh, you will, will you?" Vargus laughed harshly and looked over at Hief. "That is rich, really rich."

"Vargus," Bester pleaded again, looking concerned.

"Lieutenant," Vargus said ominously. "They have already been dealt with in a *permanent* manner. What would you say if I told you that I handled them myself?"

Lan was rocked by the man's words. His shock was followed by anger. By rights those men should have been judged by the legion and not subject to vigilante justice, no matter what they had done!

"Those three…" Vargus continued and seemed to struggle for a word before continuing, "shits…lie in a shallow grave."

Lan broke eye contact with Vargus and looked down at his own hands for a moment. He did not as yet have children. He had sisters and knew, without a doubt, that if something similar had happened to one of them, he would have done as Vargus had.

"I would have done the same," Lan admitted in a low voice, looking back up at Vargus, meeting the angry father's gaze. He needed their help, but the council also had to understand vigilante justice could not be accepted. "That said, I will not tolerate any future vigilante justice. Should a legionary cross the line, I expect you to report his transgression. I can promise he will face legion justice, which is not known for its mercy."

Vargus said nothing for a moment, as he continued to look intensely at Lan, then the heat seemed to leave him in a rush. Exhaling heavily, he leaned back in his chair and drummed his fingers on the table before speaking.

"This one has balls," Vargus commented to his fellow councilors before turning back to the lieutenant. "Lieutenant, I think I could almost like you…almost."

"Enough of this," Quintus ordered sternly, looking over at Vargus with a reproachful look. He then turned back to Lan. "Lieutenant, there are people we must speak to and consult before we can commit to any direct support. However, should you wish to pay our people for services rendered...we will not object. In fact, we will spread the word that you are paying for fair labor."

"We will give you an answer concerning our decision to fully support you or not...soon," Hief added with a note of finality.

He could understand it, considering what the valley had been through, particularly after hearing about Vargus's daughter. After a moment, he nodded in understanding. He had gotten something, which was better than nothing.

"You should also know that we have decided to mobilize our militia," Quintus added, almost as an afterthought.

"Militia?" Lan asked, attempting to hide his surprise and failing. He had not been aware that the valley had any type of military force. Neither Cannol nor any of the other garrison officers had mentioned one. Had the young man who had just left been part of that militia? Lan suspected so and that worried him. Surely the garrison officers would have mentioned a militia had they known one existed. This meant the council had concealed its existence, which was concerning. "The valley has a militia?"

"Yes," Quintus continued. "We have four hundred and eighty men currently under arms, with the ability to call up another four hundred and eighty should we feel the need to do so. We are not as helpless as we appear."

Lan was thoroughly stunned. Four hundred and eighty was the number of a full strength cohort. Though the empire had long since abandoned the cohort system in favor of companies and regiments, it meant that the valley's militia was infantry-based. He had to get a message to the captain as soon as possible with this news. Those men could be very useful to the defense of the castle. On the other hand, if the council decided to oppose the empire and side with the rebels, things could get dangerous.

"Lieutenant," Hief said, abruptly changing the subject. "Bester here told of the eagle. Is it true about Captain Stiger recovering the lost eagle?"

"It is," Lan replied, disconcerted at the abrupt turn of the conversation. "You know of the eagle and the 13th?"

"Son," Hief chuckled in a fatherly manner. "The legions have been garrisoning this valley for the last ten years. I ask you…how could we not have heard the tale of the famous 13th?"

Lan nodded. Of course they would have heard the tale of the Vanished. The 13th was all but legend and this being the region she was said to have been lost in, the legionaries from the garrison would have spoken about it.

"Do you believe the eagle is real thing?" Vargus demanded.

"I do," the lieutenant said.

"Do you believe it genuine, on your personal honor?" Hief questioned. The councilman leaned forward, seemingly very interested in the lieutenant's reply. *Why is my honor being called into question? What is going on here?*

"On my personal honor, I believe it to be the 13th's Eagle," Lan repeated. "Captain Stiger recovered the eagle in the company of an elven ranger and paladin of the High Father. There is no doubt in my mind that it is genuine."

The councilors glanced at each other. A silent communication seemed to pass between them, as if they had just confirmed something. Lan wanted to know what this was all about but feared that he could not come right out and ask.

He could not risk alienating these people. Captain Stiger had explicitly warned him about that. They badly needed to enlist the valley's support and Lan did not wish to rock the boat, particularly now that he knew they had a large militia at their disposal. He glanced once again at Vargus's marked forearms and knew with certainty where the scars had come from. Vargus had to be the commander of the militia.

"Why are you questioning my honor?" Lan asked, in the heat of the moment surprising himself at being so brash. Was it his supposition that Vargus was a military man that spurred him on? "Why is this so important to you?"

"Is it also true Captain Stiger is related to General Delvaris?" Vargus asked, ignoring Lan's question. There was no trace of the lingering anger in Vargus's voice. If anything, the man's voice seemed tinged with awe.

"The captain says it is true," Lan stated, knowing that his questions would remain unanswered unless he pressed the issue. He was unwilling to do so. "As he is a Stiger, I have no reason to question either his claim or his honor. Besides, the Delvaris name is not exactly venerated in the empire."

"As in only a fool would willingly lay claim to it?" Vargus barked out a laugh. "Lieutenant, I think I could almost like your captain too."

"Very well, lieutenant," Quintus said with a heavy breath that almost seemed to Lan one of relief. "You have given us a lot to discuss and consider. Councilman Bester will travel to the castle tomorrow to hammer out an agreement with you. We will also get back to you with our decision soon."

"Thank you for your time." Lan stood and shook hands with each councilor. Vargus, grip firm, held the handshake a moment longer than seemed necessary. Perhaps it was another test. Lan was tired and eager to start back to the castle. The meeting and wine had only added to his fatigue.

He grabbed his cloak and exited the tavern, intentionally leaving the golden talon behind.

The cold air struck him hard and he pulled his cloak tightly around him and closed the door. Mills and Sulla stood to attention, saluting. Lan pulled on his gloves. He looked up. The moon was high in the sky and it was becoming very cold.

"Mount up," Lan snapped. His breath frosted in the cold night air. They untethered their horses and he pulled himself up onto Storm, saddle leather creaking as he shifted position to get comfortable. Looking back on the tavern, he caught a glimpse of Vargus's daughter, Jenna, peeking out a second floor window and down into the street. Their eyes locked for a fraction of a second before she retreated from view. Lan felt sorrow for the poor girl. Perhaps, he considered, he could help make amends for what had been done to her. He decided to think on it. Lan pulled his horse around and gently nudged Storm into a slow, careful walk down the unlit street, headed out of town, his thoughts troubled, by the negotiations and Vargus's daughter.

CHAPTER SIX

MARCUS SAT CROSS-LEGGED on his camp blanket, which he had carefully laid out on the cold but dry ground of the scout camp. The rainy season was over. The ground was now firm and hard. Marcus and his team had cleared the camp of its carpet of autumn leaves and debris. They had made this secluded spot their home, at least for a precious few hours, as they rested and recovered.

The air was bitterly cold, with strong gusts of wind periodically blowing through the forest, stirring up the fallen leaves and shaking the trees. Even at a distance of two forested miles, they were far too close to the road to risk a fire. Instead, the scouts had only their blankets to rely on for warmth. It was a hardship to be sure, but such was the way with the legions. You either cut it or you did not. Those who could not were almost always weeded out during basic training and their initiation into legionary life.

Todd was taking his turn sleeping, snoring, while Davis and Marcus worked on manufacturing arrows. Though they received a regular supply, so active was their pace that they were always running short. It was the reason why each scout carried the tools to make their own.

Though arrows could be made from a number of woods, Eli insisted they make theirs from shoots of dogwood, which in the Sentinel Forest was difficult to locate, but not impossible. As a result, any free time that was not spent sleeping was generally devoted to the manufacture of spare arrows, a monotonous yet relaxing activity.

Neither spoke as they toiled away, cracking out arrow after arrow. While they worked, they were careful to keep watch and listen. They chipped away rough edges and smoothed shafts with small files, careful to make sure every shaft measured between twenty-four to twenty-seven inches in length. Once the shafts were ready, they were fitted with four-bladed iron heads. The fletching they were using came from a goose they had taken down the day before, in a small lake a few miles off the road. A week ago, the fletching had come from a pheasant that had made for some good eating. So proficient had they become that, upon completion, each arrow represented about ten minutes' labor and, if their aim was true, would account for one rebel.

Marcus had selected the location for the scout camp. It was an isolated spot, located in a stand of thick brush, nearly at the base of the foothills, presaging the mountain range that surrounded Vrell. Though the scouts felt relatively safe, they regularly paused in their work to listen, straining for any hint of the enemy. Eli had taught them to be vigilant.

"One who is careful lives to see the next dawn," Eli was fond of saying. "One who is careless can only be lucky, but is not wise."

The enemy skirmishers had grown in number over the past few days. At times, they were thicker than fleas on a mangy hunting dog. The result of such numbers was predictable. The scouts were pushed farther and farther from the road and away from the rebel column of march, meaning that their fight was now with the enemy's skirmishers.

Marcus and his team had increasingly found themselves struggling to get within hearing distance of the rebel column, let alone missile range. Rebel scout teams had also grown in number, quality and boldness. It had been a rude shock to learn these men were well-trained, aggressive and bold. There had already been several savage and brutal encounters where one party had stumbled across the other.

Marcus sighed heavily as he worked to smooth out a shaft. He had lost his first man today. Mosch had been his friend and was one of the originals from the 85th whom Eli had trained. He had been a good scout and someone Marcus felt he could rely upon to do his job. It pained Marcus to think that his friend had fallen. Worse yet, they had been forced to leave his body behind, pierced by an arrow through the thigh. The arrow had torn through an artery and in moments his friend had bled out.

Marcus felt guilty about not retrieving the body, as he knew that Mosch, a follower of the old gods, had wanted his remains to be cremated according to his beliefs. Marcus had considered slipping back after nightfall to attempt to recover the body, but Eli had expressly forbidden it, saying that the gods would understand.

A life in the legions accustomed one to loss and Marcus had seen men die before. Death was always a close companion. However, this was different. Mosch was the first man Marcus had lost under his command. He felt as if it were his fault, although he knew that Mosch had just been unlucky. Everyone understood that the gods could be fickle, one moment dispensing luck, the next taking it away.

Marcus needed to put this behind him, for in a few hours, he and his team would be abandoning this camp and pulling back to rejoin Captain Stiger and the main body, which had come up in preparation for striking at the rebels.

Ever since the rebels had pushed out large numbers of skirmishers and brought up better quality scouts, their advance had sped up considerably, eating up the miles with each passing day. The time for harassment raids, designed to sow terror, chaos and confusion, had passed. Hard fighting lay ahead.

Captain Stiger had ordered most of the scouts back to the main body. A handful under the direct command of Eli had been excluded from this order. These few would hit the enemy one last time. Their purpose was to cause a gap to form between marching rebel formations so that the lead formation would become isolated and without ready support. To accomplish this, Eli was going to hit the second marching formation just as the rebels were preparing to break camp and start the day's march. The raid would be prolonged and pressed, making it much more dangerous for the scouts involved. Marcus felt guilty that he was not going to be with them, but orders were orders. Besides, he was confident the captain would have some hot work for him and his boys.

Davis finished and looked up expectantly at his corporal, who was carefully inspecting his last arrow for flaws. Satisfied, Marcus placed the arrow in his quiver and returned his tools to his bag.

"I will take watch," Davis said quietly, breath steaming in the frigid air. "You need sleep more than I."

Marcus nodded gratefully and went over to where Todd slept. He laid out his blanket and then placed his bow, quiver and short sword within arm's reach before lying down fully clothed. He used a rolled-up, empty woolen sack for a pillow and then wrapped the other half of the blanket around him. He shivered despite the blanket, which wasn't thick enough.

Another uncomfortable night, Marcus thought morosely. Losing Mosch today had dampened his spirits. He understood he could not allow it to keep his spirits down.

Sleeping on the cold, hard ground without the benefit of a warming fire sounded awful, but in truth it was really not so bad. Marcus thought back to the scared kid living moment to moment in the wretched slums of Mal'Zeel. He had not known where his next meal would come from or who would try to knife him for what little he had. Life on those streets had been hard.

This is much better than I had it in the capital, he thought, gazing up through the sparse canopy at the silent stars as Todd continued to snore. The priests of Bhallen taught that the stars were suns, very much like their own, just much farther away. Marcus figured it was like the ships that anchored off the coast for the night. You could see the ship's light, there to warn others, small in size, but the ship was there just the same. Those strange suns had worlds of their own, the priests had claimed. Marcus had always found that concept difficult to believe. Staring up at the heavens, he wondered. *What if they were right?*

Is it possible those worlds are like this one? Marcus's eyelids grew heavy as the exhaustion slowly took him. *Or are they very different?*

He yawned deeply and turned on his side. He was soon fast asleep, snoring softly alongside Todd.

CHAPTER SEVEN

FORMED FOR BATTLE, Stiger stood slightly behind a double line of men over two hundred strong. Half were from the 85th and the other half were Lieutenant Brent's boys from the 33rd. Breath visible in the frigid early morning air, the men were silent and grim-faced. Shields were held to their sides, bottoms resting on the ground. Swords remained in their scabbards until the order was given to draw.

The sun, rising to their backs, broke through a cloud and shone down on the silent formation. Armor, freshly polished, glinted brightly under the sunlight as a cold gust of wind stirred the men's red cloaks and caused the banners to flap slightly. Behind the formation, and in front of Stiger, stood the standard-bearers for the 33rd and the 85th. The Tiger pelt draped across the 85th's standard made it stand out. When the enemy saw it, it would be remembered.

From his position, Stiger could see the entire line.

For a moment he found it difficult to breathe. The men looked simply magnificent. They had that perfect appearance, the stuff that heroic tales and legends were made of. It was an image that children and glory-seeking officers dreamed of when they thought on war. Those more seasoned and experienced, such as Stiger himself, knew better, and yet the captain still felt his heart stir in pride. These were his men, even those of the 33rd, and it was his honor to lead them forth into battle.

Stiger sucked in a deep breath, breaking the spell of the moment and stepped through the formation to the front. He walked along the line, inspecting the men with his critical eye as he went. Lieutenant Brent followed two steps behind, nervous but quiet. Occasionally Stiger would stop to straighten a piece of armor or tug on a strap. He was putting on a show for the men, demonstrating that he had not a care in the world other than their perfection.

He glanced over at Brent as he conducted the inspection. This was Brent's first real action and Stiger well understood the wild mix of emotions the man was feeling, from dread to excitement and back yet again. Brent showed promise. In the coming days, he would likely be on his own, leading men into battle. He had to inspire confidence. So, Stiger was making efforts to model for the lieutenant how a proper officer should conduct himself prior to going into battle. He hoped Brent was paying attention.

"Lieutenant," Stiger snapped. "If you will, kindly inspect the second rank."

"Yes, sir," Brent responded with a sharp salute, stepped by the first rank and set about his inspection. Stiger had intentionally given the young officer something to do to take his mind off of what was coming.

If only I could distract myself so easily, Stiger thought to himself, glancing in the direction of the road.

Stiger had positioned the men just over the crest of a steep hill, on the reverse side, away from the Vrell Road and hidden from view. The crest of the hill was roughly two hundred yards from the road, which traveled at this point between two steep hills. This small stretch of road was the place Stiger had selected and concentrated his men for his first powerful strike at the enemy.

Having handed the rest of the inspection off to the lieutenant, the captain placed himself in the center of the formation, behind the line but in front of the standard-bearers. The men were as ready as he could make them and in only minutes, they would be going in. The rest was up to the gods... *And my planning,* he added to himself.

"They should be coming shortly," Brent stated the obvious, breaking in on Stiger's thoughts as he stepped through the ranks, having finished the inspection. There was a nervous edge to his voice. Stiger understood that the lieutenant was filling space to avoid thinking on what was ahead. Nothing in Brent's experience could truly prepare him for what was coming, which was also true for many of the lieutenant's men. That was one of the reasons the legions drilled hard and continually. When untested and even tested men were faced with the most difficult of circumstances, they tended to fall back on their training, which at times had been literally beaten into them.

"I would expect so," Stiger responded quietly but firmly. He was also feeling the uneasy tension that presaged a fight. The last-minute worrying he suffered through was a torment in and of itself.

The rebel advance force was made up of what was estimated to be around five to six enemy companies, numbering somewhere over a thousand men, perhaps even two. It was difficult to get an exact count because the rebels did not march as a legion would, but instead walked in large groups and bunches. Regardless, Stiger was outnumbered and the 'what ifs' had begun tormenting him as he reviewed his plan, looking for oversights or mistakes.

He had devised a three-pronged ambush, the first of which was designed to bring the rebel column to a complete halt, pinning it in place at its most forward point. Then he intended to chop it neatly in half, cutting off and trapping around five hundred rebels, which he would then work to eliminate. To accomplish this, he had to force the other half of the rebel column back, or at least hold it off long enough to complete the destruction of the isolated and trapped part, before retiring farther back down the road toward Vrell and the start of his defensive corridor.

The job of bringing the rebel column to a halt had fallen to Lieutenant Ikely, Stiger's second in command. Blocking the road ahead, Ikely had a force that numbered around two hundred and was made up of the other half of the 85th, along with the rest of the 33rd. The captain had intentionally mixed companies with his own. This was to give the untested 33rd some additional backbone the first time they went into action, for the captain knew he could rely upon his own company to stand firm.

Brent's men, like the others of the garrison, had received a refresher training program over the last few weeks, but it was not as thorough as the one Stiger had put the 85th through. The captain hoped it had been enough to remind them of who they were. Only the test of battle would tell him more about the men of the 33rd.

Ikely's orders were to hold, no matter the cost. To give him every advantage possible, Ikely was dug in behind a fortified line that cut clear across the road. His position would be difficult and costly to overcome. When the rebel advance parties encountered Ikely's line, they would be presented with a ten-foot trench and behind that a twelve-foot earthen rampart topped with a wooden barricade for added protection.

The rebels would be compelled to halt, scout Ikely's position and then take time to make a decision on what to do. In Stiger's estimation, the rebels would either deploy to assault Ikely's position or attempt to flank it. The defensive line not only blocked the road, but also stretched into the forest on both sides. Like the others they had built, it ran a full quarter mile in length. To make the job more complex for the enemy, caltrops had been laid in the forest around the edges of the defensive line.

Whatever the rebel commander decided to do, whether it was a direct assault or a flanking movement, would eat up time. Even if he just sat there and watched Ikely in an indecisive sort of way, it suited Stiger just fine. It all came down to time and this was something Stiger did not intend to give the enemy.

On the other hill, opposite from Stiger's position, the captain had positioned another two hundred under the command of lieutenants Banister and Peal. This force was made up of the 95th Imperial Foot and the remnants of Captain Aveeno's command. They were similarly hidden on the reverse side of their hill and out of view from the rebels.

The central part of Stiger's plan was to keep the enemy from discovering his hidden assault prongs. The captain had unleashed nearly all of his scouts, along with some extra men to work the sides of the road, beginning about a half mile before the ambush point. These would have already directly engaged the rebel skirmishers, and pinned them down, sucking them into a protracted fight for control of the flanks. If it worked, which it seemed to have done, the rebel column of infantry would arrogantly continue to march forward, oblivious to the fact that with every step forward, they were pulling farther and farther ahead of their protective skirmish screen. This would deprive the enemy commander of his eyes, allowing both of Stiger's ambush prongs to go unnoticed and undetected until it was too late. Stiger was waiting for the enemy column marching by on the other side of the hill to come to a halt. When it halted, he would know they had encountered Ikely's line.

Since the enemy had only ever encountered harassment attacks, Stiger hoped their commander would not suspect a larger ambush lying in wait along his flanks. Ikely's fortified line was also meant to distract. He wanted the enemy commander's attention focused exclusively on cracking Ikely's line and not thinking on his flanks. Why come out and fight when you had a perfectly good fortified defensive position to hold? Regardless, Stiger would not give him very much time to think about the risk to his flanks.

Stiger held a second, smaller force, just a handful of scouts, in reserve. He would commit these when the enemy column came to a halt. These few, according to Eli, were the best of his best. Stiger would use them to strike the enemy directly to the front of his position. Their job was to harass the halted column until they provoked a response.

Stiger expected the enemy, deprived of skirmishers, to deploy to force the scouts back and away from the road and up the hill toward his position. When the enemy pushed, Stiger had instructed the scouts to give ground grudgingly, fighting the entire way...until they reached the crest of the hill. It was at this point they were to break and run in a panic, drawing the enemy after them and right into Stiger's waiting ambush, which would, at that point, push off hard, crest the hill and then drive right down to the road below. He hoped to catch the enemy disordered and unprepared.

Banister and Peal were to watch for Stiger's prong to kick off down the hill. Once Stiger was committed, they were to advance down their side of the ambush. The idea was for both assault prongs to slam into the rebels along the road, overwhelming them as the two pincers snapped closed.

For better or worse, Stiger was committed. He had no other choice, no matter what happened. Although the rebel force he was about to attack was most likely double his size, they were strung out along several miles of road and the captain meant to hit them smack in the middle. The ambush spot was narrow and confined, allowing little room for the rebels to deploy their entire force, while Stiger would be able to concentrate his.

To further pad his chances, Stiger had dispatched Eli with the rest of the scouts to attack the next rebel formation, farther back along the road. Eli was to time it so that he hit them right as they were preparing for the day's march. In this way, Stiger hoped to create a large gap to form between rebel marching formations. With luck, it would work and the second rebel marching formation would not be in a position to render assistance to the first when Stiger sprung his ambush.

And so Stiger worried, concealing his anxiety from the men. The plan sounded complex but was in reality fairly simple…as long as everything went according to plan. Stiger had seen the Rivan pull a similar move to great effect, and the captain saw no reason not to borrow from them. So far, things seemed to be working as expected, which was unusual and concerning, for in war nothing ever went according to plan.

Stiger's attention was drawn to the crest of the hill, where a scout appeared. The scout made his way slowly and carefully over the crest so that he was not seen by the enemy below. Once over and shielded from view, he spotted the captain and hurried over to him. The men in the ranks stepped aside and allowed him through.

"Sir, beg to report. The enemy column has come to a halt. I reckon company strength, just over the other side of the hill. They have dropped packs and yokes. I didn't see any skirmishers and they don't look like they are expectin' any trouble either, sir," Todd said, saluting fist to chest.

"Corporal." Stiger turned toward Scout Corporal Marcus, who stood waiting patiently with a group of five scouts. They had arrived a few hours ago and were critical to the plan succeeding. Wearing leathers and boots and carrying short bows, they contrasted starkly. "Take your men in."

Marcus began to move even before the captain had finished speaking. He and his men stepped through the ranks and climbed the short distance to the top of the hill. In moments they were over the top and gone from view.

It won't be long now, Stiger thought grimly. He forced himself to project a calm countenance for the benefit of the men. As was his custom before going into battle, he bowed his head and offered a brief prayer to the High Father, asking for a blessing of success and a personal request to spare as many of his men as possible. He then made sure to commend his spirit into the hands of the High Father.

Prayer complete, he glanced once again along his double line of men to make sure everything was in order. The trees in the step-off area had been intentionally cut back to allow the men to form an uninterrupted line in preparation for the attack. Once Stiger gave the order to push off and his men reached the crest of the hill, they would be back in the forest again, where the trees had been left as they were. The tree line was bound to break up his formation. However, Stiger was counting on surprise to counter the disorganization the forest would inflict upon his assault line.

He tightened the straps on his helmet so that they bit into his skin. Nothing could be heard from the other side of the hill, where his scouts had undoubtedly gone in, striking at the unsuspecting enemy as soon as they were in range. The minutes crawled by and then, suddenly, Scout Corporal Marcus appeared on the crest of the hill, bow in hand. He turned and fired two arrows in rapid succession back down the other side. The rest of the scouts began to appear on the crest. They paused briefly to loose a smattering of arrows. The rebels could now be heard, crashing through the forest as they neared the crest, along with a lone agonized scream as an arrow bit home. It sounded to Stiger as if a large number were charging up the hill.

"Draw swords!" Stiger ordered, pulling his own out with a hiss. He felt the familiar tingle coming and going so quickly it was a wonder he had not simply imagined it. Up and down the line, his men drew steel. Stiger glanced down at his sword and wondered if it would speak today. *Well?* he asked it silently. The sword remained silent.

"Front rank!" Stiger called loudly. "Shields front!" Instantly, the shields of those men in the front rank snapped up from the ground and were presented forward.

"Here they come, boys," Stiger called in a strong, steady voice that was filled with confidence and steel. The sound of the enemy crashing through the forest grew louder. "Stand strong! Stand tall! Fight like Tigers!"

The scouts bolted from the crest, appearing to run in a mad panic. The legionaries in the ranks stepped aside, parting their shields to let them through. Once safely through the lines, breathless from their exertions, the scouts turned back toward the crest of the hill, bows nocked and ready.

First one, then two and abruptly a large number of rebels, perhaps as many as a hundred, appeared on the crest with a roar, charging over the top in headlong pursuit. The great mass came to an abrupt and uncertain halt, having emerged into the clearing to find a heavy line of imperial legionaries waiting, shields at the fore.

Stiger knew that his men presented an impressive and shocking sight. A handful of rebels, caught up in the moment, continued to charge right into the shield wall, where they crashed upon the shields with solid thuds and explosive grunts. Those foolish few were rapidly cut down.

"Tigers, advance!" Stiger roared at his men, for even though they were mixed with men from the 33rd, in the captain's eyes all were Tigers today. The nervousness and tension left him in a rush, as it always did when the moment arrived. Grim-faced, he was intent on doing his duty. He would teach these rebels a lesson they would not soon forget.

"HAAAAH," the legionaries roared as they began a slow and steady march to the crest, just feet away. One veteran began to rap his sword upon the inside of his shield in a strong steady rhythm. In seconds the entire formation was rapping their swords in a steady, ominous beat. More rebels appeared on the crest of the hill. These also stopped, standing around in shock, uncertain what to do.

"HAAAAH!" The legionaries shouted again, this time louder. The distance between the two groups closed rapidly, with the steady tromp of many feet in unison and the ominous beat of sword on shield. Arrows began to whiz over the legionaries' heads. Two rebels fell, each clutching at arrow shafts that protruded from their chests. The advance continued along with the steady, ominous beat.

At first, a single rebel turned and fled, disappearing back over the crest of the hill. Shortly, he was followed by another and another and yet another. In a great mass, the rebels turned and ran. The crest of the hill, which moments before had been chock full, was now bare.

A handful of heartbeats later, Stiger and his men reached the crest. The forest spread out before them and ran right down to the road, around two hundred yards away. Crashing through the trees and undergrowth, the rebels were fleeing full-tilt for the road. Men ran, pushed past others, shoving their fellows aside in a bid to reach safety. A number, having caught a foot, fell, only to scramble back up and in mad panic continue their flight down the hill. Those rebels who had still been climbing stopped, shocked at the sight of their fellows crashing back through the forest toward the perceived safety of the road. The advancing legionary line came into view. These rebels hesitated a moment in disbelief and then they, too, turned and fled.

Stiger's men started over the crest and began to advance slowly and carefully down the hill, stepping around trees and brush, each man trying to remain in position, in line. Sergeants and corporals called out to specific men, ordering them to close up or keep up. No matter how hard the men tried, the trees rapidly began to break up Stiger's formation. The captain well knew it would only become worse the farther they advanced down the hill, eventually making any shield wall impractical, at least until they reached the road and could reform.

Taking in the rebels crashing down the hill in a mad dash, the captain understood what must be done, but that did not mean he had to like it. The rebels were running for the safety of the road and the momentum of the pursuit had to be kept up. Otherwise the enemy might reform. When Stiger's disorganized line of legionaries emerged from the forest, he might be met with a strong rebel line and some very difficult fighting.

"Charge!" Stiger roared, hating himself for giving the order. Instantly the men roared a battle cry and, breaking ranks, began moving down the hill at a much quicker pace. Careful to make sure that neither sword nor shield became entangled in the brush, they made their way down toward the road.

"Hit 'em hard, boys!" Stiger called, moving rapidly down the hill, his men screaming their war cries at the enemy as they ate up what remained of the slope down to the road. Following shortly behind his men, Stiger turned slightly to Brent, who looked anxious but at the same time caught up in the moment.

"When we get down there, it's going to be chaos," Stiger shouted at the lieutenant, dodging around a tree. "By the gods, keep your head and look for trouble spots, then take initiative and get yourself involved. Battles are won by the officers keeping our heads and providing direction. Understand me?"

"Yes, sir," Brent replied nervously, voice tinged by the excitement of the moment and the pent-up release of the stress he had been feeling. His eyes were a little wild, but he swallowed and nodded his understanding. "I will keep my head, sir. I swear it!"

"Good man," Stiger shouted over the din of the men's battle cries and continued down the hill, careful of where he placed his feet and shield. It would not do for the men to see their captain trip and fall like some clumsy fool.

It was then that Stiger's men reached the road and slammed into the rest of the enemy column. Surprised at the sudden appearance of their fleeing comrades and even more shocked at the roaring hoard of legionaries who came charging out of the forest, they backed up, unsure what to do. They devolved instantly into a terrified mob, as the legionaries tore into the column. A good number simply threw down their arms and ran up the opposite hill in an

attempt to escape. Others, in small groups led by officers
and sergeants, kept their heads, drew swords and fought
grimly, for only two fates waited them at the hands of the
legionaries, death or life as a slave, if they were lucky enough
to be captured.

Men screamed, shouted and cursed. There were cries
of fear, rage, excitement, ecstasy, triumph and agony.
Above it all was the unmistakable clash of sword on sword
or sword on shield. There seemed to be fighting everywhere as the captain emerged from the tree line. A rebel,
seeing an officer, charged straight at the captain, screaming madly, battle-crazed. Stiger pulled his shield up and
slammed it forward into the rebel's body, shield boss
catching the man square in the chest with an explosive
grunt. Stiger felt the blow communicated painfully to his
arm. The shock of the blow forced the air from the rebel's
lungs and the man's sword clattered uselessly along the
edge of the captain's shield. Stiger pulled the shield aside
slightly and stabbed the dazed rebel in the stomach, giving
it a good, vicious twist before yanking the blade back. The
man choked in agony as his stomach was torn open and
his guts spilled to the ground in a heap at his feet. The
rebel dropped his sword, staring in shock at his innards,
which hung down to the dirt of the road. Stiger slammed
his shield into the man once more. He dropped like a
stone and did not stir.

Breathing heavily, and perspiring despite the cold, the
captain took a step back and tried to make sense of the fight.
Most of the fighting had moved past him, his legionaries carried forward a few feet by the impetus of their charge even
as the rebels recoiled back. There were several small groups
of determined-looking rebels who had banded together and
were desperately struggling against the better-armed and

armored legionnaires. Stiger's men were methodically cutting them to pieces.

An arrow whizzed by the captain's head, striking a rebel in the back as the man was attempting to flee the battlefield. Stiger turned and saw Marcus, along with another scout, peppering targets of opportunity.

"Corporal," Stiger shouted, waving his sword to get the scout's attention. "Shoot at the organized groups!"

Marcus nodded, scanned the chaos and picked out a group of men who had decided to stand and fight. This group was trading blows with several legionaries. Within seconds, Marcus and the other scouts moved closer, shooting arrows into them, careful not to hit friendlies.

Stiger looked up and down the road toward Vrell, studying the battle as it expanded and grew as the combat spread out across a wider area. He had attacked along small stretch of the rebel column and had effectively sliced it neatly in two. The enemy in front and behind were clear of the fighting and as of yet remained untouched. They looked surprised and shocked at the sudden development before them. Stiger knew it was only a matter of time before they overcame their shock. Their officers would soon begin organizing their men and, if he was not careful, things could get sticky.

A rebel made a break from the press. He saw the captain blocking his path to escape, and charged forward, sword raised to strike at the enemy officer before him. Stiger made to brace himself for the attack and raised his shield. At the last second, the captain calmly stepped aside, catching the rebel off balance. Stiger stabbed the man deep in the side. With no armor, his sword had no difficulty penetrating, punching easily through the man's leathers. Warm blood exploded over Stiger's sword arm and shoulder. Stiger's sword grated off bone as the rebel's momentum carried him a few steps by the captain. He collapsed in a heap. Stiger stepped up and stabbed the rebel in the throat to make sure the man would not rise again.

The captain turned back to the chaos of the fight. He had to bring order to this mess and he had to do it sooner rather than later. He looked around for Brent to help him begin ordering the men. The lieutenant, who had been with him just moments before, was nowhere to be seen.

Stiger noted that with every passing second there seemed fewer rebels on their feet. The slaughter was terrible to witness and appeared very one-sided, at least until Stiger noticed a handful of legionaries down, their scarlet cloaks standing out. Some were wounded and writhed in agony, others were still and unmoving.

"Sergeant," Stiger called to Blake, who was just a few feet away. The captain put the wounded and dead out of mind. He would worry about the cost later. The sergeant finished off a rebel and seemed absorbed in the moment, slamming his shield into another, who fell backwards and was stabbed by a legionary to the sergeant's right. The man screamed as two more legionaries stepped forward and dispatched him under a flurry of jabbing blades.

"That man was mine!" Blake roared, enraged at the legionaries. "Go find your own!"

"Sergeant," Stiger shouted again, finally catching the man's attention. Blake stepped back and over to the captain, breathing heavily. The sergeant's face and chest was covered in blood. "Are you okay?"

Blake looked down at himself. He cracked a grin at the captain. "Someone else's!"

"Start organizing the men," Stiger ordered, relieved the sergeant was uninjured. "We need a rear guard along the road and another up ahead. It won't take the bastards long to get their act together and pinch us."

Blake nodded, turned and physically grabbed corporal Beni, who had just killed a rebel not two feet away, and began shouting orders at him. Together the two began swearing and shoving men about, getting those near at hand organized as the fighting on this portion of the road started to peter out. Two lines began to form, one up the road and one down it, as the corporals, sergeants and Stiger began the work of restoring order.

The last of the rebels broke and made a run for it, rushing up the opposite hill in a bid to escape, with a number of legionaries hot on their heels. The corporals and sergeants shouted and cursed at the men to get them to come back. Most sheepishly listened, others caught up in the excitement of the moment continued.

Looking around, Stiger was elated. He had scored a quick success at minimal cost. Still, he knew he had only cut the enemy column in half and there was more yet to do. He was in a dangerous position and needed to act fast to control it before the rebels could take his initiative away. The facts were simple. One portion of the rebel column was now isolated and trapped against Ikely's and Stiger's position. The other portion in the direction away from Vrell could either attack or fall back. Stiger looked up the road away from Vrell. An enemy company was forming lines not more than two hundred yards away. This was not good. They did not look like they intended to fall back.

"Right then, Corporal Marcus," Stiger shouted over to the corporal, pointing with his bloodied sword at the rebel company. "Get your scouts together and start putting fire on that rebel company. Don't give the bastards a chance to breathe!

"Form up!" Stiger shouted at those not already in the battle line. "Damn you! I want a line here yesterday or you are all on report! You will be digging shit out of the latrines for a month...so help me! Form up!"

The enemy company would shortly be ready to move forward and Stiger only had around thirty men formed to face at least two hundred. The sergeants and corporals were working frantically to turn the disordered mob of legionaries into two ordered lines, one facing toward Vrell and the other away in the direction of the enemy company. Legionnaires were spread out all across the battlefield, exhausted from their charge and fight, but elated over their sudden victory. There was even some looting going on, which enraged Stiger further and yet slowly the rear guard was becoming stronger as more and more men joined it.

Stiger wondered what was happening with the enemy in the direction of Vrell. From what he could see, the rebels there still looked to be disordered. Should they manage to get organized, Stiger could find himself getting hit from both sides at the same time. It could get ugly very fast. Sergeant Blake was actively forming the line in that direction, which left Stiger to handle the immediate threat from the rear.

It was at that moment he realized, with no small amount of surprise, that Lieutenant Peal and Banister's force was missing! They had not yet arrived. They were supposed to have gone in when he did. He looked up the hill in their direction and saw nothing.

What in the Seven Levels happened to them? Stiger asked himself as he wiped blood from his sword on the tunic of a dead rebel.

A scream of pain drew Stiger's attention back to the rebel company. There was no time to worry about Peal and Banister. With deadly accuracy, Marcus and the other scouts had begun shooting arrows into the rebel company. Faced with a growing line of legionaries and being taken under missile fire, the rebels looked to Stiger, uncertain. He had the feeling that if he pushed at them a bit they might collapse.

Stiger shot a glance at his line. He figured he had around seventy men in a single line facing an entire rebel company. Stiger's strength was deceptive due to the line's length, and lack of a second rank. It made the legionaries look more numerous than they actually were. The force he wanted to destroy was the one behind him, trapped by Ikely's command. To get to them, he needed to deal with this threat first.

"Prepare to advance!" Stiger roared, at his legionaries, who seemed startled by the order. "Forward!"

Surprised or not, the men obediently started forward toward the rebels.

"Shields front!" Stiger roared, falling in slightly behind the men. "Tighten up that line there! We're gonna push them, boys! We gonna push these bastards off the field and back where they came from!"

"HAAAAH!" The legionaries roared as loud as they could. "HAAAAH!"

With each slow, methodical step, the two lines came closer together. As the distance closed, rebels continued to fall to the scouts' missile fire. A few seconds later, the missile fire ceased as the scouts loosed the last of their arrows.

Stiger glanced back to check on Blake and was relieved to see that the sergeant had a solid double line facing the other way, prepared to deal with any threat from that direction should it materialize. Stiger spied Lieutenant Brent with the sergeant. Satisfied that things were well in hand, the captain turned back to the fight he was about to enter.

"Lock shields!" Stiger shouted as they approached to within just a handful of feet of the enemy. The shield wall went up with a resounding thunk.

The rebel officers and sergeants were screaming orders at their men in an attempt to steady them and keep them ordered. A few took nervous steps backward. The rebels were armed with a wide variety of swords, no armor and, worse, no shields. Outnumbered or not, Stiger hoped this rabble would be no match for the heavily-armored legionnaires.

A second or two before the two formations could close, the rebel ranks collapsed as their morale broke. The rebels turned and fled in panic, throwing down their swords and casting aside their packs and anything else that might hold them back. Another rebel company, which Stiger had not seen, had been formed up directly behind this one. They, too, dropped their weapons and ran.

Stiger's eyes widened. Beyond, the road was clear. Eli had been successful!

"On them!" Stiger roared and his men surged forward, cutting down all they caught, which was not as easy as it seemed. They were heavily encumbered by their armor, shields and swords, and the rebels were not.

Stiger watched the rout for a moment and grinned. It would be some time before those two enemy companies could be reformed. He could now focus his attention on destroying the rebels trapped between him and Ikely's line. Unlike this bunch, they had nowhere to run.

He turned around to see what was transpiring on the other end of the road that had become a battlefield. Where a few minutes before it seemed as if the enemy had not been organized on that part of the field, he saw Brent and Blake leading a holding action against a large, organized rebel force. The fighting looked desperate and hard as the enemy struggled to break through the thin formation of legionaries.

The enemy commander must have realized what had happened and turned at least two entire companies around. In desperation he had flung them at the legionaries. One of the rebel companies was attempting to flank, and Brent had formed his men into a hasty box. He would need help and soon, Stiger grasped, or this entire venture might come to naught. As he was about to turn back to try to reform his men a second time, there came a thunderous shout, which exploded from the hill to his left. The second prong of his ambush, late to the party, was finally moving!

Lieutenant Banister, waving his sword in the air, was leading the men down the hill and through the forest toward Brent's position. Stiger breathed a huge sigh of relief as he watched the charging legionaries slam into the surprised rebels. With the second force of the assault prong having arrived, it was clear there was no longer any hope for the trapped enemy to break out.

After a moment, Stiger turned back to look for a corporal. His men were chasing the routed rebels up the road, cutting down and slaughtering any they caught. There was no way they could be easily reformed.

"We need to get the men reformed," Stiger yelled, having caught Corporal Durggen's attention. "We need to reform the men. I want a line to hold this spot long enough to destroy the enemy we have trapped."

"Yes, sir," Durggen acknowledged. "I will see to it."

Stiger nodded, turned and jogged toward the fight.

CHAPTER EIGHT

L IEUTENANT IKELY STABBED forward with his sword, striking a rebel solidly in the chest. The man was unarmored and the sword penetrated, digging deeply with the thrust, slipping between two ribs. Warm blood washed down Ikely's sword and onto his hand and arm, with spray splattering across his face. He jerked the sword back and with a scream, the man fell over the edge of the barricade into the defensive trench below.

Almost immediately, another took the man's place, climbing up and over the edge of the barricade. This rebel, screaming madly, hurled himself bodily forward and over the barricade, toppling to the dirt of the rampart. Ikely pushed forward and struck out, sword taking him in the side as he stood. Groaning, the rebel dropped his sword, fell to his hands and knees and tried to crawl away, mortally wounded. Ikely kicked him roughly in the arm, knocking him down and then stabbed again, this time in the lower back. The sword slid deep and the rebel screamed. Ikely yanked his sword out, and brought his arm back to strike again.

The body of a legionary crashed heavily into the lieutenant's side, knocking him roughly backward and ripping his shield away. A sword lashed out before Ikely could recover and jabbed him painfully in the chest. His armor deflected the blow, but the powerful nature of the strike stole his wind. Shaken, Ikely staggered a couple of steps. In a growing haze, he attempted to parry the next blow, which he barely managed. He took another step backward, struggling to breathe, hoping to gain some room and recover before it was too late. But his opponent, a huge man, was on him in a flash. From behind him, Ikely could see additional rebels making it over the barricade.

Ikely's vision began to gray while he struggled desperately to fend off the attack. He missed a parry and took a hard slashing strike to his shoulder, his left arm instantly going numb. Once again, his segmented armor saved him from a killing blow, but it was still agonizing. Unable to catch his breath, he collapsed to his knees. In desperation, he struck out with his sword at the rebel's unprotected legs. The man jumped with a curse, easily avoiding the clumsily swung blow.

Abruptly, the lieutenant's lungs began working and he could breathe sweet, fresh cool air. The rebel roared a battle cry and struck again. Still on his knees, Ikely brought his sword up to block the blow, which rang loudly with the meeting of the blades. The blow was so powerful that Ikely almost lost his grip on his sword. His hand was left tingling from the impact. As the man pulled back to strike again, the lieutenant pulled his dagger out with his free hand and as the rebel drew back to strike, Ikely let it fly. The blade struck the unarmored man in the chest with a meaty thwack. A shocked expression came over his opponent's face as he looked down on the dagger protruding from his chest. The big rebel staggered backward as Ikely came to his feet. The lieutenant lunged forward with his sword and stabbed the rebel in the neck, blade punching right through and exploding out the back. Blood poured from the wound and the man's mouth, which was open in a silent scream. Ikely could feel the blade grate against the spine as he jerked the sword back and out. The rebel collapsed, twitching on the dirt, then he lay still.

Ikely looked up and wished he still had his shield. It lay several feet away amidst a number of rebels who had made it up and over the barricade. He counted at least seven. They were forcing his men back, with more pulling themselves up and over with every minute that passed. He was about to enter the fight again, when, roaring a battle cry, Sergeant Ranl charged forward, leading one of the reserve files. The file slammed hard into the breach. The rebels reeled under the impact of shields and swords. One rebel was hit so hard by a shield he was bodily picked up and launched backward over the wooden barricade, disappearing from view with a scream. It was hot work, but quickly done and within seconds, the breach was contained. Those rebels who had made it over were down and dispatched.

"Are you all right, sir?" Ranl asked once the danger was over. The sergeant assessed the lieutenant anxiously. "That was mighty close there for a moment, sir. Do you mind letting us grunts get in on some of the action, sir?"

"A little too close," Ikely breathed, still winded, clapping the sergeant on the shoulder to keep the man from seeing how badly his hands were shaking. He did, however, note the tone of rebuke in the sergeant's voice. "Yes, I declare that was a little too close for comfort."

He took a deep breath, steadying himself before studying his defensive line. All across it, his men seemed to be holding the rebels back. Ikely had seen this trouble-spot and had rushed over to try to bolster the defense while calling for one of the reserve files to push forward. In hindsight, he should have waited. Rushing in had almost cost him his life, but it had also perhaps helped to contain the breach long enough for help to arrive.

A legionary, five feet away, abruptly cried out as a steel-tipped arrow penetrated his shoulder armor. Both Ikely and Sergeant Ranl turned to look. Clearly in agony, the man dropped to his knees, clutching the shaft of the arrow in his hands. Sergeant Ranl quickly directed a man to help him back to the aid station in the rear.

There was no time to worry about the wounded and Ikely turned away, more concerned with the fight. Although greatly outnumbered, his men were holding their own. The enemy had made two attempts to storm and overwhelm his defensive line. This had been done at great cost to the enemy. Eventually, given time, the rebel commander would attempt a flanking movement to get around and behind him. The lieutenant smiled grimly at this. He rather suspected the rebels would not have the time to do so. Captain Stiger should have launched his ambush, cutting the rebel column in two and leaving this group isolated and trapped in a position to be destroyed.

Breathing much more easily now, Ikely stepped carefully back up to the barricade and glanced over the edge. The noise of battle had slackened considerably. The rebels, in a great mass, were pulling back. He watched them mill about uncertainly, until their officers and sergeants started shouting orders. Ikely realized they were beginning to reform for what appeared to be preparation for a third attempt to storm his line. Glancing down into the trench below, he was appalled the enemy commander was considering another attack. The rebels had left a great number of bodies down there and not all were deceased. The wounded cried out and pleaded for help, or at least Ikely imagined that was what they were doing. He could not understand their language. Still, it was awful to hear their pitiful wailing.

His attention was drawn from the trench back to the road. A fresh company of rebels had been brought up to bolster the ranks of those who had already made two tries of it. He estimated that there were at least five to six hundred rebels directly in front of his position. That meant he had around ten to possibly twenty minutes before they were ready to attempt another assault.

A flight of arrows thwished overhead in the direction of the rebels. He watched the arrows fall amongst the fresh rebel company. Three men were struck and fell to the ground, crying out in agony. He turned to look at his archers, spread out along the top of the wall. There were fifteen of them, all volunteers from the cavalry, who had been put through a hasty archery course by one of the scouts. They had been loosing arrows nonstop ever since the fighting had begun. Though not as skilled as Eli's scouts, they were making their presence felt. Ikely had made sure that the archers had an ample supply of arrows so that there would be no danger of running out. He wished he had a supply of short spears with which to hurl at the enemy as they began their next assault.

He would have even settled for a few of the javelins the captain had ordered, which had been manufactured by the castle's smith. Why the captain would prefer such obsolete weapons was beyond him. As he looked across the battlefield at the enemy gathered to his front, he considered that even an obsolete weapon could find use. Captain Stiger had stated that he was saving the javelins for when they were really needed. Shrugging, the lieutenant had neither short spear nor javelin, so such thoughts were pointless. He had to make do with what he had on hand and those were his archers.

Fighting was exhausting work and he was parched. Though the air was frigid, he was drenched in sweat from his exertions just a few minutes before. He had hardly noticed until now.

"Make sure water gets distributed to the men," Ikely ordered Sergeant Ranl, who had followed him up to look over at the rebels.

"Yes, sir," Ranl said, wiping someone else's blood from his face with a soiled rag. "I will see to it."

There were a number of dead rebels along the top of the parapet where the breach had occurred. There were also a few legionaries down, some wounded and others beyond help or already dead.

"Have the bodies moved back," Ikely ordered when he saw a legionary stumble over one. "Make sure the bodies are not thrown over the wall and into the trench. There is no point in making it easier for our enemies to get up and over the wall by giving them step stools."

Sergeant Ranl nodded in understanding. He moved off as Ikely continued to observe the enemy, keeping a careful watch on the few enemy archers who had moved forward. He crouched down to make himself less of a conspicuous target as an arrow thudded into the barricade just a few feet away.

Then he placed a hand along the top of the barricade. The movement caused his shoulder to ache terribly. He reached inside his armor and rubbed at the sore spot. Nothing seemed broken. There was no blood, but his shoulder and arm hurt. Quickly looking over the armor itself, he saw was a good sized dent where he had been struck. Come morning, he rather suspected, he would have an ugly bruise.

"Corporal Smith," Ikely called to the man who led the reserve file, which had minutes before rushed into the breach with Sergeant Ranl.

"Sir?" Corporal Smith turned. He had also been watching the enemy while his men had crouched down behind the barricade or moved down the slope of the rampart.

"Pick four men and send two to each flank," Ikely ordered. "They are to explore beyond our lines to make sure the enemy are not attempting a flanking movement."

"Yes, sir," Smith acknowledged. He immediately set about detailing four men to the task. Within seconds, the four were on their way.

"Drink, sir?" a legionary asked, drawing Ikely's attention away from the enemy. The man had come up with a bucket of water and a ladle. A couple of hundred feet back, a small stream ran directly behind the defensive line. Ikely took a drink as another flight of arrows thwished overhead toward the enemy. He savored the cool water a moment before gulping it down. He hadn't realized how thirsty he was.

"Sir!" a legionary next to him exclaimed, pointing in the direction of the enemy.

With a splash, Ikely dropped the ladle in the bucket and turned back to look at the enemy. Where a moment before they had been organizing for another attempt on his lines, they now looked disordered and confused. It took the lieutenant only a moment to realize the cause, which he was confident was Captain Stiger's ambush.

"Corporal Fisher," Ikely snapped at the nearest corporal, "find Sergeant Ranl and inform him we will be going over the top and into the enemy. Corporal Smith, begin passing the word that every man is to make himself ready and move up to the wall."

"Yes, sir," Corporal Smith responded and began spreading the word, which was rapidly communicated across the line. Ikely gave it a couple minutes and watched as his men began moving forward toward the barricade, even the reserve files, careful to keep low and out of the view of the enemy archers.

He looked around for his shield and spotted it. He retrieved it and then returned to the wall and continued to study the enemy. Where a few minutes ago they had been preparing to send in a third assault wave, now there was no indication that was even a consideration. The enemy commander could be seen at the far end of the battlefield, where the road disappeared around a bend. He was mounted on a magnificent white horse, surrounded by officers who were gesticulating excitedly back up the road and away from Vrell.

"Ready shields!" Ikely roared, shouting up and down the line as he stood, shield to the front to protect against arrow shot. "Shields!"

Careful not to expose too much of themselves, the tired and weary men grabbed their shields and presented them toward the enemy as they stood up behind the barricade, ready to make their way over.

Ikely returned to studying the enemy. They were clearly becoming more confused and disordered by the moment. It had to be the captain's ambush! The lieutenant's orders were to attack when the enemy gave up assaulting his position and turned to the rear to deal with the ambush. Beyond the rebels to his front, he could see nothing, as the road turned a bend a few hundred yards away. He rapidly considered his options.

This was only his second fight since he had joined the legions. It was by far the largest and had been the most difficult. If he ordered his men over the wall at this moment, he would be technically exceeding his orders, as the rebels had not quite turned to the rear. However, they looked like they might panic, as any sense of order seemed to have completely devolved. He was concerned that he might fail in his duty, but at the same time he was also equally worried that he might screw up by not following the captain's orders to the letter.

Should he wait or should he go? Captain Stiger was not here and the ultimate decision lay with him, as did the responsibility for his actions. He turned, looking up and down the line once again. The men looked ready and he wanted to give the order. It seemed like the right thing to do. Corporal Fisher returned and looked expectantly at Ikely.

"Spread the word to all corporals that we will be going over the top," Ikely decided. During one of their many late night talks on the march to Vrell, the captain had cautioned him about doubting himself too much.

"When you see an opportunity," the captain had said, "take it! Many are afraid to try and that can cost you the battle."

"Once over," Ikely continued, resolved, "we will form a shield line beyond the trench and then advance. We advance only after we have formed a shield line. Got that?"

"Yes, sir," Fisher, a veteran, responded grimly, understanding the risk.

The captain's orders had anticipated that the rebels would pull back several hundred feet before Ikely sent his men over the wall. With the enemy so close, going over the wall would be extremely risky. The legionaries would be vulnerable the moment they went over the top and struggled to climb out of the trench beyond the earthen rampart. Still, Ikely considered, his orders had assumed the enemy would be ordered and organized.

"Good man," Ikely responded and nodded for Fisher to go. Within five minutes, the corporal had returned, along with Sergeant Ranl. In that brief span of time, the rebels had become even more confused. Officers and sergeants were shouting orders, but their men did not seem to be listening. A few rebels had even bolted for the safety of the tree line. The enemy commander had disappeared, having ridden back up the road away from Vrell, presumably in the direction of the captain's ambush.

"Sergeant," Ikely said, feeling the full weight of command on his shoulders. "I want you to handle our left flank. I will take the right. We will go over the top, climb out of the trench, form a shield wall and then advance upon my orders."

"Yes, sir," Sergeant Ranl said, saluting crisply. He trotted off toward the left flank. Ikely moved over to the right and waited for the older sergeant to get into position.

Ikely's family had sent him to the legions to add to the family honor and prestige. So far he had served with honor, yet until this moment he had not faced a test like what was now before him. His moment had come. He would not only serve his family this day but also the empire.

"Over the top!" Ikely roared and the men surged up and forward. He followed, his shoulder crying out in pain as he carefully climbed over the top of the barricade. Slipping down the other side, into the defensive ditch below, he landed on a body and just barely missed being skewered by a sword that had its sharp end pointing upward.

The trench was filled with rebel dead and badly wounded. As the lieutenant caught himself, his hobnailed boots landed hard on the torso of a rebel, who cried out in pain. The lieutenant ignored him and instead focused on scrambling up the other side of the trench. He discovered that pulling himself out was more challenging than he had expected because of the weight of his armor and his throbbing shoulder.

"Form up!" Ikely yelled as soon as he had dragged himself out of the trench. He drew his sword. "Form up! Get those shields out! Dress that line!"

He began shoving men forward and into position. This was the moment when he and his men were most vulnerable. He was taking an incredible risk coming out from behind his fortifications before the enemy had quit the battlefield. Should they hit him, his men would be unprepared and trapped with a trench and earthen wall to their backs. But what seemed to take ages in reality took only a couple of minutes. His men formed up into a line, two ranks deep.

Satisfied, Ikely turned to see what the enemy was up to. The rebels were in an even greater state of confusion now that the legionaries had come out from behind their fortifications.

He had placed himself directly behind the line and though he had told Ranl he would take the right flank, he found himself nearer to the middle of his line. He saw no point in moving farther to the right. It was time to renew the fight while he still had the enemy before him.

"Draw swords!" Ikely shouted, pulling forth his own, his voice cracking due to hoarseness. Up and down the line, swords were drawn with a hiss. Ikely looked left and then right to ensure all was ready. Satisfied, he looked forward at the enemy. "Advance!"

"HAAAAH!" nearly two hundred legionaries from the 33rd and 85th roared at the enemy. "HAAAAH!"

"Front rank! Shields to the front!" Ikely bellowed and as one, the long rectangular shields, uniform to the legions, came up and into place.

The rebels managed to form a weak line to face the armored wall that was inexorably marching toward them. Without the benefit of either armor or shields, the rebels had little chance. Ikely hastily glanced left and right to make sure the line was properly aligned and then the two lines met.

Shields hammered at the rebel line and short swords, the perfect tool for this kind of close-in work, darted out, jabbing, stabbing and finding soft, unprotected flesh. Men screamed, yelled and cursed. Enemy swords hammered away uselessly on legionary shields, creating a tremendous cacophony.

"Push them!" Ikely shouted, impatiently pacing up and down the line. "Use your shields! Push them!"

With each fallen enemy, the line advanced. Whenever an enemy fell beneath their feet, the second rank made certain the rebel would not rise again to strike at the legs or backs of their comrades as the line pushed forward one half step at a time.

"Get that man back!" Ranl roared, indicating a legionary who had been wounded in the sword arm and had dropped his weapon. The man was moved rearward and the legionary behind him in the second rank took his place in the first.

"Rotate," Ikely shouted, which the sergeants and corporals picked up and repeated. The first rank abruptly stepped back. The second rank stepped forward, fresh and ready, shields interlocking. The men who stepped back, breathing heavily, took up the second rank's position.

"Keep at 'em!" Ikely shouted as the rebel line began to crack and buckle, breaking up as they were forced steadily backward. "Hit them with your shields! We have them!"

"Legionary Teg!" Sergeant Ranl shouted in an enraged voice. "Use your sword properly, man! You are not some dandified gladiator. You are a legionary and a killer. Killers jab and stab!"

Having been called out, Teg returned to proper form and focused on the rebel to his front. He moved his shield slightly and jabbed out. He was rewarded with an enraged cry as his sword bit home.

"Good boy!" Sergeant Ranl boomed. "We will make a legionary of you yet."

Moments later, what was left of the rebel line collapsed and the legionaries surged forward into the mass of the confusion beyond. Legionaries rushed forward madly, screaming and yelling, killing all they came across. It took only a handful of seconds, but the enemy, as one, turned and fled the field, streaming off in all directions in an effort to escape the slaughter. It was at that moment that the real killing began.

CHAPTER NINE

"**WELL MET, LIEUTENANT,**" Stiger growled, coming up to Ikely. From head to foot, Ikely was covered in dried blood. His armor was dented and scratched and he had an ugly bruise forming along his left cheek. He walked gingerly. Stiger thought he looked exactly like the kind of officer the legions preferred, one who led by example and never hesitated to get into the thick of the fighting. He was proud of him. The lieutenant had the makings of a fine officer.

Ikely offered his captain a tired smile.

"It is good to see you too, sir," he said, taking Stiger's offered hand. "I would say the High Father was with us this day."

"Seems very possible," Stiger agreed, turning to gaze across the aftermath of this part of the battlefield along a half-mile stretch of narrow road. Everywhere he looked there were bodies, mostly dead rebels. Legionaries were combing through the dead and taking what valuables they could find. Loot would later be collected by the sergeants and corporals, assigned a value and then distributed according to legion custom. Anyone caught failing to turn over any loot would be subjected to punishment. Swords, weapons and armor were also being collected and stacked in piles. What was useless for the legions would be dumped in a small pond a few miles away. Stiger was determined to leave nothing of value for the enemy.

What they would leave behind were plenty of bodies.

The wounded legionaries were being helped back to the aid station. Any of the enemy that were discovered wounded received a quick thrust and were put out of their misery. They could not and would not spare any effort to treat them. A line of rebel prisoners, under heavy guard, was being marched back toward Vrell to be sold as slaves.

"I will offer my thanks to the gods," Ikely commented, gazing around at the carnage. Stiger could imagine that Ikely had never seen anything like it. Stiger, on the other hand, had. He was only too familiar with such scenes. He was a soldier and this was the life he had chosen. For Stiger, the aftermath of the fight represented service to the empire. There was no nobler pursuit.

Looking over the prisoners being marched rearward, Stiger did not much mind the opportunity to enrich himself from their sale and contribute to the pensions of the men. What concerned him was the possibility that these prisoners might complicate his defensive plan. He needed every able man and yet the prisoners would require a guard detail. He scowled slightly as he watched them march by to uncertain futures. Unlike the bandits he had ordered executed, it somehow seemed wrong to put the surrendered rebels to death. Perhaps it had been a mistake to take prisoners. Perhaps not. Only time would tell. Of course, any sale would have to wait until he linked back up with the southern legions.

Stiger had no idea how and when that would be. He hoped Eli's two scouts, dispatched as messengers, had made it to friendly lines and that the empire knew he intended to hold Vrell.

Best not to worry about what is out of your control, Stiger thought irritably. *It is better to focus on the task at hand.*

He had no idea how many of the enemy had fallen, only that it had been a considerable number. Darkly, he wondered how many of his legionaries he had lost. Later this evening, after the rolls were taken and the wounded counted, he would learn the butcher's bill.

"Sir," Lieutenant Banister came up. The man's left forearm was wrapped in a hastily applied bandage that was already soaked through with fresh blood. He looked to be in considerable discomfort. Banister was also dusty and blood-spattered, like Stiger, Ikely and the rest of the men.

"Lieutenant," Stiger nodded in acknowledgment. Despite his victory, Stiger's thoughts clouded over as he took in Banister. It troubled him greatly that the other prong of his ambush had waited so long to go in. The delay had in all probability caused additional casualties and that made Stiger angry enough to spit. Though when the second prong had finally gone in, they had completely shattered the rebel attempt to break out, which perhaps had made up for the delay. There had been no time to ask the cause of the delay until now.

"What took you so long?" Stiger asked grimly of the lieutenant.

Banister looked away briefly, clearly uncomfortable. He cleared his throat, then after a slight hesitation, he drew himself up and looked the captain square on.

"When the action began and your men charged," Banister explained, giving a formal report, "I am afraid Lieutenant Peal ordered the men to retreat, sir."

"He did what?" Stiger snapped, tiredness forgotten in a rush of anger. His blood boiled. He could not believe what he had just heard! Banister was essentially accusing

Lieutenant Peal of cowardice in the face of the enemy. Such accusations were not lightly brought. If convicted through a trial of his peers, the punishment meant execution.

"As we were about to go in, sir, he gave the order to retreat. Well, really run for it," Banister continued, clearly deeply uncomfortable under the captain's intense scrutiny. "I was forced to countermand that order; however, the damage had been done. I am afraid it took me some time to reform the men."

"I see." Stiger fell silent. His mood had soured. Stiger had never been one to abide cowards, nor understand them. He scowled deeply at the thought of what he must now do. "What was the lieutenant's reasoning for giving such an order?"

"I am not entirely sure," Banister admitted, taking hold of his wounded arm for support as a spasm of pain wracked him. Despite the cold, sweat beaded his forehead. "I believe he may have become unnerved, sir."

"Where is Lieutenant Peal now?" Stiger asked angrily. Peal's apparent cowardice could have cost them the fight, had things gone differently. Officers must always set an example for their men. Peal would now become such an example, just not the one the captain had intended for him to make when he had given the man a second chance.

Pending a trial, Stiger would be forced to order Peal's arrest and confinement. Worse, he did not have the time for such nonsense. A trial would have to wait until they returned to Castle Vrell and were safe behind its massive walls, with winter well underway and the fighting concluded for the season. Only then would Peal be made to answer for his actions. Stiger kicked irritably at a rock, which rolled a few feet before it connected with the torso of a dead rebel.

"I regret to inform you that Lieutenant Peal did not survive the battle, sir."

Stiger's eyes narrowed suspiciously. "What exactly happened to him?"

"I—ah—thought it prudent to send Sergeant Boral after the lieutenant," Banister explained. An uncomfortable hesitation followed that seemed to speak volumes. "While I was reforming the men, the sergeant found him slain, sir. Unfortunately, no one witnessed how he died, sir. Sergeant Boral believes that the lieutenant encountered rebel skirmishers and fought his last battle."

Stiger felt the explanation weak. Though it was possible that enemy skirmishers had slipped through…Stiger did not believe a word of it. He could easily guess at what had occurred. Boral had more than likely dealt with the coward himself, perhaps even on Banister's orders. The captain considered his possible actions. He kicked at another loose stone in frustration. It was not a satisfactory state of affairs.

The men would speculate on Boral's actions, perhaps Banister's too, which was even worse. Such acts usually led to more trouble and might encourage future action against officers who were unpopular. Stiger was reminded of the assassination attempt on his own life by legionary Bennet. Though he had spared the man's life, to make an example, this was far different.

Boral had been extremely helpful in the last few weeks and Stiger had grown to like the man. He wasn't exactly sure how he wanted to handle it, for any action he took against Boral might have repercussions on Banister. He could make direct issue of it, but in truth, Boral and perhaps Banister had saved Stiger from dealing with an unfortunate and unpleasant affair. The captain was tired and worn out from the fight. He decided to think on the matter further before taking any action.

"See that his body is recovered," Stiger ordered of Ikely. "Since the lieutenant is unable to answer for himself, he will be buried as befits a legionary officer."

"Yes, sir," Ikely responded. "I will see to it, sir."

"We will take all of our fallen from the field," Stiger added after a moment's further thought. "The rebels' bodies remain where they are. It will serve warning as to what they can expect."

Ikely and Banister nodded. Banister had begun to shake slightly from the fatigue and pain.

"Banister," Stiger said, gesturing at the man's arm, "get yourself to the aid station and have that seen to."

"I will, sir," Banister replied with a nod. "Once I have seen to my men."

The wounded lieutenant stepped off in the direction of his men. Stiger and Ikely watched him go. Neither said anything for several seconds.

"Sir," Ikely said tiredly, breaking the uncomfortable silence. He drew himself up and offered a smart salute, a large smile plastered on his face. "Congratulations on your victory. We really cut them to pieces."

Stiger gazed across the field once more. It was a good, solid and complete victory. The rebel advance column had been thoroughly smashed and those he had trapped had been destroyed, as he had intended. Though there were many more rebels where these had come from, he had given the enemy a bloody nose.

Stiger nodded, returning Ikely's smile. "Excellent work on your end too. I expect a full report on your actions later this evening."

"Sir," Lieutenant Brent hurried up to them. Stiger had left the lieutenant supervising the cleanup of the ambush site, a quarter mile up the road and away from Vrell. The lieutenant's armor was streaked and spattered with blood and his face was dust-covered like everyone else's. "Lieutenant Eli'Far sent a scout to report the enemy is on the march and should be here in three hours, perhaps more. Eli has also broken off his fight and should be joining us shortly."

"Well, then," Stiger said, and looked up at the sun, which was almost directly above them. By his reckoning, it was slightly past noon. "Let's get our fallen off the field and the men behind our fortified line. We can give the men a well-earned rest and get them fed. I suspect it will be close to dusk by the time the enemy arrives. I rather doubt they will attack us until tomorrow, especially when they see the surprise we have left them."

"Sir," Brent asked surprised. "Do you mean to hold?"

"No," Stiger admitted. "I do not. We are only looking to delay them. I expect that we will pull out sometime in the morning."

The men had performed wonderfully. Before he asked more of them, they needed rest and some time to recover. He would allow them that and in the early morning hours, well before daylight, he intended to pull the bulk of his men back, leaving a number of scouts to man the fortification. To them would fall the job of convincing the enemy that the fortification was fully manned. With luck, the rebels would be forced to deploy and make an assault, eating up valuable time. The scouts would naturally leg it as soon as that happened.

A few miles down the road, Stiger's defensive corridor began and continued nearly the entire way to Castle Vrell.

The defensive corridor stretched over forty miles in length. Clearing the road would take effort and that translated into time.

Ikely turned abruptly to gaze upon the line of rebel prisoners being marched off. An odd expression slid onto his face and he suddenly turned back to Stiger with a lopsided grin.

"Sir," Ikely spoke up, "I've just had a marvelous idea."

Chapter Ten

BLAKE APPROACHED THE prisoners. Huddling around a fire, the group numbered around thirty. They were under a watchful guard. Having run during the fight four days prior, the prisoners had been recently taken by Eli's scouts. They had been found wandering, hopelessly lost in the woods. Blake saw that they had just been fed. Two of the guards were collecting empty bowls. The prisoners looked miserable, weary and beaten.

The rebellion was over for them and their futures were far from certain. Having rebelled against the empire, they would probably end up as slaves, most likely either working a plantation or in a mine. Such a life was a terrible existence, where lifespans were measured in months and not years. A lucky few might be selected for the gladiatorial schools, where they would have a chance to live well, earn fame and possibly freedom, should they prove good enough. If they were unlucky, they would be nailed to a cross and crucified as an example to others. The prisoners understood this. The empire did not tolerate rebellion.

Corporal Beni had been placed in charge of the guard detail. Sergeant Blake sauntered up to him and the corporal nodded a friendly greeting. Having seen something in him, Blake had taken the large man under his wing and arranged for his promotion to corporal. Since that time, Beni had worked hard in his new role, proving the sergeant's decision a correct one.

The sergeant scratched his stubble as he looked over the wretches, considering them. Any and all prisoners taken represented a future pension investment for him and the men. What he was about to do would perhaps see that investment lessened somewhat.

"This bunch giving you any trouble?" Blake asked with a glance at the prisoners.

"Naw," Beni responded in a bored tone. "After all they've been through, they seem to be a pretty meek lot."

"Do any of 'em speak common?" Blake asked, glancing over at Beni, with a curious look.

"Not that we can tell," Beni said, looking sourly over at the ragged group of prisoners. "Pretty ignorant bunch if you ask me."

Just days before, these ragged and dirty prisoners had been doing their level best to kill Blake and his fellow legionaries. If it weren't for the prospect of selling them off and increasing his pension, Blake would have been more than willing to execute the bunch and move on.

He smiled thinly and walked around the prisoners, casually studying them. The prisoners either averted their gaze or eyed the sergeant warily. Having made a full circuit of the group, Blake turned back to Beni.

"Not a very sanitary group, are they?" Blake commented, wrinkling his nose at their stench.

"No, sergeant, they are not," Beni replied sourly. "They don't seem to have heard of a bathhouse, let alone a latrine. Seven Levels, we had to show them where to shit."

"I see," Blake said, considering the prisoners for another moment before looking over at Beni curiously. "So they know what a latrine is?"

"They do now," Beni barked out a laugh. "Had to beat it into two of them before the rest understood."

"Perfect," the sergeant said to Beni. "Mind if I borrow a few to dig some fresh latrines?"

"You are welcome to them, sergeant," Beni responded in a bored tone. Blake had not really been asking for permission. "I doubt they will prove any good, though."

"I have a work detail that needs to be done," Blake announced loudly to the prisoners. He suspected a few could speak the common tongue. "Anyone who speaks common will live through the day and avoid being nailed to a cross."

Five of the prisoners looked up, naked and abject fear in their eyes. Blake smiled broadly. Here were the very boys he wanted. Looking them over, he decided they would do nicely. All five were big, strapping young men. He was confident that prior to their capture they had been full of piss and vinegar.

"If you boys speak common, then stand up," Blake ordered in an impatient tone. The five stood, with the other prisoners looking on with apathy. "Right then, you five come with me."

"Teg," Blake motioned to one of the guards. "You're with me. Keep a watch on these bastards."

The sergeant led the five prisoners, with Teg trailing along, in the direction of the road. All around them legionaries toiled away at various tasks, preparing for the arrival of the enemy, who Blake knew were somewhere around ten miles off.

The defensive line had been started weeks ago, but it had not been finished, as they had run out of time. The legionaries were now working feverishly to complete the work. The line boasted a ten-foot-deep trench and ten-foot-high earthen rampart. Logs had been set vertically along the outward side of the rampart, creating a crude barricade, which would provide the legionnaires manning the wall with some protection.

To the front of the defensive line, along the road, the forest had been intentionally cut back around sixty yards. Three hundred yards in the direction of Vrell, the road was neatly blocked with fallen trees and marked the start of the captain's defensive corridor. The captain planned to make a stand here and it showed through the activity of the men.

A company of legionaries, looking extremely smart, with a standard-bearer to the front, marched by, up the road, and away from Vrell. The formation passed through the central gate of the rampart, which stood open.

Blake and the prisoners were forced to wait until the company passed, hobnailed sandals making an impressive crunching sound as they marched by in perfect unison. Freshly polished armor gleamed and glinted under the sunlight. The company made a remarkable sight.

Once clear, Blake led them across the road and along the back of the fortified line that was nearly complete. Several legionaries gave the prisoners and the escort an odd look before returning to their work. They were clearly wondering where Blake and Teg were off to with the prisoners.

They passed one group that was busily stacking javelins every few yards. Another was carrying field stones up to the top of the rampart to be piled up neatly, leaving small piles every few feet. Others were busily finishing up work, smoothing out the top of the rampart or placing stakes in the trench, along with many other jobs that needed doing.

Blake led the prisoners to an area where the work, for the most part, had been completed, along the end of the defensive line's right flank, which reached out into the forest. The trees at this point behind the line had been neatly cut back, but not those before it. There were very few legionaries about. Several shovels lay on the ground.

"I know you are ignorant and shit where you like," Blake stated in a disgusted tone. "We, on the other hand, do not. We are civilized you see. You lot will dig me some latrines right here in this spot. That is a trench for men to shit in. Understand me?"

"Yes, sar," one of the prisoners said in heavily-accented common and then spoke rapidly to the others in their own language.

"We dig hole here?" Another prisoner asked, pointing at the ground where the shovels lay. "Here?"

"Right," Sergeant Blake replied and then marked out what he wanted. "You dig here, four trenches about this size, three feet deep. You do a good job and you get to live out the day."

The five prisoners stepped forward and took the shovels. They began digging furiously. Teg gave the sergeant an uncertain look, clearly unsure what was going on.

Why put the prisoners to work on latrines that are not needed? Blake could read the question in Teg's eyes. When Blake was sure the prisoners were not watching, the sergeant turned his head, looking meaningfully at Teg, and winked.

"Is that the seventh?" Blake asked, gesturing behind the legionary, who turned to look. Another company was marching through the work parties, following the path of the other company that had passed some time ago. Teg looked back at the sergeant, who slowly winked once again and then rolled his eyes at the legionary, as if to say *stop being the village idiot.* Blake knew full well Teg knew that there was no seventh company.

"I think you might be right," Teg answered slowly as understanding dawned.

"Bought time the general brought up the reserves," Blake continued in a bored and semi-disinterested tone. "Let someone else do some heavy lifting for a change."

Teg cast the sergeant a long look before replying. He turned back to watch the company march up the road and into the woods, disappearing from view. "That's what, two more fresh companies today?"

"I would hazard all of second regiment is being brought up," Blake continued just loud enough for the latrine diggers to overhear. "With them rebels only a few miles up the road, the general must be planning a right party."

They heard hooves behind them and turned to look into the forest. Emerging from a trail that had been cut into the woods for logging came a full escort troop of cavalry. At its head was a rider holding a standard topped with an imperial eagle and another holding the standard of the 85th, complete with tiger's pelt.

Teg took a step back in surprise. A general rode behind the standards, complete with general's armor and the signature blue cloak, which signified his rank. The legionary blinked. Blake shot Teg another covert wink. The general was none other than Captain Stiger, clearly dressed up in General Delvaris's kit. The prisoners continued to dig but cast nervous glances in the direction of the mounted group, which rode carefully around the work party and the holes they were digging.

Blake and Teg both snapped to attention, saluting as Stiger rode up.

"Sergeant." Captain Stiger pulled his horse to a stop. He addressed them in the aloof haughty style that was commonly used by the aristocracy when they spoke to those of a lesser social standing. "I see you are putting the scum to work."

"Yes, General," Blake responded with a shrug. "Something useful, even if it is only digging latrines. Saves our boys some labor."

"General Stiger." Lieutenant Ikely, who had been trailing behind, pulled up next to Stiger. The lieutenant's horse shifted uncomfortably. Ikely leaned over slightly to speak and lowered his voice, though they were close enough that the prisoners could still hear what was said. "Colonel Lan is waiting for you at headquarters, sir. Might I remind you he has a long day ahead of him and an even longer march if he is to flank the enemy?"

"Very correct, lieutenant," Stiger responded, kicking his horse forward. "It is time we moved on. Carry on, sergeant."

Teg and the sergeant watched Captain Stiger and his party ride toward the center of the line and the road. They were silent for several moments. There was only the sound of the prisoners' rhythmic shoveling.

"A great man," Teg ventured, "that General Stiger."

"I bet the general has got a surprise or two in store for your rebel friends," Blake said to the prisoners. "You boys did not figure on running into an entire legion, freshly arrived from the North, did ya?"

The prisoners said nothing but continued to dig, not even daring to look back at the sergeant. Blake laughed harshly at them before turning back to Teg. "They thought this here campaign would be an easy one!"

"I think their friends are in for a nasty surprise," Teg said, getting into the act. "General Stiger is one of the best."

"That he is, lad," Blake confirmed with a nod. "That he is."

They turned back to watching the prisoners work and were silent for a time. Another company marched through. It was the same men marching by each time. They were far enough away that he was sure the prisoners could not tell the difference. Only someone who had served with the legions would notice the telltale signs. Each time the company came through, the standard-bearer and standard were changed out and the men's marching order was shifted around.

"Blake," sergeant Boral called over in a friendly manner. The other sergeant was supervising a nearby work detail that consisted of four men. They were smoothing out the top of the earthen rampart and were packing down the dirt so that it provided a level surface for the defenders behind the barricade. They were standing around a spare post that had originally been intended to be used as part of the barricade. "Can you two help us lift this post? We need to move it out of the way. Damn thing is devilishly heavy."

"Sure," Blake called back good-naturedly. He started over and looked back over at Teg. "Let's go help."

"What about them?" Teg asked with a jerk of his thumb at the prisoners toiling away. The latrine diggers were working up a good sweat, despite the cold air.

"What about them?" Blake asked stopping and turning to look back at the prisoners without a hint of concern.

"Sergeant, they could run," Teg protested. "I don't think the general would be too happy if we lost some prisoners."

"Out here?" Blake scoffed, gesturing at the forest around them, then turned serious. "You boys run and we will hunt you down. Being nailed to a cross will be the least of your concerns. Understand?"

There were several wide-eyed nods at that as they stopped work briefly. Blake gestured for them to get back to digging. The prisoners hopped to it, feverishly digging away at the budding latrine trenches, not daring to look back up.

"See," Blake laughed harshly. "They are sheep. They won't run. Besides, they were stupid enough to get lost the first time. I doubt that they will make the same mistake twice. Hell, that there forest is thick as they come. It was pure dumb luck we found them anyway."

"If you say so, sergeant," Teg answered uncertainly.

"I do," Blake replied in a growl before starting over to help Boral. "Come on, lad. Let's get this over with."

Teg followed Blake over to Boral and his detail. As soon as they got there, one of Boral's men pointed back toward the prisoners.

"Sergeant," the legionary said laconically. "I believe some of your prisoners are escaping."

"Are they now?" Blake turned slowly and saw that three of the five were making a mad dash for it. The other two just stood there, watching the others leg it, afraid to make a run for it too.

"Let's give them a moment, kind of a sporting head start," Blake said quietly to the group and shot Teg another wink.

"After them!" Blake roared, having waited for around ten seconds. "Don't let them get away!"

Blake, Boral, Teg and the legionaries ran after the escaping rebels, who plunged deeper into the woods, running for their very lives. The legionaries made a show of pursuing the fugitives, following them into the forest, calling loudly and intentionally driving them in the direction of the main rebel army. After a few minutes, Blake made the others give up the chase. He was satisfied that the prisoners thought they had made a clean getaway. The direction the prisoners were heading led back to the rebel army. Two of Eli's scouts would now shadow the escaped prisoners. If needed, the scouts would dog their heels, getting close but never close enough to catch them, ensuring they continued in the correct direction.

As they made their way back, Blake hoped that nothing went wrong and the three escapees managed to reach the rebel lines. With luck, they would report on what they had seen and heard. Perhaps the enemy general would believe he was facing an entire legion and play it more cautious. If not, well then, with the loss of those three, his pension had just taken an unwelcome hit.

CHAPTER ELEVEN

"I SEE YOU finally managed to get yourself promoted," Eli stated with a smirk as he walked up to Stiger's campfire. The night air was cold and a short while ago a few flurries had fallen, only to melt where they landed. The fire was well-fed and crackled loudly, providing sufficient heat to keep those seated near it relatively warm.

Stiger looked up from the campfire to Eli. Several cut logs had been placed about the fire. Stiger was seated on one of these. Ikely, on another, offered Eli a friendly wave in greeting. Stiger smiled at his friend, whom he had not seen for the last two days and then only briefly after the ambush.

"My father would be so proud," Stiger said sarcastically, tapping General Delvaris's breastplate with his pipe. "Don't you agree?"

"All I can add is that the emperor seems to have finally come to his senses." Eli grinned a full, open-mouthed smile. He stepped up to the fire and took a few moments to warm his hands before selecting a seat to Stiger's right.

"Just promise me that if it comes to a decision on succession, you back the son most likely to succeed to the throne?"

Ikely's eyes widened with that comment and he darted a careful look to his captain. Such talk concerning the Stigers was dangerous business. Stiger, for his part, shot a sour glare in Eli's direction, but said nothing in reply. As usual, he declined to become engaged in such talk. He was confident it only amused Eli more so.

"I think he looks particularly good in blue," Ikely commented, cracking a smile and clearly steering the conversation away from dangerous ground. It was Ikely's turn to receive a sour look.

"You know, it was all his idea," Stiger explained to Eli, throwing a small stick he had been playing with into the fire. "Surprisingly, he actually made sense for a change and suggested that I must continue to wear General Delvaris' kit in the event an enemy scout inadvertently makes it through your screen and spots me. It would be confirmation for the enemy that a general was present. Can you believe that?"

"Very sound reasoning, Ikely," Eli commented with a closed-mouth smile. "By the way, also very becoming. It looks like it was made for you."

Stiger did not like the implication of that. General Delvaris's armor did fit well, a little too well, almost as if it had been made for Stiger and not his long-deceased relative. The thought made the captain more than a little uncomfortable. When he had donned the general's armor, he had half expected the sword to speak, but it had remained silent. Normally, if one heard voices, it was not considered a good sign. Glancing down at the sword resting against his log, Stiger wondered for a moment if he was going insane.

"We even allowed a few prisoners to escape, having, of course, seen the great and powerful general himself," Ikely explained with a flourish.

"Indeed," Eli chuckled, amused that the captain and lieutenant were pulling one over on the enemy. "Surprisingly, I believe your ruse may actually be working."

Stiger looked up at that, eyes narrowing. "How so?"

"The rebels have become a great deal more cautious in the last day or so," Eli explained. "Their advance has slowed and they are pushing out double the number of skirmishers. Their scouts are also thick as the fleas on one of those mangy creatures your family calls hunting hounds."

"Those are good dogs!" Stiger protested with mock indignation. "How dare you accuse my family of breeding mangy dogs!"

"If you say so," Eli replied skeptically before returning to the matter at hand. "Since the ambush, it has become increasingly hazardous for my scouts. I am afraid there is not much more we can do other than act as your eyes."

"How far back are they?" Stiger asked. He had known that there would come a point when his scouts would no longer be able to effectively raid the enemy. It seemed they had reached it sooner than he would have liked.

"The lead enemy column is camped about five miles from this spot," Eli answered casually. "They have made very little progress today."

"I think they received our message," Ikely chuckled. "We gave them a good one, right to the nose."

"The ambush was nothing more than a large skirmish," Stiger replied, and Ikely sobered with this statement. "The rebels have deeper reserves than us and it is dangerous to underestimate them."

"How many men did you lose in the ambush?" Eli asked of Stiger.

"Thirty-two dead and another forty injured," Stiger responded grimly. "It would have been worse had we faced a better-prepared enemy."

"Be careful what you wish for. Farther back in their line of march, the rebels have formations of some quality," Eli reported. "They wear scale armor and appear much disciplined. I believe part of their slow progress has been to shift forward some of these formations."

"You are just full of good cheer," Stiger breathed, taking out his tobacco from a bag. He filled the pipe with the last of his good tobacco and used the end of a small twig to light the pipe. He puffed up a good burn and took a moment to savor the rich flavor. An additional store of tobacco had been recovered after the ambush. It seemed one of the rebel officers had a taste for the weed. Despite being inferior in quality to the good eastern stuff that Stiger preferred, he had claimed it for himself. After tonight, he would have to resort to the captured tobacco.

"Troops from the southern kingdoms, perhaps even the Cyphan Confederacy?" Ikely postulated, eyebrows raised. "Our initial interrogation of a few of the less ignorant rebels seems to confirm that the confederacy is behind the rebellion. A few even claimed the confederacy marches with the rebels."

Have they finally committed to war with the Empire? Stiger wondered, taking a pull on his pipe. Beyond the empire's southernmost province, across the Narrow Sea, lay the Cyphan Confederacy. It had long been suspected that the confederacy had stirred up the rebellion in the hopes of slowing imperial growth and ambition. In some quarters, war was even considered inevitable.

"It is possible," Eli admitted with a shrug.

"I guess we will find out eventually," Stiger exhaled heavily before taking another pull off of his pipe. "The enemy should reach our defensive line tomorrow then?"

"At their current pace, yes...by the early afternoon. Their scouts should be in sight of the line by morning though," Eli added after thinking on it. "Expect the rebel commander to have a report on your position by noon. They have just too many scouts for us to stop them all."

"How many have you lost so far?" Stiger asked.

Ikely, as was his nightly ritual, had pulled out a piece of wood he had carefully selected and began chipping away at it with his service dagger. Every evening he meticulously formed small wooden figurines of the gods. He left these the next morning, where he had bedded down for the night. Highly superstitious, the figurines were prized by the men and every morning, without fail, someone was lurking to scoop them up. Ikely never complained and it had become Stiger's belief that the lieutenant wanted the men to have the little figurines. It seemed to be his way to spread the good word.

"Seven so far," Eli said with great sadness. "One from the 85th and the remainder from the garrison companies."

"One of ours?" Stiger asked. "Who?"

"Mosch," Eli replied. "He was lost before the ambush, in an encounter with a group of rebel scouts."

"We have been lucky so far," Ikely said as he continued to work on the figurines.

"How so?" Stiger asked, looking over at his lieutenant.

"The men from the garrison are nowhere near as well-trained as our company," Ikely explained, still chipping away at the wood, shaping it to his will. "Should we get into a bind, they could very well fail us at a critical moment."

Stiger nodded in agreement as he breathed out a long stream of smoke. "My intention is to not put them in that position, but stack our chances so that we have every possible advantage when I commit them."

"I know," Ikely said with a quick glance at his captain before looking back down on the figurine he was shaping.

"We have to keep in mind that the rebels will have a few surprises for us too."

His lieutenant was quite correct and he knew he could not let his guard down. He would have to be careful and alert to the enemy's intentions.

Stiger broke the silence. "Once we fall back on the castle, we will have the winter to train the garrison companies up and get them into proper shape."

"Sir, dispatch just arrived." Blake stepped up to their fire and saluted. He handed it over to the captain.

"Thank you, sergeant," Stiger responded, looking at the dispatch. It was from Lan. "I will have a reply later this evening."

"Sir?" Blake asked and Stiger looked back up questioningly at the sergeant, pipe clamped between his teeth.

"What is it?" Stiger asked.

"I have an accounting tallying what we recovered from the enemy," Blake said. "There had been so much of it, especially since we captured four enemy wagons, that what with my other duties, it has taken four days to compile a complete list."

"Ah…yes," Stiger nodded. "Swing by this evening around ten bells and we shall go through it."

"Yes, sir." Blake drew himself up, saluted and left.

Stiger took the dispatch and opened it. He read through it quickly, tilting the dispatch toward the fire for added light. Lan reported that Councilman Bester had arrived at the castle and the negotiations had begun. The lieutenant felt that they were well on their way toward an agreement that hopefully would secure a longstanding peace between the garrison and the residents of the valley.

Several days back, Stiger had learned about the valley's militia. None of the garrison officers had known and that was a worrying sign. It bothered the captain that the council had concealed its existence, which meant they had never fully accepted imperial rule. Typically, militias were nothing to be seriously concerned about, but with a rebel army marching on Vrell, the last thing the captain wanted to deal with was a second armed enemy, no matter how inept, in the valley behind him.

Taking another puff off of his pipe, Stiger returned to the dispatch. Lan ticked off the items he had agreed to and went on to explain his reasoning behind each one. He had also listed a few of the more contentious points and the council's thinking. One of those Stiger could absolutely not agree to: allowing the civilians to bring legionaries to trial and the right to then punish those convicted.

The captain well understood the council's reasoning and desire to bring legionaries to justice; however, he could not allow it. Imperial law forbade local interference in legion affairs. Should a legionary break the law, the offender would face legion justice. This usually meant the local commander decided the guilt or innocence of the accused and type of punishment, if any was warranted.

Stiger carefully folded the dispatch and placed it in a pocket. Later this evening, he would reread it once more and then write a detailed reply, which he suspected would take some time. Together with Sergeant Blake's report, the evening promised to be a long one.

"I must go," Eli announced, abruptly standing.

"So soon?" Stiger asked, though he was not surprised. It was difficult to keep Eli in one place at the best of times, especially when he had work to do.

"Unfortunately." Eli grinned, a closed-mouthed smile. "I am due to meet Marcus shortly. I want to get a better look at those formations the enemy is bringing up. Besides, I have had a strange feeling these last few days and I want to have a more thorough look at the enemy. Something doesn't feel quite right."

"Strange feeling?" Stiger asked, not liking the sound of that. "Care to explain?"

"I...I wish I could." Eli hesitated seeming to be unsure what to say, which in and of itself was highly unusual. "This forest is old and I have a feeling it is trying to tell me something."

Stiger said nothing but watched his friend. Ikely had stopped his carving and was also looking at the elf. Stiger felt Eli looked conflicted. The elf tapped his foot in irritation and then plunged ahead.

"My people can both speak and listen to the forest," Eli explained. "You know this. What you probably do not know is that occasionally we can catch glimpses, or perhaps you might call it feelings, of others in the forest."

"Others?" Stiger asked surprised. "What others? Elves?"

Eli turned to the fire, gazing into the blazing depths. "That...has always been debatable."

"Debatable?" Stiger questioned. "What in the Seven Levels does that mean?"

"Some of my people," Eli continued, in a way that made it seem he was very uncomfortable speaking on the subject, "believe that we can catch glimpses...though to be fair, it is not quite an image...you could almost call them the emotions of others through the forest. There is another faction that believes very strongly that this is simply a collective memory of the forest, a look into the past, if you will. It is extremely rare."

Stiger had thought he understood Eli fairly well. His friend always seemed certain and confident. When Eli did not know the answer to something, he began searching until he found it. This, however, was something altogether different. Stiger was being allowed to see a mystical side of Eli's people that few outsiders were ever permitted to glimpse.

"How long have you been feeling this way?" Stiger asked quietly.

"Ever since we left Vrell," Eli answered, turning back to look upon Stiger. His friend bit his lower lip, his perfectly-formed face clouded with worry.

"Are you sensing other elves?" Stiger asked.

"There are no other elves," Eli said firmly.

"Who then?"

"Is the forest trying to warn you of something?" Ikely asked, almost at the same time the captain had asked his question. Eli turned to look on Ikely, eyes very intense.

"Yes," Eli said quietly after a moment. "I believe you are on to the root of the matter. Yes…the forest is trying to warn me."

"Of what?" Stiger asked.

"I do not know," Eli said plainly, shoulders slumping. "There has been no time for a proper commune."

"Well, that is not very helpful." Stiger took another pull on his pipe and exhaled slowly. "You will tell me if you learn anything more?"

"Yes," Eli said.

Stiger understood it had likely taken a lot for his friend to tell him this much.

Eli's eyes lit up. "Think how easy things would have been had you chosen a life with Miranda."

Stiger exhaled a stream of smoke slowly, as he considered his friend. Eli was intentionally changing the subject.

"Doesn't the emperor have a younger sister by the name of Miranda?" Ikely asked, having returned to his whittling.

"How is he doing?" Stiger asked, declining to take the bait. "Your new scout corporal?"

"Marcus?" Eli asked, eyebrows raised, gathering up his bow and kit.

Stiger nodded, taking another pull on his pipe. He blew it out long and slow as he watched Eli.

"I suspect he can feel the life-beat of the forest," Eli said quietly, slipping his quiver over a shoulder.

"He's that good, huh?" Stiger looked up in surprise. Eli nodded.

"He will one day make a fine ranger," Eli explained wistfully. "That is, should he survive this campaign..."

Ikely had stopped his carving and sat there looking between the two. After a moment, he shook his head and returned to shaping the wood.

"Once this mess is over with," Eli said, "you may wish to make special arrangements for him."

"You mean for Marcus to be transferred to the rangers?" Ikely asked of Eli, this time not bothering to glance up from his work.

"It would give him an opportunity to become more than he is," Eli said. He moved to leave.

"Take care, my friend," Stiger said to Eli, who nodded and stepped out of the firelight.

Stiger took another puff on his pipe and stared into the depths of the fire. Eli had given him a lot to think on.

CHAPTER TWELVE

MARCUS HAD BEEN waiting for Eli in the agreed-upon spot. It was a small clearing surrounded by larger trees, bordered by low level scrub brush. The clearing was mostly free of the brush that grouped up haphazardly in this portion of the forest. It was a very isolated spot, which is why Marcus had chosen it. Anyone attempting to sneak up on him would have to pass through the scrub and to do that silently would be nearly impossible. Only someone with Eli's skill level could have done it.

Eli was late, which was not unusual and Marcus was far from concerned. The lieutenant always had more on his plate than he could handle, but he somehow managed in the end. When the lieutenant finally arrived, they would set out to take a careful look at these new formations the rebels were bringing up. They appeared to be better organized, armed and led. Todd, who had first seen them, said they were *professional*.

The night was very cold. It had dropped to near freezing. Despite the cold, Marcus had not set a fire. That might have drawn the attention of the enemy. It was dark, but the nearly full moon occasionally broke free of the clouds and through the trees provided a bit of illumination to see by.

Marcus was not terribly cold, as he had donned two of his service tunics to provide some modicum of warmth. He had friends who, when the temperature dropped far enough, would wear as many as three or four tunics at the same time. The legions did not provide much in the way of cold weather clothing. When in the field, simple legionnaires had to rely upon their tunics, cloak and blanket. Truth be told, Marcus felt he was becoming inured to the cold.

He was kneeling on the forest floor, waiting patiently. Over the past few days, it had been rare to have some time to himself. Since he now had that time, he set out to enter that deep meditative state to which he had become accustomed, to feel the forest. With each and every try, it was becoming easier. Almost immediately, he was able to enter that state and he could literally feel the forest around him. It seemed to embrace and welcome him, as if it were aware of his presence, which was a somewhat unsettling thought. For a while, he just felt the forest about him and around him, enjoying the feeling. Then he became aware of something intangible that he could sense far off in the distance, something hovering on the very edge of the forest, far to the south. It was an awareness, an alien presence. He began to reach for it with his mind and then abruptly stopped. Something was wrong, dreadfully wrong.

He became aware of a disturbance. It was as if the forest itself was sending him a warning. *Danger!*

He dropped out of the meditative state and his eyes snapped open. He was careful not to move a muscle. His bow, with a full quiver, lay in front of him, within reach, as did his short sword. Marcus dared not go for it. Something warned him not to.

He could almost feel someone observing him from behind. For some reason, he was quite sure it was not Eli. Whoever it was meant him harm. Marcus was sure of it. How he knew, he could not say. He listened intently and then he heard it, a faint sound like someone nocking an arrow and drawing back to loose.

He rolled to the right, more sensing the twang of the bow than hearing it, as the tension on the bow was abruptly released. This was followed near instantly by a THWISH of an arrow passing by extremely close to his face, so close he could feel its passing. As he rolled, Marcus pulled his dagger from his boot, coming up into a crouch. Instinctively, he let the dagger fly in the direction he thought the arrow had come from. Though he could see nothing in the dim moonlight behind the scrub brush, he heard a solid meaty thwack, followed by a grunt. There was no accompanying scream of pain. About to reach for his bow, he sensed…almost felt as if another arrow was about to be shot from somewhere in the darkness and he dodged left, away from his bow. THWISH… an arrow flew into the empty space where he had been a fraction of a second before and embedded itself into the soft forest floor with a quiet thump.

This last arrow was from a second shooter! Marcus knew he was in serious trouble. Whoever was out there was good, perhaps too good. They had approached him unheard and unseen and that, with the scrub brush around the clearing, should have been near impossible!

"Sasha'haleen," a voice shouted abruptly. A figure exploded into the clearing between Marcus and the bowmen. Marcus, in mid-dodge, turned to confront the attacker, wishing he still had his dagger, when he suddenly realized it was Eli.

"Sasha'haleen," Eli shouted once again. "Tarato sleeth ta'doshi."

There was a moment of silence. Marcus froze, unsure what to do. About to move for his bow or sword, for it was better to be armed than not, Eli abruptly turned to him.

"Do not move," Eli ordered quite firmly, switching back to common. "Do not move, for both our lives depend upon it!"

Marcus froze, looking back at Eli, who was suddenly illuminated in moonlight as the clouds parted. The scout tried to peer into the brush, but in the gloom he could see nothing.

"Sasha'haleen ta'doshi," another voice called out in what seemed to Marcus not directed at him and Eli, but others beyond his sight. How many were out there? How had they gotten so close that he had not heard them?

"Etra'to saleesh," the voice continued. "Etra'to saleesh hamash."

Seeming to materialize from the darkness, a man cautiously emerged from the scrub brush that surrounded the clearing, with a nocked bow aimed squarely at Eli. Eli tilted his head slightly to an odd angle, which once again reminded Marcus that the lieutenant was not human. Human necks just did not bend like that.

Eli said something in the language he had spoken moments before. The one with the bow replied and Marcus abruptly realized the bowman was a she! He glanced at Eli, unsure what he should do. Eli's complete attention was on the woman and the lieutenant looked to Marcus very much like a coiled spring, ready to explode into action.

She turned and said something back into the forest in the same tongue and slowly lowered her weapon. Two additional figures materialized from the darkness. Both were larger and clearly male. One was nursing his shoulder, where Marcus was sure his knife had landed. That much Marcus could make out in the moonlight.

"For the moment, we are safe," Eli said, turning back to Marcus, slowly relaxing, the tension leaving his posture.

"Do not make any threatening moves or reach for your weapons."

"Who are they?" Marcus asked, carefully straightening up from the crouch he had been in.

"Elves," Eli replied simply, returning his attention to the female, who seemed to be their leader. In the darkness Marcus could not make out their features too well.

"Your people?" Marcus gasped, startled. "What are they doing this far south?"

"These are not my people," Eli responded in a strained tone. "There should be no elves this far south."

Remain silent, Eli rapidly signed with his fingers. *Danger about.*

Eli turned back to the other elves, whereupon they began a rapid-fire conversation in what Marcus took to be elven. While Eli conversed with the leader, the uninjured male elf began to attend to the one Marcus had wounded.

Desiring to help, Marcus moved for his pack, where he had a needle, thread and some bandages for tending to wounds. Instantly the clearing became silent and filled with tension. The female had her bow up, aimed at Marcus, with an arrow nocked. The scout froze and slowly turned toward Eli, who was looking at him with an alarmed expression.

"I have needle, thread and bandages in my pack," Marcus explained to Eli, who then translated to the leader. She eyed him oddly for a moment before nodding once and lowering her bow. The tension faded as Marcus quickly retrieved what he needed. He handed it over to the elf treating his wounded comrade, who took it without a word of thanks.

Marcus stepped back to Eli, who had continued his discourse with the leader, speaking at length before turning to the scout.

"We will have a fire," Eli announced to Marcus, as if it had been decided.

"This close to the enemy?" Marcus asked skeptically. Until recently, he would never have dreamed of questioning an officer. Eli had taught him to question everything.

"They have guaranteed our safety," Eli stated. "Let us gather some firewood."

Within a short while, a small fire was started and soon they were all seated about it on the ground. In the firelight, Marcus discovered that the leader was stunningly beautiful. Her face, perfectly proportioned, was framed with long, straight, red hair. Her skin was smooth and pale. Her up-tilted eyes were a deep hazel in color and her ears, pointed like Eli's, poked ever so slightly from beneath her hair. Marcus felt her slim nose seemed almost delicate. She was so perfect that it made Marcus's heart ache to simply look upon her. He wanted nothing more than to protect her from danger. The other two elves looked similar to Eli but slightly different. Their manner indicated they were confident and sure of themselves.

While Eli and the female talked, Marcus sat cross-legged on the ground. Unable to comprehend their language, he settled for observation.

These elves were dressed in loose-fitting deerskin tunics and pants, in forest greens and browns, which were designed to blend into the background. Each carried bows that were similar to the ones Eli and Marcus carried, but slightly larger and more powerful-looking. Their arrows were held in small skin quivers and, from the length of the ends, appeared to be around four to six inches longer than the arrows the scouts used. They also wore swords. Beyond that, they carried no pouches, packs or haversacks. The lieutenant being the only elf he had ever known, Marcus did not know if this was how the High Born normally moved about the forest, perhaps even living off of the land. After a moment, he disregarded that thought. He rather suspected that they had dropped their packs before closing in on him.

Having witnessed what Eli was capable of, Marcus was more than a little nervous that these elves seemed allied with the rebels. More concerning was that just minutes before, they had tried their very best to kill him. Now they sat about a small fire, almost appearing peaceful.

"Ah—Lieutenant?" Marcus spoke up, abruptly realizing something that chilled him to the core.

Eli looked over questioningly, with a raised narrow eyebrow.

"There are more of them out in the trees, sir," Marcus said quietly. "I can feel it."

The leader cocked her head slightly at Marcus and fixed him with an intense and seemingly ageless hazel-eyed gaze that sent shivers down his spine. Once again, he felt like a strange bug being studied by a child.

"Yes, I know," Eli responded carefully. "We are in no danger from them, at least for the moment."

"You feel forest?" The leader addressed him directly for the first time. She spoke a soft, broken common that the scout found fascinating and attractive. Her eyes never left him. He tried not to squirm under her gaze. It was difficult to think clearly.

"I do," Marcus replied quietly, admitting it aloud for the first time, even to himself.

Eli looked back over at him sharply, but said nothing.

"Well met, ranger," she said, with a nod of respect. "I am Taha'Leeth."

"Well met, Taha'Leeth," Marcus replied politely and nodded his head respectfully. "I am Marcus."

She flashed him a brief smile filled with needle-sharp teeth before turning back to Eli.

The two elves spent some time in discourse before Taha'Leeth breathed out a heavy breath. Then began a long period of talking where the other two elves joined in, at times gesturing and pointing excitedly. Marcus had no idea what they were discussing, but after a time, he felt somehow the danger had passed. Perhaps it was the smiles and meaningful looks that the elves began sharing.

Eventually, several hours later, Taha'Leeth stood. Eli stood as well, dousing the fire with dirt from the forest floor. The darkness returned, but not quite as deep as it had been before. Dawn was fast approaching and the gloomy early morning light was beginning to show. Eli motioned for Marcus to stand and grab his kit. Stiffly, Marcus got to his feet.

"What's going on?" he asked, picking up his kit, including sword, bow and quiver. He secured his sword. He was careful to make no threatening moves as he did so, lest the elves get nervous. But they paid him little heed.

"We are being permitted to leave," Eli stated firmly. "They will not trouble us, nor will they continue to interfere with our fight against the rebels."

"Lieutenant," Marcus said, eyeing the three elves. "Aren't they working with the rebels?"

"They were," Eli admitted grimly. "No longer."

Taha'Leeth said something to Eli in elven, to which Eli replied and offered a respectful nod, which almost seemed to Marcus as if she was thanking him.

"Farewell, ranger," Taha'Leeth addressed him once again and offered him a nod of respect.

"Farewell, Taha'Leeth," Marcus replied, with a respectful nod in return. He also nodded to the elf he had wounded, who smiled in reply and patted his bandaged shoulder gently, as if to say it was no big deal. With that, the three elves turned and left the clearing as silently as they had come. They melted into the gloomy pre-dawn light as if they had never existed.

Eli turned and led Marcus back into the forest. Though he could not see them in the darkness, Marcus could feel the eyes of many other elves on him. Eli set a punishing pace in the direction of their own lines. He seemed in a hurry to get back.

"Eli," Marcus asked after a bit, struggling to keep up. "What happened back there?"

"I will not speak on it to you," Eli said, rather harshly, having abruptly stopped. "You will not speak on it to any other. Is that understood?"

"Yes, sir," Marcus replied, wondering how he had offended the lieutenant, whom he had considered a friend.

"It is a matter between the High Born," Eli stated, softening his tone.

"Eli," Marcus said carefully, thinking of the beautiful Taha'Leeth. "Do you think you could teach me elven?"

"Yes," Eli said with a grin and turned to go. "Sho'ha means hurry. The enemy will attack in strength this morning. Now, we hurry to warn the captain."

Marcus frowned. That did not sound good. Another thought occurred to him. "Why did she called me 'ranger'… what was all that about?"

"Taha'Leeth did not call you ranger," Eli said, turning back, a proud look on his perpetually youthful face, lit softly by the dim gloom of the early morning light. Eli pointed a finger at the scout's chest. "She *named* you ranger…"

With that, Eli set off again, leaving a stunned Marcus behind. To be named a ranger by one of the High Born meant he was one!

"Sho'ha," Eli called from ahead. "We must warn the captain!"

Managing to gather his wits, Marcus broke into a run and followed.

CHAPTER THIRTEEN

"HOLD!" STIGER SHOUTED to his men. The line was under intense pressure. The noise of the fight was overwhelming. Men screamed, shouted oaths, cursed and cried out in agony, exultation and pain. Shields hammered against shields, swords clashed and swords struck shields... Choking clouds of dust from the road were being kicked up into the air as hundreds of men struggled against each other in a confined space. Wounded fell beneath the immense press of the line and were crushed under foot by comrades and enemies alike.

"Hold, damn you!" Stiger shouted, pacing up and down behind the line. This was the first real test for his men and they were performing well. "Show the bastards legionary steel! Stab, don't slash! It takes two inches of steel to kill. Close order now, lock those shields!"

Stiger stopped pacing and looked across his line, which was three ranks deep. His men were being heavily pressured, but they held and it was clear they were giving better than they were receiving. Directly behind the center of the line stood the standard-bearers for the 85th and the eagle.

Lieutenant Banister and his company held the right and, to his left Brent held the other side. From what Stiger could see, both flanks were in very good shape. It was the center that was at risk.

They were fighting on this field because Stiger had sprung a hastily-organized ambush about a mile to the front of his defensive line. The ground he had chosen to fight on was a large open area. It was good ground, with a slight rise on which Stiger's men were positioned. The forest had been cut back on both sides of the road, where, years before, a farmer had once lived and worked the land. The sloping fields were long overgrown and the men on both flanks were forced to fight amidst waist-high brush and overgrowth. The abandoned farmer's house, long ago collapsed, was to his right and behind.

The fight, which really could only be described as a serious skirmish, had been going on for the past hour and a half. Stiger had surprised and rapidly destroyed the enemy's lead company, only to have them rush up additional forces before he could properly disengage. He had meant to strike fast and then fall back upon his prepared defensive line. To his chagrin, it had not worked out that way.

The current slug fest was threatening to turn his quick victory into a solid defeat. The captain figured he was facing close to a thousand rebels, with more coming up the longer the skirmish dragged on. Over the heads of his men, he could see yet another rebel company marching onto the field several hundred yards behind the enemy line. He would have to shortly disengage and that would be tricky, since it meant he would be making a fighting withdrawal back to the defensive line where Lieutenant Ikely was positioned with close to two hundred fresh men.

Fighting withdrawals were difficult to manage, especially when outnumbered, as he was now. The best bet would be to leapfrog his companies back, each taking a turn at rearguard. With the enemy dogging their every step, it would be dangerous, difficult and costly work. It was something he was loath to do.

He began studying the enemy to his front as his mind worked out the details for a withdrawal. The enemy force assaulting the center of his line, at least three companies strong, was better trained, armed and kitted-out than the rebels he had faced to date. These men were equipped with short chainmail shirts. They carried small, round shields and were armed with large, curved swords. They also had discipline and it was that quality that was making the fight so difficult. *Are these the soldiers Eli spoke of that the enemy brought forward? Are they soldiers of the confederacy?*

Stiger's men were, however, better armed and armored. Their legionary short swords were the perfect tool for this kind of close-in work. In the press of the front ranks, the rebels were having difficulty getting sufficient room to use their larger swords, which were meant for slashing and not stabbing. Stiger's legionaries had no difficulty jabbing out with relentless ruthlessness from behind the cover of their curved, rectangular-shaped shields. The enemy seemed to be paying a heavy price. Though in time, Stiger well understood that numbers would tell. The enemy had deeper reserves than he did. Once his men tired, the enemy would be able to overwhelm him.

As Stiger was studying the enemy directly to his front, it occurred to him that the rebels on the flanks were of the same type he had previously faced, poorly equipped and armed. It was the reason his flanks were holding up so well! *I wonder how their morale is? If I push them...will they break?*

He looked around for a runner and spied Eli no more than ten feet away, directing the scouts. There were no more than ten of them and using their bows, they were peppering death down onto the rear ranks of the rebels.

This entire affair had begun when Eli had arrived with a warning that rebel scouting parties had found the defensive line early and that the enemy was making a forced night march to launch a surprise attack at first light. Why none of Stiger's forward scouts had reported the enemy movement, the captain did not know, but he suspected the worst and immediately swung into action.

Recalling the field in which they were currently fighting was good ground for an ambush, Stiger had figured that he would give the rebels a surprise of his own. He had intended to surprise the enemy and smack them hard before retiring backward to the safety of his defensive line.

"I need two of your scouts!" Stiger shouted over the noise, hustling over to his friend. Eli nodded and called over Davis and Todd.

"Davis," Stiger ordered, "I want you to find Lieutenant Brent over there and, Todd, locate Lieutenant Banister. Tell them, as soon as practical, I want them to go all in. They are to push forward into the enemy formations directly to their front. They only need to push the enemy to break them. Once broken, they are to collapse on the middle from the flanks. It is important that they collapse on the middle! Understand?"

Both scouts nodded, saluted and dashed off in opposite directions. Stiger stepped back toward the line. Sergeant Blake and Ranl were moving up and down behind the line, shouting orders and occasionally swapping out the front rank to give men a brief break. The wounded, if able, staggered and crawled back behind the line in ones and twos toward the aid station, which was back at the defensive line, a mile to the rear.

"Straighten that line there!" Stiger shouted. "Use your shields properly!"

The pressure on his front rank was increasing. He needed to relieve that pressure before the enemy was able to crack his line. Thankfully, he had a secret weapon and figured now was the best time to use it.

"Third rank!" Stiger shouted, cupping his hands. "Ready javelins!"

The third rank took two steps back, raised their javelins and drew the long, specially-weighted weapons back. Stiger had hoped to save this surprise for later, but he no longer had a choice. Looking left and right, he confirmed that the third rank was ready. The javelins had arrived over a week ago and the men had been practicing non-stop.

"Javelins release!" Stiger shouted and instantly, with a chorus of heavy grunts, the third rank threw their deadly weapons up into the air. The javelins flew upward to arc and then fall, crashing down like wave upon the rebel company. There was no hiding from the long-pointed, deadly missiles. Even if a shield were raised, the iron heads punched right through and then the shank bent, rendering the shield useless. Men screamed, died and were wounded as the javelins struck home. The pressure on the front rank slacked as the rebel ranks recoiled briefly.

Stiger smiled. He had just become the first legionary commander in over three hundred years to use javelins in battle. The legions had long abandoned the weapon, which Stiger felt had been a mistake. The captain himself had been on the receiving end of a javelin toss on more than one occasion, courtesy of the Rivan. The effectiveness of the javelin, frequently a one-use weapon, had impressed him. The soft shaft or shank of the spear was intended to bend upon impact so that the enemy could not return them in kind, unlike a short spear.

"Second volley," Stiger called. "Release at will."

A second ragged wave of javelins flew at the enemy, who, now aware of the danger, could do little to protect themselves. Javelins pierced shields, armor and unprotected flesh with ease, killing some outright and wounding and maiming many others.

The sound of the battle on Stiger's right abruptly rose in pitch, followed by something similar on the left side. Both of his flanks, whose orders had been simply to hold moments before, went forward with a war cry and shout, pushing the enemy physically back, one step at a time, struggling through the brush and undergrowth. Shields locked together, parted for the inevitable jab at unprotected flesh, followed by a half-step forward, the rear ranks helping to push the front. It was a powerful drive and the rebels, caught by surprise at the suddenness of it, fell by the score.

The enemy on both flanks staggered under the weight of the slow but steady advance pushing them backward. Stiger cheered his men on as he carefully watched his own line. He needed at least one flank to break to be able to pull back. On the left, the enemy held for a moment more, then buckled and fully collapsed, turning as one and running rearward in great confusion. On the right, the enemy held on stubbornly.

Stiger watched anxiously as Brent struggled to get his men reorganized, for many legionaries had broken ranks to chase after the fleeing rebels. Stiger caught a glimpse of what looked to be a rebel officer going down under a flurry of swords before he returned his focus to the center.

Slowly but surely, Brent's lines reformed and the lieutenant began wheeling his formation around to hit the center from the side. The movement took time, but was well-executed. The enemy commander in the center must have seen what was happening and understood he was facing certain disaster, for the pressure on Stiger's line abruptly eased. A moment later they began, in good order, to pull back.

"Sergeant Blake!" Stiger shouted, cupping his hands to his lips. "Sergeant Ranl! We will advance upon my word!"

Both sergeants acknowledged and began issuing orders to the corporals, getting the company ready to push forward. Stiger could see his men were tired and weary. However, they were legionaries of the empire. Nearly every day they were worked, drilled or exercised to near exhaustion. This, combined with rigid discipline, was designed to deliver unquestioning obedience and make one tough soldier, an incredibly formidable opponent. This was the legion's secret. It was the reason why legionaries endured the fatigue of battles better than their enemies. Stiger had trained these men and there was no doubt in his mind they would do as ordered.

"Advance!" he shouted, waving his sword in the air. His men stepped forward and began to advance upon the enemy. Within seconds, both lines were once again back in close contact. The fighting intensified and the rebel company was forced to halt their backward movement. Brent's force pushed home into the flank of the enemy, slamming into it. At the same time, the enemy force on the right side, pushed by Banister, abruptly collapsed. The rebels ran for the rear in panic. Moments later, like an accordion, the center company pressed from the front and one flank folded and broke.

Stiger breathed a huge sigh of relief as his men began to slaughter the disorganized enemy. He closed his eyes briefly and offered a prayer of thanks to the High Father. It was time to withdraw.

There were fresh enemy companies coming up and it was only a matter of time before they moved forward and he found himself once again tightly engaged. He could not afford to let his men get too far out of control. He called out to Blake and Ranl to reform the men who had surged forward after the fleeing enemy. The sergeants and corporals got to work, blowing their whistles. The 85th slowly began to reform. But the 95th and 33rd under Banister and Brent were completely disorganized as they chased down the enemy from the field.

What I wouldn't give for some good legionary horns, Stiger thought, for when fighting in larger formations, the legionary was trained to listen for horn calls, such as a recall to reform.

Stiger looked about for Eli to send runners to both lieutenants when, suddenly, there was a loud explosive roaring to the right. He turned and blinked in astonishment, not quite sure he believed his own eyes.

From amidst the fleeing enemy, a large ball of fire rose up into the air and then fell into the middle of Banister's company. There was a terrific explosion, with men thrown bodily into the air while others were blown apart, arms and legs flying. A gout of flame shot up into the air from where the ball of flame had landed and within a stone's throw, the concussive force threw men flat.

Shock settled across the field, as men from both sides simply stopped what they were doing and looked in utter surprise. Another massive ball of fire arced up into the air before falling amidst Banister's men with a terrific explosion.

Banister's company, a moment before in pursuit of fleeing rebels, broke. Men scrambled to their feet and, screaming with fear, ran for their lives. Stiger's men and those of Brent's company began inching backwards. The enemy, already in a state of panic, continued their flight from the field, while those enemy companies having freshly come up simply stopped and watched the show.

As the last of the broken rebels cleared the field, a tall, out-of-place-looking man wearing brilliant red robes was left standing alone. He had a long black beard that was neatly braided and his jet black hair was tied back in a long ponytail. He held forth a hand up and away from his body. His red-robed sleeve slipped back to reveal a heavily tattooed forearm. A ball of fire formed in the man's palm. It began to smoke heavily as the ball of flame grew in size and intensity. The fire smoked a dark black, as though it came from burning pitch or oil. A moment later, he jerked his hand and the ball of flame was released. It seemed to leap forth, reaching skyward before losing velocity and falling back to earth amongst Banister's fleeing men. The ball of fire touched the ground with another terrific explosion and concussive blast that knocked those nearest from their feet.

Still in shock, Stiger stood motionless. The enemy had a wizard! Wizards never got involved in battles! It was an unheard occurrence.

How do I fight a wizard? Stiger asked himself, completely unprepared. He was about to call for a general withdrawal, when there was a flash from his peripheral vision, as Eli darted by. The elf pushed roughly through the ranks, nocking an arrow to his bow as he did so. Once in the clear, he brought his bow forward, pulled back, aimed for a fraction of a second and let go. The arrow flew true.

The wizard's hand was once again afire and stretching forth to release yet another deadly ball of flame when the arrow struck home, easily piercing the wizard's red robes to lodge deep in the man's right side.

The wizard staggered, eyes wide with shock and pain, both hands reflexively going to the arrow shaft that protruded from his side. As his flaming hand touched it, there was a deep thump as the spell was abruptly released.

This was followed by a horrible scream as the ball of fire exploded upon the wizard, engulfing and consuming him. The scream lasted but a few heartbeats before his lungs burned and he could issue no more sound. He fell to his knees as the fire burned away skin, flesh and then muscle. So hot was the inferno that in mere moments it had burned itself out, leaving only a pile of ash where once there had been a living, breathing wizard.

A stunned silence descended upon the battlefield, followed a heartbeat later by a hearty roar of approval from the legionaries. Stiger's shoulders sagged in relief. What had looked like certain defeat only moments before had turned to victory. He took another deep breath and stood tall. The battle was far from over.

"Sergeant Blake, Ranl!" Stiger snapped in his loudest parade-ground voice. The newly-arrived enemy company was still there and another was coming up behind them. "Reform the men!"

"Yes, sir!" Blake responded.

With the help of the corporals, the sergeants began to reform the company. Brent was also reforming his company. Shattered, Banister's company had fled the field, leaving behind only their dead and wounded. Stiger did not have time to think of them.

Once both companies were formed up, Stiger ordered his and Brent's to advance a short way and form a line to cover the field while details worked quickly to remove the wounded and dead, which took just shy of thirty minutes. The enemy, though they formed a line of battle, watched from a safe distance as Stiger's men worked. They did not advance onto the field, but remained where they were, silently watching the legionaries go about their work. Had they moved forward, Stiger would have immediately called for a withdrawal, but they did not seem inclined to do so.

Lieutenant Banister was one of the wounded. He had been badly burned and having seen the man's wounds, Stiger doubted the lieutenant would survive the night. Once they had collected and removed the dead and wounded, Stiger's company marched off the field first, followed shortly by Brent's. They moved off smartly in the direction of Vrell and Ikely's defensive position, where they could rest and reorganize.

The men were exhausted from the fight. Stiger could see it as they marched wearily down the road. Eli trotted up and fell in next to him. For a while they were both silent, Stiger brooding upon the fight and the significant losses he had suffered. The loss of Banister himself was major, since he was short of good officers. They may have won the fight and bloodied the enemy yet again, but at what cost? Then Stiger recalled that the losses could have been far worse had it not been for Eli's skill with the bow.

"Nice shot," he said to Eli amidst the rhythmic crunch of many sandaled feet. "Very timely too."

"He never saw it coming," Eli agreed with a self-satisfied, full-toothed smile directed at his friend. "He never saw it coming."

CHAPTER FOURTEEN

S TIGER SAT BEFORE the fire in front of his tent. Eli was out checking on the enemy. Ikely was making the rounds, as he was the duty officer this evening. Brent was seeing to the wounded. Alone with his thoughts, the captain was mulling over the day's skirmish. He had lost over forty men and another thirty-three injured, most with severe burns. The enemy had suffered far more heavily, but that did not make him feel any better. Stiger could ill-afford any losses. The rebels, however, could.

He had given the enemy two good bloody noses. Yet, what with the wizard, the enemy had given him one as well. Stiger still had difficulty coming to grips with that. Wizards were supposedly solitary individuals who pursued their own interests and cared little for the concerns of others, let alone those of nation states. They were dangerous and best left alone. How had this one come to band together with the rebels?

He rubbed at his tired eyes as he tried to make sense of it all. A paladin, Castor, the rebels, a strange band of elves and now a wizard! He felt as if he was becoming caught up in something that he did not fully understand. It was maddening! He ran a hand through his hair, matted and dirty from wearing his helmet for most of the day. He badly needed a bath and itched terribly. *What does it all mean? Why Vrell?* The answer kept eluding him.

Eli had been vague on the subject of a band of elves he and Marcus had encountered, just hours after assuring Stiger there were none in the south! He had simply said that they were not of his people. His friend would say nothing more.

Apparently, just prior to the enemy's attempt to pull off a surprise attack, these elves had been responsible for eliminating most of Stiger's advance scouts. Had Eli not arrived with word of the rebel's unexpected movement, Stiger might have found himself caught flat-footed.

The captain frowned in irritation. Eli insisted the elves would no longer trouble Stiger's men nor continue to work with the enemy. Unfortunately, the damage had been done and that had hurt the most. Stiger had lost the majority of his scouts, men he badly needed as his eyes. With fewer scouts, his ability to pull off ambushes and counterpunches was significantly reduced. It certainly made things more dangerous.

"It is a matter of the High Born and best left that way," Eli had stated, a pained look on his perfect face. "I cannot discuss this any further."

Stiger wondered if Eli would not say more because he chose to or whether he was in reality forbidden from doing so. Only once before had Stiger run into a similar wall with Eli and his elven brethren, which was why the captain was leaning toward the latter explanation. The more he thought on it, Stiger was sure this was a topic Eli was prohibited from discussing with non-elves. Regardless, it was frustrating and when Stiger had the time, he intended on having a serious conversation with Eli. He would demand an explanation.

A strong, chilly wind blew through the forest and Stiger shivered. Even without the wind, the night air was bitterly cold. He was in a foul mood and it was becoming fouler by the moment. He prodded the fire before him with a stick to flare it up and then hurled the stick into the blaze. He pulled his cloak tighter about himself for an added measure of warmth. Winter was nearly upon them. Lan had even reported that the first snow had hit the pass the day before, although the two inches that had fallen had subsequently melted by noon.

After the fight, he had pulled back to the defensive line that Ikely had been holding. His men were tired. They all needed a rest and he also had to deal with Banister's company, who had fled from the field.

The legions were not terribly tolerant of units that broke and retreated from battle. By rights he should make an example of them. Decimation, the killing of every tenth man, would be an appropriate punishment. Under any other circumstance, he would have felt justified punishing the unit, but he just could not bring himself to do so. Ever since Captain Aveeno had murdered their commanding officer, the 95th had been commanded by a junior officer, Lieutenant Banister. When they broke, they had been under magical attack from a wizard. Such a thing, to Stiger's knowledge, had never occurred before and therein lay the heart of the matter. Had it been the 85th, instead of the 95th on the receiving end, Stiger's men might have run as well.

So, short of officers and men, he did the only thing that made sense. Stiger had broken up the 95th, assigning half to the 33rd under Brent and the remainder to the 85th. The company's standard had been returned to Castle Vrell, where it would be boxed up. When contact was reestablished, the commanding general of the south would make the final decision on whether to reactivate the 95th.

Stiger's thinking shifted away from the 95th and back to the enemy. His defensive position was formidable and blocked the road, stretching out into the forest on both sides. The ground beyond the flanks was broken and rugged. It would be very difficult, but not impossible, for the rebels to pull off a successful flanking maneuver.

Stiger meant to allow the enemy to come up, deploy and assault his new position before giving additional ground. Then, he would fall back to the next prepared position several miles down the road and into his defensive corridor. With each movement backward, Stiger got closer to Vrell and the safety of the castle walls.

Stiger suddenly tensed. Where a moment before there had been no one, a short, squat man in night-black robes was now standing by the fire. The man carried a staff with an oddly-formed hunk of crystal mounted upon its top. It looked like it had once had a shape but had partially melted. The firelight made the crystal sparkle with refracted light. Stiger reached for his sword, which was lying by his side.

"I mean you no ill will, captain." The man spoke in a deep, husky voice that was tinged with an unfamiliar accent, yet he spoke the Common tongue fluently. "I am here to talk…only talk. I assure you."

Stiger grabbed his sword and, in one swift motion, drew it from the scabbard, standing as he did so. The tingle was electric and for a brief moment, the blade glowed an intense blue before fading away. In surprise, Stiger almost dropped the weapon.

"Guards!" His personal guards were only feet away. Ikely had insisted that two men stand watch over the captain at all times. Stiger was now grateful he had given in to Ikely's insistence on a protection detail.

Unfortunately, there was no response from them.

"They will not come," the small man said, which was followed by an unnerving maniacal giggle. "They cannot and will not hear you."

Chilled by the statement, Stiger took a step back, sword held at the ready. His eyes searched for his guards. They were not to be seen. Stiger blinked. The camp beyond the captain's fire was strangely dark and ominously silent.

"Had I meant you harm, you would already be sleeping with your ancestors," the man said, his manner becoming dangerous. "Though I readily admit that sword you carry is somewhat special and might complicate matters a bit. As I understand it, General Delvaris deserved only the best. Has it spoken to you yet?"

"What?" Stiger asked, confused, eying the intruder carefully.

"No matter," the small man said with a negligent wave of the hand. "As I said, I mean you no harm. You have my... ah...yes, my word of honor." He giggled.

"Who are you?" Stiger asked. He did not like this one bit. The man knew to whom the sword had belonged and that the weapon could speak! He was standing by the firelight, but Stiger could not clearly see his features. It was as if the light was afraid to touch his face. Something very unnatural was afoot.

"I am The Master," the man said, which was followed by another strange giggle. "The Master...it still sounds so not right to my ears. You may call me Ogg."

"What do you want?" Stiger asked as the small man stepped closer, his face abruptly becoming clear, as if the light was no longer afraid. The captain sucked in a breath. Ogg was not human! The face was too wide and the eyes set too far apart. The nose and brow were also far too large. Though short, he was wider than a man had a right to be.

"Want?" A strange expression passed across his unnatural face. "That is an interesting question. Really interesting,

I must admit. One day, when the time is right, I may even tell you."

"Why are you here?" Stiger growled, becoming angry at the cryptic responses. "What are you playing at?"

"Those are also good questions." Ogg took a seat before the fire on a large log next to the captain's. He leaned his staff against a leg and shifted forward to better catch the heat from the fire. Stiger noticed that Ogg's hands were short and stubby. He also had an extra finger!

"You…you are a dwarf!" Stiger exclaimed.

Ogg looked up at him with a very sour expression. "Some of my people would not wish it were so."

"You are then," Stiger stated, absolutely convinced. "You are a dwarf?"

"Though your word usage is potentially offensive… you are accurate in your assessment." Ogg turned back to the fire. "We call ourselves the Dvergr. In our language it roughly translates to People of the Legend."

"What do you want?" Stiger asked, not daring to take his eyes from Ogg, though his heart was racing. Eli had been right all along.

"Back to that again, are we?" Ogg asked, looking up from the fire. "Put that sword away. Let us converse like civilized beings instead of savages. You imperials do claim to be civilized?"

Stiger hesitated a moment as he considered. He indeed believed that, had Ogg wished it, he would be dead. He gave a shrug, sheathed his sword and took his seat once again before the fire. As he did so, he took another look around the camp. It was still dark beyond the light of his campfire. No others could be seen, which was damn odd. Moments before there had been hundreds of campfires before as many tents, with legionaries preparing to bed down for the night. Now he could see no one, not even his guards, who had stood watch not more than ten feet away.

He made a show of pulling out his pipe. From a small pouch, he filled it with some of the captured tobacco, took a moment to light the pipe then puffed up a good burn.

"How can I help you, Ogg?" Stiger asked conversationally, blowing out a long stream of smoke. Two could play at this game.

"That is the correct question," Ogg replied, which was followed by another giggle. "See, we are becoming acquainted, which is my purpose."

"Acquainted?" Stiger responded with a grunt, taking a deep pull from his pipe.

"Though," Ogg said after a slight hesitation, "you should have asked how we can help each other?"

Stiger said nothing. Obviously the dwarf had come for something. He would eventually get to the point. So, Stiger decided to remain silent until he did. As a result, the two did not speak for a good while, each lost to his own thoughts. Strangely enough, as he smoked away, Stiger no longer felt as lonely as he had minutes before.

"My people are gathering their warriors," Ogg breathed after some time. "They are preparing to drive you imperials from the valley."

"What?" Stiger asked, sitting upright. Had he heard the dwarf correctly?

"My people really do not like your people. Well, to be fair, we don't like anyone, even our own at times," Ogg explained. "But your people brought Castor's influence into the valley and my people mean to cleanse it."

"I was not responsible for that," Stiger stated firmly, taking the pipe from his mouth and jabbing it in the dwarf's direction. "I had a hand in removing that filth."

"I know that," Ogg admitted, turning his gaze back upon the fire.

"Do your people?" Stiger asked. "Do they know?"

"Not yet," Ogg explained, which was followed up with another little maniacal

giggle.

"Tell them!" Stiger growled angrily. "By the gods, I will tell them! Give me the chance!"

"I may take you up on that," Ogg said, looking back at him. "My people are hard-headed. At times they hear only what they wish to, particularly our leaders. Sometimes words are just not good enough."

"Then why tell me?" Stiger asked bitterly. This all seemed to be a cruel jest. Was having to contend with one enemy not enough? How cruel the gods could be! "Why give me this warning?"

"Unity, honor and friendship," Ogg replied simply, offering Stiger a small, tight smile.

Stiger held Ogg's gaze. He had heard those words before. Then it hit him. Eli had read those very words off of the monument in the valley.

"The monument to the 13th!" Stiger exclaimed, snapping his fingers. "Those words were inscribed there."

"They are the heart and soul of the Compact," Ogg said sadly, then giggled. Stiger was beginning to wonder if Ogg was altogether sane. "You should thank General Delvaris. I am repaying a debt long owed, but still yet to be fully paid."

"I don't understand," Stiger spat. "Explain what you mean!"

"You were lucky today," Ogg said flatly, changing the subject, looking back at the fire. "I watched your skirmish. You were very lucky. Yes, very lucky."

Stiger frowned at the abrupt change in direction of the conversation.

"Years of playing with power tends to convince wizards that they are omnipotent and infallible," Ogg continued, eyeing Stiger as he said this. "I can assure you we are not, as you so aptly learned today. Stick a knife in me or shoot me with an arrow and I will bleed just as you would."

Stiger went cold. Though he had suspected it, the dwarf before him had just admitted to being a wizard. He felt like pulling out his sword again but restrained himself. Ogg held the power here and not he.

"So, you can be killed as anyone else," Stiger growled, almost as a challenge.

"Yes," Ogg agreed with a dangerous glint in his eye. "Unless, of course, I am prepared for such eventualities. I can assure you, I am unlike that weak-minded fool your elf struck down."

Thinking on what Ogg had told him, Stiger slowly leaned back and took another long pull from his pipe. He slowly blew out some smoke as he considered what he wanted to say next. It seemed as if, with the rebels to his front and the dwarves to his rear, he was truly screwed.

"So, Ogg," Stiger said, taking another pull. "What now?"

There was no response. Stiger looked over at the dwarf wizard, only to find him gone, disappeared, as if he had never been. He looked around, searching. Beyond the fire-light stood his two guards and beyond them the fires of the legionary camp, which shone brightly in the darkness. The sound and noise of the camp returned with an abruptness that surprised him. He shook his head in bemusement then turned his gaze back to the flames, his thoughts far more troubled than they had been just moments before.

CHAPTER FIFTEEN

L AN STEPPED OUT from the keep and into the castle courtyard as the first of several wagons, converted into ambulances, arrived. The cold air hit him immediately and he pulled his cloak closer about himself. In the confines of the courtyard, the wagon clattered loudly across the granite paving stones. The seriously injured lay in the beds, while those who could sat upright. Some were able to walk alongside or behind the wagons, blood-soaked bandages a testament to the intensity of the fighting.

The large supply wagons were not known for their comfort. Bouncing and jostling from every rut or bump in the road, they were a torment for those already in unbearable agony. He could hear the cries and moans of the wounded as the wagon pulled to a stop.

Some would survive and recover, returning to their respective companies. Others would recover, crippled for life, only to be discharged with a meager disability benefit. These poor unfortunates would be returned to Mal'Zeel. Likely they would end up living a life of idle squalor, dependent upon the grain dole and their disability payment, which would inevitably go toward cheap wine and the occasional diseased whore.

"Lieutenant," Sergeant Arnold greeted him in his normally gruff manner and pulled his wagon to a stop. He offered the lieutenant a lazy salute. Lan reflected that even being offered a salute was a far cry from what he had gotten from the sergeant a few weeks back, when they had first met. It seemed he had earned a little respect from the veteran.

Sergeant Arnold himself was an anomaly in the legions. He had received a near-crippling injury to the knee. The man could barely get around and yet instead of being discharged for his disability, he had been assigned to supply and teamster duty. This typically only occurred when the man had performed a feat of intense bravery or completed some important service. Though the sergeant, like most of his rank, wore several phalera, which signified his honors fairly earned, Lan had difficulty seeing that side of the man.

Several troopers stepped to the rear of the wagon to begin the careful unloading of the wounded. Others guided those who could walk toward the keep. Lan had ordered a hospital ward set up on the second floor. The garrison had not warranted a surgeon and as such, the wounded were at the tender mercy of the company surgeon's mates, men trained as medics or, as they were called in the old tongue, medicus.

They were trained to perform minor procedures, such as the sewing up of injuries, basic wound care and the tending of those who were ill. Unfortunately, they were not trained for surgery or the care and mending of those seriously injured. Worse, there were only six of them in the entire garrison, with only one remaining at the castle. The rest had gone forward with Captain Stiger.

Once word had reached the castle that wounded were on their way, and that some cases were extremely serious, Lan had asked Councilman Bester to send for anyone trained in surgery. With luck, the two valley doctors would arrive within the next few hours.

"How many?" Lan asked grimly, glancing at the covered wagon from which he heard moans and cries. Unfortunately, or fortunately, depending upon one's point of view, the wagons could only travel two miles into the forest. Captain Stiger had excluded the last two miles of road from his defensive corridor. So it meant that the wounded were hand-carried many miles on litters, or litters pulled by horses, until they could reach the wagons. Over a hundred of the cavalry had been designated as litter-bearers and sent forward to help return the injured.

"Around forty poor wretches," Arnold answered tiredly. "Including, unfortunately for him, Lieutenant Banister."

"Banister?" Lan asked with some surprise.

"He's in the back," the sergeant said, jerking a thumb.

"Oh, great gods," Lan breathed, realizing that if the lieutenant was wagon-bound it was a serious injury. He stepped around the side of the covered wagon to look and was horrified by the sight that greeted him. Because of the severity of his burns, he was only able to recognize Banister by his armor. Officers typically wore more ornate armor, greaves for their legs and with their swords secured to their left side instead of right like the rest of the rank and file.

Lan stood there for a moment, staring at the wreck of a man that Banister had become. Banister looked to be unconscious, which was in all probability a blessing for the man.

Looking at him, it was hard to see how he had managed to live long enough to be brought to the keep. The skin on his arms, legs, and hands had burned away. The skin on his face had burned off, leaving a mass of ugly red and black twisted and blistered flesh. Banister's eyelids had been burned off, along with his lips, allowing his undamaged eyes and teeth to be seen in their entirety. Banister's armor looked to have partially melted and at points fused with the twisted flesh, especially around the helmet. Both the sight and smell of burned flesh was strong and incredibly nauseating, to the point where it was nearly overpowering. Lan felt the bile in his throat rise and struggled to hold it down. He had seen men die before, either by sword or arrow. Yet never like this. Then he remembered something he had heard as a child.

"Paladins can heal," he whispered almost to himself.

"What was that, sir?" a trooper asked, having set a litter down on the ground in preparation for the unloading of the wagon and carrying the seriously injured into the keep.

"Send for Father Thomas, man, and hurry," Lan ordered.

The trooper saluted and dashed off for the keep.

"Do you know what happened?" Lan asked of Arnold, who had struggled down from the wagon and had limped to the back.

Two troopers carefully lifted Banister out of the wagon and down onto a waiting litter. One of the men staggered a few feet away before falling to his knees and retching.

Looking down upon on the hideous creature laid out before him in horror, Lan could not imagine how Banister had been so badly burned.

"I was told a wizard got him," Arnold said. "Poor bastard. No one should have to go like that."

"Wizard?" Lan asked, aghast. He had gotten a terse note from the captain that they had had a skirmish and a number of wounded were on their way back, but not much else about the fight itself. "Are you sure?"

"Yeah." Arnold spat upon the flagstone. "From what I heard, he burned a lot of good men before the captain's elf took the bastard down."

Lan was about to ask more questions when he saw Father Thomas emerge from the keep. The paladin rushed over, brown robes aflutter and his expression concerned. Without a word to Lan or Arnold, he immediately knelt down before Banister and placed a hand on the man's badly-burned face. The paladin closed his eyes and bowed his head. His lips moved in a silent prayer. Several troopers stopped to watch. Lan refrained from ordering them back to work for fear of disturbing Father Thomas.

Banister stirred slightly and moaned with agony, lidless eyes looking around wildly, before becoming still as he fell back into unconsciousness, seemingly more at ease. A dribble of blood ran from his ruined mouth. After a time, Father Thomas opened his eyes and looked up at Lan with an incredibly sad look.

"I am afraid he has walked too far down the path to the next world," Father Thomas announced. "There is nothing to be done, other than to ease his pain and make his last hours comfortable."

Lan bowed his head in sadness and offered a prayer to the High Father. He asked that Banister's passing be free from pain. The man had served the legions honorably and deserved better than the agonizing death he now faced.

"Back to work," Lan snapped at the idle troopers.

The men jumped and continued their work, unloading the wounded from the wagon, setting each out on a stretcher. Another burned man was set down next to the mortally stricken lieutenant. This man's left arm and side were badly burned. Someone had removed his armor and he wore only his service tunic, or what was left of it. The tunic had been burned through and the skin beneath was an ugly mass of twisted and burned flesh.

Father Thomas wiped Banister's blood off his hand with his robes and moved over to the man as he was laid down upon the granite flagstone. The man looked up at the paladin with tears of pain in his eyes. His forehead glistened with sweat and he shook terribly. Fever had taken hold, which was not a good sign for someone who had been burned. It meant infection had set in and that meant death was a close companion.

"Please make the pain stop," he begged, tears running down his face as he shook uncontrollably. He was doing his best to keep from screaming his agony to the world.

"What is your name, son?" Father Thomas asked in a soothing tone, squatting beside the man.

"Legionary Paulus," he replied, tears streaking down his face. "Milk of the poppy! Please. It hurts terribly."

"There...there... Paulus you say," Father Thomas spoke soothingly and then quoted from the holy book. "Bless the High Father and forget not all his benefits, for burn for burn and wound for wound, who forgives all of your iniquity, who heals your faithful body and soul, who redeems your life from the pit and crowns your soul with steadfast mercy and love."

The paladin placed a hand on the man's forehead and closed his eyes. Almost immediately the legionary closed his eyes and seemed to completely relax, slipping into a deep slumber. The feverish shaking stopped as well. A solitary tear rolled down his face as he took a deep breath and began to snore.

There was an intense flash of light that came from where the paladin's hand touched Paulus's forehead. Lan took an involuntary step backwards and shielded his eyes with his hands. The flash of light faded as quickly as it came, leaving Lan and Arnold blinking away the spots.

"By the old gods...a miracle," the grizzled old sergeant exclaimed in awe.

Lan sucked in a breath and gave a shallow whistle. Where a moment before Paulus had been terribly burned, now there remained unmarred skin that looked a deep angry red, as if freshly sunburned. The snoring continued from Paulus as the paladin sat back before standing, a tired look in his eyes. A couple of the stretcher-bearers, having witnessed the healing, fell to their knees, offering up prayers to the High Father.

"Just the High Father's blessing," Father Thomas stated wearily and then looked down at the man he had just healed. Something clenched in Paulus's hand apparently caught his attention. He bent down and retrieved it and held it up for examination.

"The High Father's image," the paladin said, showing the small wooden figurine to Lan and Arnold as he looked kindly down upon the sleeping legionary. After a moment, he returned the figurine to the man's hand. "Lieutenant Ikely's good work, I assume."

Lan and Arnold shared a surprised look.

"Are there many more?" Father Thomas asked.

Sergeant Arnold nodded as two more wagons clattered into the courtyard.

"Around forty," Lan said, struggling to keep the emotion from his voice. He had never before witnessed such a healing, but after having seen it, he wondered how he could ever again doubt the High Father's existence.

"Have the wounded moved into the hospital ward," Father Thomas said. "I will tend to them there."

"Yes, Father," Lan responded reverently. Though they did not have a surgeon available, with the paladin's help he hoped many more would be saved.

"I will require at least five assistants," the paladin continued, "bandages, thread, fresh tunics and clean water too."

"Bandages?" Lan asked surprised. He had expected Father Thomas to be able to heal most of the wounded.

"I will likely not have the strength to heal them all, only the more severe cases," Father Thomas explained with a faraway look. "Each healing taxes my strength greatly and...I feel called."

"Very well," Lan said with a slight frown as he watched the paladin look in the direction of the castle entrance. "You will have all that you require. If you need anything further, please ask."

"I will, my son," the paladin responded. "I will do what I can, but I must leave tonight or at the very latest in the morning."

"Tonight?" Lan asked, frown deepening. Surely he would be needed for the wounded. "Why?"

"The High Father calls me away," the paladin said, focusing back on Lan. "I will do what I can, then I must go."

"I see," Lan said. It seemed the doctors would be needed after all.

"Father," Arnold spoke up a little hesitantly. The paladin turned to look on the grizzled supply sergeant.

"Yes?"

"Father," Arnold said, hesitating. "Do you think you might be able to look at me bum knee and fix it?"

Father Thomas looked the sergeant up and down, considering him for a moment. The sergeant did not make the most presentable man and Lan felt Arnold was suddenly conscious of that. The sergeant tugged nervously on his stained tunic, straightening it under his armor.

"When was the last time you spoke on your sins, my son?" the paladin asked, eyeing Arnold closely.

"My sins?" Arnold barked out a harsh laugh. "Father... I've not been a good boy for a long while. I've not been particularly religious-like too."

"I see," the paladin replied. He nodded to himself, as if he had suspected as much, before turning to walk back to the keep. He stepped aside to allow a stretcher-bearer pass.

"Ah, Father," the sergeant called after another slight hesitation. Father Thomas turned back, a bushy red eyebrow raised in question. "Will you…ah…be kind enough to hear me sins?"

"Come to me this evening with an open heart," Father Thomas replied in a grave manner. "I will hear your sins and so will the High Father."

The grizzled old sergeant swallowed, almost as if he was afraid and then gave a curt nod of acceptance. "I will come."

"We will see together if there is forgiveness for your transgressions," Father Thomas said. "Have no fear. The High Father is merciful. He is loving in his blessings, especially so on those willing to repent, as long as they are open and honest with themselves."

Lan and the sergeant watched the paladin go as another wagon full of wounded pulled into the courtyard. The lieutenant looked down upon Paulus, whom Father Thomas had just healed and then at the mortally-wounded Banister, who was resting peacefully. He felt a great sadness well up in his heart, for a good man would soon pass from this world.

Sergeant Mills came up and cast an uneasy look upon the mortally-wounded commanding officer of the 95th. There was no expression to the veteran's face.

"Who is it, sir?" Mills asked of Lan.

"Lieutenant Banister," Lan replied sadly.

"Poor sod," Mills said.

"Sergeant," Lan ordered. "Father Thomas will be tending to the wounded. He requires five good men to help. See that he gets any medical supplies he requires and that all of the wounded are issued with fresh tunics."

"Yes, sir," Mills responded. "I will see to it."

Lan looked down sadly at Banister. He would take it upon himself to provide the death watch for the man as he passed from this world to the next. No one should ever have to die alone. "I want Lieutenant Banister moved to private quarters."

"It will be done, sir," Mills said and stepped off, calling for men to take the mortally wounded lieutenant into the keep.

Lan was silent for a moment and then became conscious of Arnold staring toward the keep, where Father Thomas had gone. He could only imagine what was going through the old sergeant's mind.

"Sergeant," Lan turned to Arnold, a slight smile cracking his face. "I believe you should find a quiet place to reflect upon your past transgressions, for I believe Father Thomas will expect an accounting that includes openness and honesty."

The sergeant looked sharply at the lieutenant, face screwing up into a scowl. "What if I forget some of me sins and cannot remember all the bad I've done?"

"Be honest with yourself and the High Father. It's not every day that you have an opportunity to be both forgiven for your sins by a paladin and potentially healed from a crippling injury."

The sergeant nodded but said nothing, a scowl still on his face.

"Your heart and soul," Lan added after a moment.

"Sir?" the sergeant asked, scowl deepening.

"I rather suspect," Lan explained to the grizzled sergeant, "that the High Father will require the dedication of your heart and soul in return for his blessing and healing."

"You might be right on that count. Never thought to be having anything further to say to the High Father."

"The gods work in mysterious ways," Lan said, turning away to look down on Banister.

CHAPTER SIXTEEN

"WHAT ARE YOU thinking?" Stiger asked bluntly of Eli, looking over at his friend. Ikely and Brent were standing nearby, watching also. Their breath steamed in the cold air. Stiger rubbed his hands together for warmth.

The enemy had inexplicably not moved forward for a week. They had remained camped just three miles away, each day simply allowing the legionaries to improve their defenses. Eli and his best scouts had even gone looking for a wide turning movement but had found no evidence of an attempt.

Then, this morning, the rebel army had moved up.

Eli looked back at Stiger and shrugged. They were both standing in the center of the fortified defensive line, looking out across the field toward the enemy, who were not yet deployed for battle.

Stiger had expected for the enemy to assault his position at first light or well before. He had close to five hundred men manning a line that stretched across the road and into the forest on both sides for over a quarter mile. On both of his flanks, Eli's few remaining scouts were operating with a handful of volunteers to keep the rebel scouts and skirmishers at bay. They were also positioned to detect and pass on word in advance of any type of flanking movement.

A ten-foot trench had been dug to the front-facing side of an earthen rampart ten feet high and topped with a wooden barricade. The barricade raised the height another five feet. To complicate the enemy's task, sharpened stakes had been planted before the trench, with the intention slowing and breaking up any assault. The only easy way to dislodge their position was to flank his line, and that would take time since the ground was rough, forested and broken up along either side.

"Do you think they plan on surrendering?" Stiger asked in jest, referring to the man walking slowly forward. He was holding forth a white flag.

"I rather doubt it," Ikely said, cracking a smile. "Though to be honest, what would we do with the prisoners? I don't believe we could manage to feed them all."

"Feeding them is only a minor concern," Stiger chuckled. "Think of the headache of hauling so many slaves back to Mal'Zeel and then spending the proceeds."

"The men would be very pleased with their cut," Ikely announced. "Sir, upon due consideration, I fully recommend accepting their surrender! It is good for morale and I am confident it would save both us and them a great deal of trouble. Besides, this entire affair can have only one outcome, that being their utter defeat. So I ask you, sir, why waste time?"

Several of the men who were close enough to overhear the exchange chuckled at the jest. Stiger was pleased with his executive officer, who had consistently shown a calm and collected attitude. The men would soon be sharing and retelling the joke up and down the line, reducing the tension created by waiting in the face of the enemy.

Yes, Stiger thought, looking over at his executive officer, *Ikely is developing nicely.*

"What do you want?" Stiger demanded of the flag-bearer, once he was within speaking distance. The man was unarmed, but wore armor that befitted an officer. He had stopped just shy of effective arrow range.

"Lord General Kryven of the Cyphan Confederacy wishes to present his compliments and requests the opportunity to parley with General Stiger," the man spoke in a heavily accented voice. "If agreeable, the parley will be held between the lines this day at noon."

"Hmmm...Cyphan Confederacy," Ikely said quietly. "I guess we now have confirmation about the driving force behind the rebellion."

Stiger nodded in agreement and turned to Ikely. "The prisoners who were questioned gave us some other name?"

"General Masmo," Ikely responded. "From the southern city of Turnbown. Seems he was a local they elected to general. Definitely not a confederacy general."

Stiger nodded before calling back out to the flag-bearer. "What are General Kryven's conditions?"

"None," the officer responded, tilting his head to one sided. "Only that it be an honorable parley. All parties may come armed."

"Very well," Stiger agreed, placing his hands on his hips, his general's cloak parting as he did so. "I will meet with General Kryven at noon, on the condition that you move your nearest men back to a distance of at least fifty yards."

"I believe the Lord General will be agreeable to such a reasonable suggestion, sir." The officer saluted, turned around and walked slowly, almost casually, back to his lines.

Stiger watched the enemy officer for a moment. *So that is an officer of the Cyphan,* Stiger thought. Likely the better quality formations that Eli had spoken about were Cyphan as well. Perhaps even the company they had faced before the wizard had shown up was one too.

"No sense in tiring the men out," Stiger said to Ikely. "Have half stand down while the other half man the fortifications. See that the men are fed, as well as rotated off the line."

"Yes, sir, I will see to it."

"Are you really going to meet with them, sir?" Brent asked, surprised.

"Why not?" Stiger replied with a shrug. "We lose nothing by talking. It only buys us more time and…there is an added bonus."

"What is that, sir?" Brent asked.

"I get to meet this Lord General Kryven," Stiger said. "Learning more about your enemy can be just as important as scouting."

"Yes, sir," Brent said.

"I think I would like to look over our defenses," Stiger announced. "Eli, with me, please."

Ikely and Brent saluted, fists to chests, as the captain and Eli left the two lieutenants. Eli followed a few steps behind as Stiger began his informal inspection. He had walked the line enough already to know that all was in order. This time was for show, to allow the men to see him calm and in control before the enemy. It was also a way to pass the time and distract himself prior to meeting with General Kryven.

Orders had been rapidly passed along and like an ocean wave drawing back from the sand, men were moving off the line to designated spots some twenty yards back. Each file had an area where not only rations waited, but a fire was kept going. Soon men would be huddled about those fires, gathering what warmth they could. Walking along the line, Stiger received a series of crisp salutes and "sirs" as he moved by.

"You have earned their respect," Eli stated after Stiger had gotten his tenth or twelfth salute. "They are yours."

"You think so?" Stiger paused and looked at his friend.

"I do," Eli said. "It borders on worship. Winning will do that."

Stiger continued on but began to study the faces of the men. He noticed how they would stop what they were doing and watch him as he passed by. It wasn't the cautious, semi-hostile and wary attitude men would normally use around feared or disliked officers. This was something altogether different and that made him uncomfortable. He had seen such looks before, in the North, directed at General Treim.

"I've been lucky so far," Stiger replied sourly, realizing Eli's assessment was correct, but not desiring to admit to it.

"It is more than that and they know it." Eli showed his teeth. "Gods blessed, they say…"

"Please don't start up that nonsense again."

"I don't particularly think it nonsense." Eli's grin grew larger at his friend's discomfort. "They may be on to something…"

Stiger shot his friend a withering look, turned and continued on. He looked over the left flank first, and spent some time speaking with the scouts posted on the edge of the line. He wanted to make sure they understood the need to be active and alert, lest the enemy surprise them and roll up the line. Satisfied, he went back and inspected the right flank, giving the scouts on the end of the line the same treatment. By the time they started back, more than an hour had slid by. Stiger was very pleased with what he had seen. His men were alert and ready and their morale was good.

"If they fight better for it, so be it," Stiger said after some time, his mind still on the hero worship of the men, somewhat discomfited by the thought. "I will use every advantage I have to win."

"You always do," Eli said and followed Stiger as they headed toward the middle of the line. The captain had intentionally placed his defensive line along the top of a slow rise that could not quite be described as a hill but was pretty close. The hills on this portion of the road were much farther back into the forest. On the reverse slope of the rise, a few yards behind his defensive line and concealed from view, were two catapults that his men had constructed.

Normally, each company hauled along two artillery pieces, usually either small bolt or spear throwers. Since Stiger's original mission had been a simple escort, there had been no need to bring along their assigned artillery.

The two catapults were an example of what made the legions so formidable. They were mostly self-reliant when it came to artillery. Each company was trained in the construction and maintenance of artillery. As long as the supplies needed were handy, any company could, at will, construct artillery.

The two machines were of the smaller type that the legions operated. Both were capable of firing four-pound ballista balls. A supply of the rounded stone balls were neatly piled next to each catapult. Stiger had been lucky in that the castle had held a good store of ball, saving his men the trouble of having to make their own ammunition.

Stiger smiled as he looked over the two machines. Defensive lines added to the morale of defending units, but Stiger had found that friendly artillery was also a morale booster. There was nothing a legionary liked to see more than friendly artillery in use.

"Corporal Durggen," Stiger called as he approached the two machines. "Is Third File ready?"

"Sir." The corporal snapped to attention and saluted fist to chest. The men of Third File stopped what they were doing and also braced to attention. They had been unloading additional balls from a wagon and piling them neatly along with the rest.

Unfortunately, when Stiger gave the order to pull back from his current position, the wagon along with the two machines would have to be abandoned. They would not be able to take them back through his defensive corridor. A few hundred yards behind the artillery, the road had been thoroughly destroyed. It pained Stiger to leave a good wagon behind, but he was consoled by the fact that it had been put to good use in the construction of this line.

"Third File stands ready, sir," Durggen said confidently.

"Excellent." Stiger made a show of carefully inspecting the catapults. "Nice work, corporal. Your men did well."

"Thank you, sir," the corporal responded proudly, puffing up his chest. "The rebels are in for one heck of a surprise, sir."

"Yes, they are," Stiger agreed. "I am sure Third File will hammer them good."

"We will, sir," Durggen affirmed. "You can count on that."

"Make sure when it is time to fall back that both catapults and the wagon are destroyed."

"I have a good supply of dragon's breath." Durggen gestured at several sealed jars and a crackling fire a few feet away. "When the time comes, nothing will be left for the enemy, sir."

Stiger nodded and continued to look over the catapults. An earthen mound had been built to stabilize and level the catapults at a slight angle against the slope. Both machines had been tested to ensure that, when fired, the balls safely cleared the crest of the rise and the top of the barricade.

Both would be able to throw their balls up to a distance of four hundred yards, which was pretty standard for machines of this size. The enemy did not know it, but they were already in range. Stiger almost grinned at the thought.

In the North, he had seen much larger machines in action against several besieged Rivan cities. One had been so large that the ammunition fired was called 'wagon stone,' because a wagon was required to haul it. Each ball had weighed around three hundred and fifty pounds.

"Carry on." Stiger was satisfied that all was in order. He stepped off for his camp fire with Eli still following. The captain's tent, along with those of the men, had already been taken down and moved back to the next defensive line, a quarter of a mile away.

Stiger's fire, which he had left at a good blaze, still burned, but low. In the cold morning air it provided little warmth. He threw on several more logs and poked it up a bit. He then sat and pulled out his pipe and tobacco. A few moments later it was lit and he was puffing away.

Eli took a seat on the opposite side of the fire. A cold, brisk wind blew hard and the sky was a heavy overcast. By the look of it, rain or perhaps even snow was likely. The fire slowly grew to a comfortable blaze and began to share its warmth. The two friends were silent, both staring into the fire.

Stiger glanced up at Eli and considered demanding answers on that strange band of elves. Would he answer? If not, how then would it affect their friendship?

After a moment, Stiger decided now was not the time. It would have to wait.

For now, he was more concerned about what was coming, but experience had taught him to remain calm and not let his imagination get the better of him. Besides, having the men see him argue with Eli right before a potential battle was not the right move. It could shake their confidence. The worst thing he could do was to show anxiety. The men needed to see him strong and confident. In short, they needed to believe that he was in control.

Stiger smoked his pipe, thinking about the future and what it held. After hearing what Ogg had to say, he had immediately sent a dispatch to Lan and warned the lieutenant to remain vigilant. The likely axis of an attack would be from the valley side. He had asked Lan not to inform the men that it would be dwarves, but instead dissidents from the valley. Stiger was unsure how his men would react to learning that there was a dwarven kingdom nearby and that the dwarves meant them ill.

Stiger had made the decision to tell no one, other than Eli, Ikely and Lan, about Ogg's visit. This might have been a mistake, but he was already facing one determined enemy and did not wish to unduly alarm anyone. He could not afford to send men back to the castle, as that would weaken his chances of delaying the enemy. It would also increase the likelihood of the enemy being able to inflict significant losses on him. No, he had decided, he would deal with one problem at a time and hope everything would work itself out in the end.

"Captain Stiger!" a jovial voice boomed, interrupting his thoughts. Stiger looked up to see Father Thomas striding over, a large smile on the big man's face. "Or should I now call you General Stiger?"

"Father," Stiger greeted. Eli respectfully stood and offered the paladin a slight bow. Stiger noticed with interest that the paladin was wearing his armor, with his sabre belted on. The man's friary robes had been left behind and instead he wore a white cloak emblazoned with the crown-shaped sigil of the High Father. "Will you join us?"

"I do believe I will," Father Thomas said, taking a seat by the fire. The captain noted the paladin's eyes dart briefly toward the captain's sword as he sat. Eli resumed his seat a respectful half second later, shooting Stiger a look of disapproval for not having stood.

Stiger wondered what the paladin was doing out here. Had he come to fight?

The last Stiger had heard from Lan was that Father Thomas had been busy searching through the castle for any remnants of evil. Stiger's mood darkened and his thoughts turned on the paladin. He had already faced one wizard and met another. Was there evil about?

"Getting colder by the day," Father Thomas said.

Stiger grabbed a wine jar that had been sitting atop the log next to him. He tossed it to Father Thomas, who caught it.

"Why, thank you, my son." The paladin smiled and took a deep pull from the jar. "Ah…the good stuff, valley made. I must say I am becoming quite fond of their wine."

"The snow can't come soon enough," Stiger remarked, glancing up at the sky. If the snow came early and began to pile up in the pass, he could pull back to the castle and wait out the winter. Until that occurred, he would be forced to delay the enemy as long as was possible.

"Lieutenant Banister passed away," Father Thomas announced sadly after a second pull from the jar.

Stiger blew out a long stream of smoke, letting it out slowly. "Though I knew him but a short while, he seemed a good man."

The three were silent for some time before Father Thomas shifted uncomfortably, as if he wanted to say something.

"You were called, were you not?" Stiger asked quietly, fearing the answer he would receive.

"Yes," the paladin confirmed gravely. "I was called here."

Could it get any worse? Stiger asked himself, hand clenching with the frustration of it all. He returned his gaze to the fire. *Dear gods, a paladin on quest…could it get any worse?*

CHAPTER SEVENTEEN

"OPEN THE GATE," Stiger ordered, pulling on his helmet and securing the chin strap. Six men stepped forward and, struggling, lifted the entrance gate, dragging it back and aside. The biting cold wind immediately cut through the opening, causing Stiger's blue cloak to flutter. The men then laid planking over the trench to act as a makeshift bridge.

Stiger looked over at Father Thomas. "Are you sure you do not wish to join us?"

"Not this time," the paladin said with a faraway look, which the captain did not much like. He rather suspected Father Thomas knew more than he was saying.

"Right then," Stiger growled, turning to Eli and Sergeant Blake. "Let's go."

Stiger strode forth from the fortification and onto the makeshift bridge of planking that had been laid over the trench. Sergeant Blake and Eli followed. Looking down at the V-shaped trench below, Stiger could readily see the ankle breakers, small sharpened stakes and caltrops that had been placed in anticipation of an enemy assault. Anyone unlucky enough to make it into the trench was in for an unpleasant surprise. He stepped around the oversized sharpened stakes that pointed outward towards the enemy and onto the field his men had cleared of forest.

Stiger had made sure the field, littered with stumps, was large enough for the enemy to be able to line up at least three companies for assault. He wanted to give the enemy enough room, thereby encouraging an assault, but not too much open space to permit their attack to become overwhelming. This was his ground, not theirs, and he intended to dictate the rules.

Of course the enemy would be able to assault the portion of his fortified line on either flank, which stretched into the trees. However, that would prove difficult, as the terrain was rugged and the forest would break up any type of organized formation. Caltrops had also been seeded around the flanks of his defensive line, along with ankle breakers and small pits with sharpened sticks, covered over by leaves.

With precious little space off the road for maneuver, Stiger was essentially inviting a frontal assault, where he had carefully created the perfect killing zone for the enemy to enter. He had learned this lesson fighting against the Rivan in the hellish forests of Abath. The only sensible move to unseat him from his current position would be to try a flanking movement and that would take time. Once detected, Stiger would simply abandon his defensive position and pull back to his next line. It was all very obvious to the captain, but was it obvious to the enemy? Stiger suspected not. He expected at least one serious attempt to force him out, which was what he wanted. The more of the enemy he killed now, the fewer he would face later.

In the middle of the stump-studded field and between the lines, the enemy had placed a small portable camp table. There were two folding camp chairs on opposite sides. Set smack in the middle of the field, the table looked out of place and forlorn. He walked slowly to the table with Blake and Eli on his heels.

A man, whom Stiger took to be Lord General Kryven and two other enemy officers were waiting. The general was seated and by all appearances waiting patiently, with not a concern in the world. The other chair was empty. The general stood respectfully as Stiger approached.

"General Stiger," General Kryven greeted in flawless common. Stiger noticed a trace of irritation on the general's face when he realized Eli was not human. The irritation was replaced by a flash of anger and vanished almost as quickly as it had appeared. "It is an honor to finally meet you."

"The honor is mine." Decorum demanded that he show respect for his enemy and he was not about to sully his honor.

"General Stiger," Kryven said. "May I introduce my aides, Captains Kevern and Ithax. Both are trusted aids and have been with me a long time."

"And may I introduce Lieutenant Eli'Far and Sergeant Blake."

"Now that we are acquainted, shall we sit?" Kryven suggested, gesturing toward the table. "Though we are currently enemies, I see no reason to not be civilized."

Stiger nodded and took his seat, as Kryven did the same. The two men were silent, assessing one another. Kryven was older, with a strong aristocratic bearing about him. He wore a rich red cloak with a matching tunic under a well-made armored cuirass, heavily and expensively engraved. A red sash ran around the middle of his chest, probably denoting the general's rank. His helmet, topped with a horse-hair mane dyed red, rested upon the table.

Kryven's hair was grayed by age, with a few wrinkle lines about the eyes and mouth. He was physically fit and looked to be a professional soldier, with a weathered air about him as if he had spent a lifetime in the field, commanding men. Stiger noted that the general's sword, larger than a legionary short sword, seemed more functional than flashy. This was a hard man, Stiger decided, whose continence bespoke of competence. He was a commander to be respected.

Glancing at the helmet resting on the table, Stiger considered removing his own, but then dismissed the idea. If there was trouble, he wanted all of his armor in place.

"You have greatly impressed me," Kryven said when Stiger said nothing. "I must admit it has been a great while since I faced someone with even a modicum of your skill. Many play at our trade, but few are masters."

Stiger nodded, accepting the compliment, but said nothing. The captain was wondering what the general was playing at. Why even bother with a parley? Kryven eyed Stiger for a few silent moments, as if weighing his opponent.

"You are a man of few words," Kryven commented, with a trace of a smile and then a glance over at Ithax. "If only some of my officers were as taciturn."

"I speak when needed," Stiger growled and Kryven's smile grew. "I see no reason to waste idle words."

"I executed several officers over their inability to keep your raiders off my column. Now I see my mistake." He nodded respectfully toward Eli, who nodded back in reply. Stiger felt that there was a tinge of anger in the man's tone. *Is he upset over losing his elves?*

Curious, Stiger remained silent. He saw no reason to reveal anything or fill the silence and allowed Kryven to continue. The more Kryven talked, the more Stiger learned.

"You have cost me near three thousand men," Kryven continued, smile fading. "Granted, they were poor quality, rebels, you call them...former flotsam of your empire... their lands now added the Confederacy. Still, your actions have forced me take direct command of my advance column and to bring up my best."

Stiger said nothing in reply. Perhaps this was why the enemy had delayed their advance a week. He got the feeling that the going would be more difficult with General Kryven in direct command. Stiger knew he would have to be much more cautious and on his guard.

"You might be pleased to know the fool who commanded the advance, I had removed, along with his head."

"General Masmo?" Stiger asked as he cracked his knuckles.

"Yes," Kryven admitted with a slight trace of irritation.

Stiger said nothing in reply.

"You do realize you have no hope of winning?" Kryven asked abruptly.

"General Kryven, I beg to differ," Stiger responded gruffly. "I realize no such thing."

"That is Lord General to you," the officer who had been introduced as Ithax hissed with offense, hand going to the hilt of his sword. Blake's snapped to his and he took a half step forward, ready to protect his captain and draw. There was a hard look in Blake's eyes. Eli remained where he stood, completely motionless. Stiger was comforted by the thought that Eli could be extremely fast. He had no doubt that, should the need arise, his friend would act without hesitation.

"He is not my lord," Stiger said firmly, not taking his eyes off of Kryven, who seemed somewhat amused. Ithax's eyes went wide with outrage. Kryven held up a hand and gestured for Ithax to back down.

"Ithax," Kryven rebuked him. "Now is not the time."

Ithax took his hand from his sword and reluctantly stepped back. Blake relaxed a fraction but remained where he was, eyes firmly fixed upon the enemy officer, all but daring the man to go for his sword.

"I tire of this game. You are no general," Kryven said bluntly, pointing a finger at Stiger. "You are Captain Stiger, regardless of that ridiculous getup."

Stiger simply shrugged. He was not surprised that the deception had failed, as it was bound to at some point.

"You had my staff quite convinced, you know," Kryven admitted, leaning back in his camp chair, which creaked. The general crossed a leg. "Your ruse worked...for a time. With the casualties we were taking, you had my staff convinced we were facing an actual legion.

"Do you know my men call you the Tiger?" Kryven asked in amusement when Stiger refused to reply. "The Tiger...a good name I think, fitting."

Stiger offered a thin smile but continued to say nothing.

"How I wish I had someone of your quality working for me," Kryven continued wistfully. "I very much doubt I could ever convince you to switch sides?"

"I am honor-bound to the empire," Stiger affirmed simply.

"I thought not," Kryven nodded with exaggerated sadness. "Even in the Cyphan Confederacy we have heard of Stiger honor."

Stiger stiffened slightly, unsure if he was being insulted. After a moment, he decided it mattered little to him. The man before him was the enemy and as such, he could expect only the very worst.

"Which is why I will make you a different sort of offer... an honorable trade, if you will."

"Oh?" Stiger asked, curious to know what the general was thinking.

"I will allow you, your company and the garrison to march out under arms, with all of your standards, including the 'lost' eagle you found." Kryven uncrossed his legs and leaned forward, placing a palm on the table. "You will have free passage back through our lines to your empire."

Stiger narrowed his eyes at this offer. Kryven knew that he had recovered the eagle. He must also know the formidable nature of Castle Vrell, Stiger realized. Had his scouts made it that far? This was obviously an attempt to quickly take the castle without additional losses. But why send so many men to take it? Vrell was a backwater. Surely there was greater need elsewhere for the forces Kryven commanded?

"I only want Vrell," Kryven continued. "The empire loses Vrell, but you get to bring home that 'lost' eagle, which should mitigate any loss of honor. Vrell is a remote and isolated valley of little consequence to anyone."

The offer was more than generous and the Lords of the Cyphan Confederacy were known to treat with honor. Stiger had no doubt that, should Kryven give his word on safe passage, he and his men would have it. However, Stiger's honor was such that it would not allow him to so easily quit the castle and valley.

"Why Vrell?" Stiger asked. "Why do you want it so badly?"

General Kryven cocked a surprised eyebrow at Stiger. "I was quite sure that is obvious. Our two nations are at war. My orders are to take Vrell and crush any legionary forces in my way."

"And yet," Stiger smiled thinly, "you are offering me safe passage to march my men under arms and with our standards back to imperial lines in exchange for Vrell. That does not seem like you are following your orders to the letter."

"No, it does not," Kryven replied smoothly. "I am simply attempting to spare both sides additional bloodshed."

"No," Stiger replied simply, not buying a word of it. There was something more going on. Though he did not know what it was, Stiger was sure of it. Kryven and the Confederacy wanted Vrell for a very specific reason. The valley must have some sort of strategic value to them. "You cannot have Vrell."

"Come now, Captain Stiger," Kryven said with a slight laugh that Stiger took to be outright irritation. "I know your total strength is under a thousand men. Your company is a 'named' unit, Stiger's Tigers, a little pretentious perhaps. Your second officer is Lieutenant Ikely and each night he carves figurines of the gods, which are highly prized by your men. I know everything there is to know about you and the forces under your command. I even know that you were sent to Vrell to escort a supply train, it being only the gods' fortune that sees you frustrating my advance."

Kryven hesitated a moment. He had become exceedingly irritated and it had shown. He took a deep calming breath before continuing.

"I shall make this plainer," Kryven said. "There is no possible way you can hold Castle Vrell once I am able to concentrate the entire strength of my army. Captain, you can only delay me from getting what I want."

"That may be so," Stiger admitted. General Kryven could only have gotten the information from prisoners he had taken, likely a scout captured prior to the last fight. The scout had most probably been tortured for the information. The thought infuriated the captain, though at the same time he understood he would have ordered the same to obtain such critical information. "However, I will see you pay for Vrell with rivers of blood."

General Kryven leaned back in his chair, an exasperated expression on his face. He shared a brief glance of disbelief with Ithax before looking back at Stiger.

"Is this the famous Stiger stubbornness?" Kryven asked, raising an eyebrow. "I believe your father is called Stalwart Stiger, due to his stubborn defense at Aetella. I have read about that campaign. Am I incorrect?"

"No, your facts are quite correct," Stiger responded curtly, irritated that his father had been brought into the conversation. Time and again, he was judged by his father's actions. Only General Treim had ever weighed him on his own merit.

"I will not take no for an answer," Kryven said after a moment of silence. "I propose we adjourn and meet in four hours to continue our discussion, after you have given this matter additional thought."

Stiger almost smiled. It was past noon and he was looking to burn time. Four more hours of inaction suited him just fine. It might even mean that there would be no fighting today and he could continue to hold the defensive line into the next day.

"I find that acceptable," Stiger agreed. "I will consider your offer."

Kryven nodded and stood. Stiger stood as well.

"Think hard," Kryven said firmly, eyes narrowed. "After what you have done to my army, some of my officers feel my proposition is far more generous than you deserve."

"I understand."

Stiger turned and walked back to his lines with Eli and Blake following. Once they were out of earshot, Stiger turned to Eli.

"He may be stalling for time," Stiger said. "I want your scouts looking for a wide flanking movement."

"If there is one, we will find it," Eli assured him.

"Good," Stiger said, stepping onto the planking that bridged the V-shaped trench. He stopped, turned and looked at Eli and Blake. "We have to be on our toes. That bastard Kryven knows what he is doing."

Once the three were back behind the fortified line, the planking was pulled in. With grunts of exertion, the gate was moved back into place. It fell with a solid thud.

"I thought that went well," Blake said, flashing Stiger a smile. "You both got along famously, sir."

"Can I call you the Tiger?" Eli asked with a full smile, filled with needle-like teeth.

Chapter Eighteen

"**A**RE YOU QUITE sure?" Braddock demanded of Garrack, standing up from his desk, where he had been working.

He had made his headquarters in Old City, buried deep in the bowels of Thane's Mountain. The house, where he had set up his command post, had once belonged to Old City's mayor. No longer did anyone live in the city, for it had become too dangerous. The dvergr who had inhabited this once grand city and now crumbling edifice to the past had long ago moved on to new homes located deeper into the mountain range. In their absence, the lesser races had moved in. Upon arrival, Braddock's war band had evicted them, cleansing the city and reclaiming it in the name of his people. Streets and markets once full were now depressingly empty. Braddock aimed to change that. He aimed to restore the Compact and win his people, the dvergr, their due.

"Yes, my Thane," Garrack responded. "We have confirmed the imperials who marched out of the valley are fighting a delaying action against another army of humans. Our estimate is this army's strength to be around twenty thousand, perhaps more. We believe they are intent on taking Grata'Kor."

This was a complication he had not planned for. In two days, his partially formed army would be on the move, dispersing to their jump-off positions. The retaking of Grata'Kor was at hand. If everything went as expected, the move should achieve absolute surprise. Once the great citadel fell, the humans of the valley, who had called for his help, would thank him. However, the implications of such a large army marching on Vrell did not escape him. Whoever held Vrell potentially controlled the fate of this world.

"How much time do we have until they reach Grata'Kor?" Braddock asked.

"Two weeks, maybe more. It may take them longer. The human in command of the legionaries is skilled. Captain Stiger is his name. His tactics have proven successful. He has inflicted a surprising number of casualties on his enemy. He has also damaged the road badly. It will take time to clear it."

Braddock let out a relieved sigh. Two weeks allowed him time enough to follow through with his plan to storm the citadel, remove Castor's filth and reclaim Grata'Kor in the name of his people. Once the dvergr army held the walls of the citadel, let this human army try to take it from him!

"Who is it who challenges the might of the Mal'Zeelan Empire?" Braddock asked, curiously. The dvergr had no real knowledge about what was occurring far beyond the borders of Vrell. Ever since they had turned their backs on the wider world, his people had remained isolated from the other races.

"I do not know," Garrack admitted. "It is possible that this army is part of the rebellion the emissary has spoken about. To confirm that, we would need to take prisoners. Such a move may reveal our presence sooner than we wish."

Braddock frowned. He did not like this at all. "Taking prisoners, I think, is not a venture I wish to risk. Perhaps after we take the citadel."

"I agree, my Thane," Garrack nodded. "It would be very chancy."

"There are, what, no more than two hundred holding Grata'Kor?"

"We believe their strength to be around two hundred," Garrack confirmed with a nod. "Nothing we cannot handle. However, if we delay further, this Captain Stiger will eventually fall back on the citadel for protection. Then we are looking at the possibility of around six hundred to nearly a thousand, and that could pose complications."

Braddock grunted at the thought. Every dvergr life was precious. He had no intention to delay the assault on the citadel, and this was further reason to push ahead. His people had nearly become extinct and he would not allow that to happen again. The thane began to pace and was silent as he thought through all angles. Garrack said nothing, but waited.

"Do you think this army could take Grata'Kor from the imperials?" Braddock asked, having stopped his pacing, looking over at his oldest friend.

"Doubtful...at least until spring," Garrack responded after a moment's consideration. "This legionary commander seems to know his business and winter is almost here. Once the first real snows hit the pass and the foothills, well, you know what will happen. Any significant movement until spring will be extremely difficult. My Thane, as you are well aware, the legionaries are skilled and disciplined fighters. Even without snow, it would likely be difficult for this army to dislodge them."

"What of our human friends in the valley?" Braddock asked. "Will they help us?"

"The emissary claims the filth that contaminated Grata'Kor has been removed by the legion," Garrack said.

"Since they feel we are no longer needed, I doubt they will assist."

"Bah!" Braddock scoffed. "How could the humans remove the misshapen one's filth on their own? I tell you, they have been hoodwinked. As it stands, I have had to bring forth some of the holy relics to help deal with the creature and its contamination."

"They are stubborn," Garrack admitted. "As you know, they claim this Captain Stiger has recovered the eagle. Maybe he even wields the sword? It is a powerful artifact, perhaps mighty enough to challenge and remove Castor's filth."

"You seriously believe that?" Braddock was familiar with the legend of Delvaris's sword, but was it strong enough to challenge the full power of a dark god?

"It matters not what I believe. The humans in the valley have begun to assemble their forces as though the Oracle's words have been fulfilled. You know what that means."

"Will they ask of you to fulfill your family's vow?" Braddock looked over at Garrack in question.

"I believe they will," Garrack said, after a moment's thought. "According to the emissary, their council is debating that very question."

"If they ask, will you break the seal?" Braddock feared the answer.

"I will be legend-bound to do as they ask," Garrack answered plainly, a look of profound sorrow on his face. "If I must, I will break the seal on the vault of the 13th."

"What if I ordered you not to?" Though he suspected Garrack's answer on this, he wanted to hear it spoken aloud so there could be no misunderstandings.

"You cannot order that," Garrack said quietly with a pained look. "Please, I beg you. Do not even try."

Braddock was silent a moment. If he attempted such a move, it would surely mean an end to their friendship, which had lasted since they were children.

"They are fools then."

"They see it differently," Garrack countered. Braddock knew that Garrack was fond of the humans, which was why he tolerated Garrack's defense of them. "They see it as a great responsibility."

"Unsealing the vault now...would be a waste," Braddock huffed.

"What if they are right?" Garrack tugged on his neatly braided beard. It appeared to Braddock as if his friend had voiced the question almost to himself. Yet it enraged the thane nonetheless.

"They are not," Braddock roared, face going red. "The time for the Last War has not come!"

"What if it has?" Garrack asked, looking on his thane gravely.

"Then we are all doomed. The Gate will open and death will come forth."

"The Oracle predicted a choice will have to be made," Garrack countered. "Do I need to recite the codex?"

"We shall move as planned," Braddock said. If he made his attack as planned, the emissary would not have time to return and make the request of Garrack that Braddock so dreaded. "The quicker the better. Once we retake Grata'Kor and restore the Compact, they will see it is not time. There will be no need to open the vault."

"Yes, my Thane," Garrack said, though Braddock could tell his friend was not convinced.

"We strike while the defense of Grata'Kor is weak and cleanse the citadel of Castor's filth. Let us see what our friends of the valley have to say when I show them the truth!"

"I think that might be not a prudent course of action," a voice hissed.

Braddock and Garrack jumped, both turning. Garrack's hand instinctively went to his sword. They had been alone in Braddock's study and should not have been interrupted without a servant announcing a visitor. Braddock saw Ogg was standing by the door, shrouded in his midnight-black robes, holding his staff.

"Ogg!" Braddock snarled in irritation and outrage at being interrupted in such a manner. Ogg, like Thoggle before him, went where he pleased. It was infuriating and lacking in proper decorum. "A knock would have been appreciated."

"The imperials are not our enemy. Should you act prematurely, you risk us all," Ogg said. As he moved toward them, the metal guard on the bottom of his staff made a clicking noise on the stone floor. "The humans from the valley are correct. Castor's contamination has been removed."

"Have you been to Grata'Kor for yourself?" Braddock demanded. "Can you tell me with certainty that Castor's contamination no longer resides there?"

"No." Ogg stopped and eyed the thane. "I have not been to Grata'Kor myself."

"Bah! It is only hearsay then," Braddock spat, shooting a doubtful look to Garrack. "You know nothing!"

"I know one who is so obsessed with his own legend he would act prematurely and needlessly risk all."

"Ogg," Garrack hissed in anger. "You go too far!"

"Do I?" Ogg took two steps closer, the metal guard of his staff clicking on the stone floor as he moved.

"I know the risks," Braddock spat back with irritation. He did not enjoy being lectured by one who was without honor and legend, even if the wizard was kin.

"I fear the humans are right," Ogg said. The hint of madness, for a moment, left the wizard's eyes. "Braddock, I feel it in my bones. The Last War is coming. Can't you feel it? The day fast approaches when the Gate can be unlocked and the way made open. Though, by your actions, we teeter on the edge of an endless night."

"Bah!" Braddock waved a dismissive hand at Ogg. "You are overreacting. Not all of the conditions have been met. The empire's representative has not declared the Compact restored!"

"Not yet, but soon. Braddock, you cannot attack these humans. In doing so, you will destroy the Compact. You cannot simply declare the Compact fulfilled yourself. It will doom us all."

"Doom us all?" Braddock was concerned with Ogg's new act. The wizard had lost his mad edge in favor of a serious one. Braddock paused, considering the wizard for a moment. He decided he would not be put off. "The assault on Grata'Kor will go forward as planned."

"I forbid it," Ogg said quietly.

"You do not tell me what I can and cannot do!" The wizard had gone too far. "I am the Thane!"

Silence settled upon the room. Braddock's gaze bored into Ogg's, daring the wizard to say more. Instead, Ogg dropped his eyes and looked down at the floor for a moment. When he looked back up, his gaze was concentrated.

"I have met their captain." Ogg gave an abrupt giggle, the look Braddock took for madness returning to his eyes. "He is honorable and with legend."

"You did what?" Garrack asked, aghast at the implications of what the wizard had done. "You revealed yourself to the humans?"

"Yes," Ogg said without a trace of concern, the madness seeming to creep deeply across his beardless face as he smiled. "I felt it necessary."

"What did you tell him?" Garrack demanded, face reddening with anger at the betrayal.

"Only that we are planning to attack them," Ogg said, with an abrupt crazy giggle as he came nearer, the metal guard on his staff clicking on the stone floor. "I made our intentions abundantly clear."

Braddock ground his teeth in rage at this base betrayal. He took a step back and bumped into his desk. "You told them we were coming for them? Why?"

"Have you no honor?" Garrack roared, enraged. "You destroy your own legend!"

Ogg stopped a moment to consider Garrack. The wizard's eyes narrowed; the madness twisted Ogg's face. "Once I chose my trade, my very own family turned their backs upon me. According to my father, I *gave up my legend the day I swore an oath to another god.* Isn't that what you said, Father?"

"I should have killed you the day you made that choice. I will correct that mistake." Garrack fumbled in his rage for his sword, intent upon drawing more than steel. "Something I should have done years ago when you dishonored the family and the clan."

"I think not," Ogg said softly, voice filled with a menace that made Braddock go cold with dread. Ogg rapped the end of his staff down hard upon the stone floor. The oddly-shaped crystal flashed brightly, momentarily blinding the thane. There was an earsplitting crack, as if the world had been torn asunder. The room rapidly filled with an unearthly fog. Braddock staggered backward. The desk he had been leaning against was no longer there. The world swam before snapping back into brilliant focus. The fog had vanished and, with it, his office. It had been replaced by a crackling campfire set in the forest sometime around midday. The cold of the early winter air hit the thane like a smack across his face.

Braddock looked up in amazement at the leafless limbs of the trees. The sun was nearly directly above. Braddock glanced around, eyes wide at the magical power that Ogg had just demonstrated. It was the kind of thing Thoggle had been capable of doing, but rarely displayed. Ogg was clearly much more skilled at his craft than the thane had believed. Braddock turned toward Ogg and saw Garrack, who was looking upon his disowned son with an expression of horror. Braddock knew Garrack had never before seen Ogg wield his craft and having witnessed it, it made the betrayal that much more real.

"What have you done?" Garrack choked.

It was at that moment that Braddock realized that he, Garrack and Ogg were not alone. A human warrior and an elf who had been sitting before the fire were staring up at them in shock. The smell of many unwashed bodies, old leather and excrement assaulted his sense of smell. Braddock glanced around and in a flash understood where he was. Ogg had transported them to the legionary commander's camp in the middle of the Sentinel Forest. He turned back to the human and elf, just as shocked as they appeared to be. The moment passed. Both scrambled to their feet and drew their swords.

"Ogg, you fool," Braddock snarled, dragging out his sword, only to have Ogg clamp his hand firmly down on the thane's forearm, preventing him from fully drawing the weapon. Braddock was surprised at the wizard's strength. Their eyes locked.

"Do nothing rash," Ogg warned. The mad look had once again vanished from the wizard's eyes, leaving Braddock questioning whether it was an act designed to further Ogg's own machinations. "You are in the middle of an armed camp, have a care."

There was a clatter and rush from behind. Braddock turned and saw several human legionaries rushing forward, swords drawn. They quickly surrounded the three dvergr. Shouts of alarm could be heard across the camp, with more men rushing forward.

"I brought you here to listen, not fight," Ogg said, hand firmly clamped upon the thane's forearm. "I will return you, unharmed. You have my word…unless, of course, you or my father do something rash. In such an event I will, in all probability, be unable to protect you."

Braddock looked over at Garrack, who nodded. Frustrated, Braddock released his sword hilt. The blade, only partially drawn, slid back into the scabbard with a hiss and click as the guard came home. Ogg removed his clamp-like grip from the thane's forearm.

"Captain Stiger," Ogg said, switching from dvergrish to common, turning to the human who had been sitting at the fire with the elf and now stood with his sword out. "I have the distinct honor to present Braddock Uth'Kal'Thol, Thane of the Mountains and Ruler of Dvergr."

There was a moment of profound silence as the legionaries surrounding the three dwarves were unable to seemingly take their eyes off the apparitions before them. Stiger exchanged a startled glance with Eli, who shrugged and grinned. Evidently, he thought this was highly amusing.

"We have not come to fight," Ogg explained with a careful look to the thane. "We have come to *talk* and *listen.*"

Stiger hesitated a moment before sheathing his sword. Eli, still grinning at Stiger, sheathed his as well.

"Isn't this a surprise," Eli said.

"Your Majesty," Stiger said gruffly, ignoring Eli and gesturing toward a log. "You are most welcome to share the warmth of my campfire."

Braddock took a deep breath. "Captain Stiger, is it?" Braddock asked in heavily accented common.

Stiger nodded in reply.

"Captain Stiger," Braddock continued. "We will be much honored to sit at your fire and share the warmth of its blaze. Before we sit, may I introduce my lieutenant, and kin, Garrack alk'Thol, my oldest friend and my personal advisor. Unfortunately, I believe you already know Ogg."

"It is an honor to meet you both, and yes, I have met Ogg," Stiger replied evenly. "May I introduce Eli'Far, elven ranger, my lieutenant and someone I also name a friend."

Braddock nodded in greeting.

"Sir?" Ikely asked. The lieutenant had approached and pushed his way through the ring of men, sword drawn and staring at the dwarves with extreme shock, as if disbelieving his very eyes. "Is everything all right, sir?"

"Yes," Stiger replied. "Lieutenant, everything is under control. Dismiss the men and kindly see that we are not disturbed."

"Ah, yes, sir," the lieutenant said, hesitating as he eyed the three dwarves with apparent awe. It was almost as if he could not believe they were real. He shot a look at Eli, who nodded in good-natured reply, almost as if saying *told you so.*

Ikely tore his gaze from the dwarves and turned to go, then stopped himself. "About the parley?"

"Remind me when it is time," Stiger ordered.

"Yes, sir." The lieutenant turned to the men who had gathered by the fire, swords out. "Sheath swords. Dismissed! Sergeant Ranl and Blake, both of you are to remain."

Swords were reluctantly sheathed and the men began to move off with curious looks directed at the dwarves.

"Is there anything else you require, sir?" Ikely asked. It was clear to the captain that the lieutenant was intensely interested in the captain's guests.

"No, lieutenant." Stiger nodded toward the defensive line. "Keep an eye on the enemy until I am finished here."

The lieutenant saluted smartly and moved off, following the men as they dispersed.

Blake and Ranl remained, standing off to the side. Stiger made no move to countermand Ikely's orders and dismiss them too. Ogg had told him the dwarves meant his people ill. Stiger felt more comfortable that the two veterans were close at hand.

"Would you care to sit?" Stiger asked, gesturing at the logs placed around the campfire. Braddock nodded and sat and then gestured to Garrack, who cast a hostile glance at the wizard before doing the same. Ogg moved to the opposite side of the fire, well away from the two sergeants and also took a seat, leaning his staff against the inside of his left leg. Stiger and the Eli sat also. An awkward silence followed.

"I understand you mean to take the castle from me," Stiger said, deciding to come right out and say what was on his mind. It was not really a question.

Braddock threw an angry glance in Ogg's direction before turning to face the captain. "Yes, we will take back Grata'Kor."

"Why?" Stiger asked in exasperation, gesturing around. "What harm have we done to you and your people?"

"You brought evil to the valley," Braddock said simply. "The empire is not as it was. Humans are short-lived and shortsighted. You have defiled the Compact and I mean to restore it."

"If you are referring to that business with Castor, we were responsible for purging that evil," Stiger said. "The agent of Castor is no more."

"How you banish agent of Castor?" Garrack spat gruffly in even rougher common than the thane's.

Stiger did not like the dwarf's tone.

"Sergeant Ranl," Stiger said, turning to one of the two legionaries. "Please be kind enough to ask Father Thomas to join us."

"That will not be necessary," Father Thomas announced, walking up to the campfire. Braddock and Garrack looked up. Eli stood and offered Father Thomas a respectful nod. The paladin stopped before the two dwarves, an expression of fascination crossing his face. He towered over the two dwarves, who had to crane their thick necks to look up at him. Stiger noted Father Thomas wore armor that, under the sunlight, shone impressively. Braddock's eyes went to the mark of the High Father's sigil. It was clear to Stiger the thane recognized it.

"I was called," Father Thomas said.

"This is why you were called?" Stiger demanded. "You were called to meet them?"

"It seems so," Father Thomas said. "Though I detect no evil here."

"What is going on here?" Braddock asked. "Explain yourself."

"Your Majesty," Stiger said, standing up once again. "May I present Father Thomas, a holy warrior in service to the High Father."

"A warrior priest?" Garrack said with a scowl. "You people call a paladin, no?"

"That is correct," Stiger confirmed.

Braddock frowned at Father Thomas. Stiger could read the questioning look in his eyes, as though he were wondering if this was some kind of a human trick. "He speaks the truth," Ogg confirmed from across the fire. "This man is a direct representative of the High Father."

Braddock looked over at Ogg in surprise. After a moment, he stood respectfully and inclined his head slightly. "I am pleased to meet one honored so by the High Father."

Stiger introduced the dwarves to Father Thomas.

"It is I who has been honored," Father Thomas said. "The High Father has seen fit to offer me his blessing to do his good work."

"Shall we sit?" Stiger asked. Braddock nodded. Once the paladin had found himself a seat, everyone else resumed their places.

"Was...was it you?" Braddock asked of Father Thomas. "Is it true that Grata'Kor has been cleansed?"

"If you mean Castle Vrell," Father Thomas nodded in confirmation. "Then, yes, Castor's contamination has been removed, thanks to the High Father."

"The true enemy of our people marches on Vrell," Ogg said. "Our enemy is not here, nor is it at Grata'Kor."

"I should have listened," Braddock said in what was clearly an apology directed to Ogg. "I have never had cause to doubt your word."

"My word?" Ogg seemed shocked by the suggestion. "Why take mine, when you can take that of the enemy themselves?"

"What do you mean?" Garrack demanded.

"Captain Stiger," Ogg said, turning to the captain. "I believe you will shortly be speaking with your enemy. You call such a meeting a parley? Is that not correct?"

"It is," Stiger affirmed. "How do you know of this?"

Ogg shrugged, as if it did not matter, and then turned back to Braddock. "Take a close look at his sword and scabbard."

Braddock paused for a moment, glancing over at Ogg, before looking. The sword and scabbard lay next to the captain. Stiger saw the thane sit up. A startled expression crossed Braddock's face.

"Delvaris's sword!" Garrack said excitedly. "The Oracle's words…"

"It would seem so," Braddock said and ran a hand through his neatly braided beard. "This changes everything."

The two dwarves slipped into their own language and spoke rapidly back and forth, both at times gesturing toward Stiger. He heard them say "Delvaris" more than once.

"My ancestor," Stiger interrupted, eyes narrowing. "What of General Delvaris?"

"You hold the sword of Delvaris. It is a powerful artifact named Rarokan. That blade was forged long ago," Braddock explained, pointing at the weapon. "You wear his armor as well. Did you take it yourself?"

"Yes," Stiger said. "I did."

"The Compact," Garrack said in common. "As foretold by the Oracle, the Compact is on the verge of fulfillment!"

"What Compact?" Stiger asked. "What are you talking about?"

"He doesn't know? How can that be?" Garrack asked in surprise.

"You did not come to Vrell to fulfill the Compact?" Braddock turned to face the captain.

"I don't even know what the Compact is," Stiger replied, "let alone know how to fulfill it."

"Much of the empire has long forgotten the Compact," Ogg stated. "Human lives pass quickly and as such, they have short collective memories."

Braddock looked intently at him. "If you do not know of the Compact, then why do you wear Delvaris's armor and cloak and carry his sword?"

"If I answer that," Stiger said, "will you explain this Compact you speak of and why it is so important?"

"I will," Braddock affirmed. "Upon my legend, I will."

"It was an attempt at a larger deception," Stiger explained. If he could win over Braddock, he could put to bed the threat posed by the dwarves. "We are vastly outnumbered. By wearing the general's kit, I wanted the enemy to think that they faced a general in command of an entire legion, instead of a few hundred. I made sure both I and the eagle were seen by the enemy. I even allowed a few prisoners to escape, having seen me in this getup along with false information about our size and disposition. The enemy had to believe the ruse so that they would advance more cautiously...slowly. My entire focus has been to harass and counterpunch, delaying their advance as much as possible, at least until the winter snows come to the mountains and then fall back on the castle and hold it until spring."

"I see," Braddock said thoughtfully as he absently tugged on his beard with one hand. "Did it work?"

"It seems it did for a time," Stiger answered. "I learned today that my enemy now knows the truth. I guess it is time I returned these relics and got back to my own kit."

"I think not," Braddock said quietly, leaning forward. "As it was you who activated, or really deactivated, the spell, the sword, armor and personal effects were meant for you and you alone. Only one from Delvaris's line could have done as you did, which was foretold by the Oracle. You have taken the first steps to restoring the Compact between the Dvergr Nations and the Mal'Zeelan Empire."

"Captain," Garrack spoke with awe, making his accent thicker. "More dan a thousand years have passed since Dvergr Nations and Empire formed Compact. You see Compact boils down to joint defense of Vrell. We built Grata'Kor and for two hundred years your empire lived up to terms of Compact, then something changed and empire abandoned valley."

Stiger absorbed this information silently, then ran his hands over the sword hilt of Delvaris for some moments, feeling the familiar tingle. After a moment he looked up, eyes alight.

"The 13th was not a lost legion," Captain Stiger breathed, snapping his fingers. "She marched south to fulfill the empire's obligation."

"During a dark time, my people requested a restoration of the Compact," Braddock continued, "and your Emperor Atticus dispatched the 13th Legion for that purpose."

"Atticus?" Stiger said, trying to remember his history lessons on the emperors. From the beginning to the current day, every child from a noble family could recite the complete list of emperors. Unfortunately, other than the man's name, there was very little Stiger could recall of Atticus.

On the other hand, Stiger did know a great deal about his ancestor and the legend that surrounded the 13th. Nothing he could recall about the legend of the Vanished involved Vrell. Stiger had not even heard of the Vrell Valley until General Mammot and Kromen had mentioned it.

Still, Stiger had always wondered why the 13th was allowed to remain on the rolls of 'active' legions. He had assumed, as many others had, that it was a way for the empire to save face. The 13th had disappeared so long ago that that line of reasoning no longer made sense. There had to be another reason…

He considered what he had just learned. Why had he never heard of the Compact? To dispatch an entire legion just to fulfill the terms a treaty hinted that the agreement held strategic importance to the empire. Had all of the emperors from Atticus down to the current been content to keep the legend alive, that the 13th was simply lost…vanished? Did they perpetuate that falsehood for a reason? Again, he wondered what was so important about Vrell. Stiger shook his head. Until recently, he had thought dwarves were mythical creatures and now here he was, conversing with three of them.

"You are planning to attack us to restore the Compact!" Stiger said finally. He had the thane, the dwarf ruler, in front of him. Surely, Braddock could call off this impending attack, particularly now that Stiger knew the empire and dwarves had been allies, or really still were in a strange sort of way that he did not yet fully understand.

"We could not allow Castor dominion over our Valley," Braddock said. "It would have been a betrayal of trust."

"What about now?" Stiger asked. "Will you still make war upon us, knowing the truth?"

"I believe I speak for my thane when I state that matters are now different," Garrack said. "As foretold, you have assumed mantle of Delvaris."

"There are some of our people," Ogg said with an unnerving giggle, "who believe the Oracle meant that Delvaris would be reborn. I believe you humans use the word reincarnation."

"You think I am Delvaris reborn?" Stiger asked incredulously, shooting an alarmed look to Eli. "That armor fits pretty well," Ogg continued with another strange giggle. "Wouldn't you agree?"

"That armor would fit anyone," Braddock barked at Ogg in irritation. "It is enchanted, or have you forgotten, you honorless dog?"

"I forget nothing, my Thane," Ogg replied, sobering. "Nothing."

Stiger looked down at his armor with concern. Like his sword, it was enchanted?

"Captain," Braddock said, drawing the captain's attention. "When I was but a youth, I had the honor of meeting Delvaris. He—"

"Wait a minute," Stiger interrupted, his head spinning at the implications. "You knew General Delvaris? That means you are, what…over three hundred years old?"

"I am a little past middle-aged for one of my kind," Braddock admitted. "Regardless of my age, you could easily pass for the general's brother."

Stiger stood up, paling. He could not believe what he was hearing. He looked over at Eli, who actually looked awed.

Awed!

Nothing awed Eli. His friend had lived a good long time and he had done and seen most everything.

"You believe this?" Stiger asked him.

"The gods move in mysterious ways," Eli said. "Though I have never met anyone who could conclusively prove they had been reincarnated, that does not mean it could not happen, gods willing."

"Though I do not believe you are Delvaris reborn, there are some of our people who will," Garrack said.

"What was Delvaris's title?" Braddock asked of Garrack, gesturing at Stiger. "You know, the one his men called him. Having assumed the mantle of command, that title would naturally be his."

"I am sorry, my Thane," Garrack said. "It was a very long time ago and human languages are not my strength."

"Legate," Ogg said quietly. "I believe the title Emperor Atticus gave Delvaris was Legate."

"That is it," Braddock said with a pleased look and then turned back to Stiger. "You are now Legate of the 13th."

Stiger almost laughed bitterly. Legate was a title that had not been in use for at least two centuries. It was absurd! How could he command a legion that existed in name only? With the rebel and Cyphan army on his doorstep, though he took all of this seriously, it was the least of his concerns. Or was it?

"As Legate of the 13th," he said after a moment, "I could declare the Compact restored and you would remain as our ally in defense of the valley? Am I correct?"

Braddock glanced at Garrack, who nodded. Then he slowly turned back to Stiger.

"As legate of the 13th," Braddock said slowly, "and direct representative of your emperor, yes, you can declare the Compact restored."

"Be warned, captain," Garrack said with a grave look. "Invoking Compact is not a thing our people take lightly. As direct representative of empire, you will be held to account."

Stiger nodded, thinking fast and hard. By restoring the Compact, the dwarves would be honor-bound to assist in defense of the valley. "If it keeps us working together as allies instead of enemies, then so be it. I declare the Compact restored."

Braddock blinked, his dark eyes filling with tears. Garrack, too, seemed moved, exhilarated and elated. The thane fell to his knees and began offering what appeared to be a prayer in his own language. Stiger glanced over at Eli, who looked grave. Stiger thought he read disapproval and caution in his friend's eyes. Perhaps he should have consulted Eli before making such a momentous decision? Well, it was too late now. There was no going back.

"Thank you, Legate," Braddock said, getting up. A tear ran down his cheek and into his braided beard. "I thought never in my lifetime to hear such words from a human. You have restored my faith in the futures of both our peoples."

Stiger pursed his lips at the display of emotion. Only Ogg seemed unaffected. Actually, the strange wizard appeared amused. The question of why the Compact was so important to the dwarves nagged at Stiger. His doubts about what he had done in haste returned. He glanced over at Eli, who looked grave. Stiger needed to learn more about the Compact, but that would have to wait. He had ended the threat from the dwarves and gained an ally in the process. He saw Ikely approaching. Having dealt with one threat, Stiger rather suspected that dealing with General Kryven would prove much more difficult.

"Sir," Ikely interrupted. "It is time."

"Yes," Ogg said in a firm tone. "Braddock, it is time you meet our true enemy."

CHAPTER NINETEEN

"ARE YOU SURE you wish to meet our enemy?" Stiger asked Braddock, looking sideways at the dwarf. Stiger had intentionally emphasized the word 'our' to reinforce to the thane that General Kryven's army was not just an enemy to the empire, but also now to the dwarves as well. Stiger felt a shiver of concern, recalling what Ogg had said about the thane meeting the 'real' enemy.

"I do," Braddock said. "I wish to put a face to the enemy who would dare to covet Grata'Kor."

The legionaries manning the defensive line were looking at the dwarves curiously. Word of their arrival had spread quickly and many found any excuse to come by and gawk. Sergeant Blake and Ranl were doing a good job sending them on their way.

"You are a man who understands defense," Ogg said, gazing about at the fortification with appreciation.

"I mean to give the enemy a hot reception," Stiger said. "If they want to reach Vrell, they will have to earn it."

Braddock nodded appreciatively, examining the elaborate defenses the legionaries had erected. Stepping up to the barricade, he looked down at the trench below and whistled.

"I would not want to fall down there," Braddock said to a legionary, who was manning the barricade.

"No, sir. It would not end well if you did." The legionary eyed the dwarf warily.

Braddock barked a laugh and clapped the legionary on his armored shoulder. The legionary almost staggered under the friendly but powerful blow.

"This is good ground you selected," Braddock addressed Captain Stiger. "An excellent choice. I approve."

"I hope the enemy likes it enough to try and take it from me," Stiger said.

"Open the gate!" he yelled as he put his helmet on, tying the chin strap in place. Looking over at the dwarves, he had a funny feeling about the coming parley. He wondered how General Kryven would react to his new allies.

Several men stepped forward and struggled, grunting with effort as they lifted the gate back and to the side, opening the way. Planking was run out, bridging the trench. Stiger, Eli, Blake, Braddock and Garrack started forward. Father Thomas had once again elected to remain behind, as did Ogg.

Garrack, realizing Ogg was not coming, stopped and turned toward the wizard with a questioning look. "Aren't you coming?"

"I believe I shall remain," Ogg said. A mad look overcame him and he grinned crazily. "I would like a word with the good paladin here. We have business. Don't worry, Father, I promise to stay out of trouble."

Garrack shot Ogg a concerned look before shaking his head and following after the others.

Stiger saw that General Kryven was waiting as before with his two officers. Seated, he was looking off to the side, legs crossed, seemingly unconcerned about the forthcoming parley. Stiger knew it was all show. As they approached, one of the general's officers, Ithax, saw them. With a start, he excitedly leaned forward to speak to the general. Kryven turned to look at them then leapt to his feet in a rage, his chair falling backward.

"Captain," Kryven said, spitting on the ground in disgust. "I see that my opinion of you was wholly wrong. You debase yourself by consorting with such animals!"

Stiger stopped several feet from the table, hand resting calmly on the hilt of his sword. The familiar tingle felt slightly reassuring. From Ogg's comment, Stiger had been expecting trouble and so he had not been surprised at the general's visceral reaction. The general appeared to recognize Braddock and Garrack as dwarves, which meant he had encountered the thane's people before. That surprised Stiger. Kryven glared furiously at the two dwarves. Any hint of the refined gentleman Stiger had met was gone.

"I have considered your offer," Stiger began but was cut off by Kryven, who waved a hand in dismissal.

"I withdraw it," Kryven snarled with hatred. "I will destroy you, captain, as I destroyed the dvergrish trash in my homeland. There will be no mercy, no quarter! For bringing these animals into my presence, I will have your head pickled and preserved as an example to all others."

Stiger scowled at this. He did not much take to threats, but that was not what bothered him. He looked over at Braddock in question. Why did the dwarves inspire such hatred?

"Where is he from?" Braddock asked Stiger.

"The Cyphan Confederacy, located to the far south and across the Narrow Sea," Stiger said, keeping a wary eye on Kryven and his officers.

"Garand Tome," Garrack breathed in shock to Braddock. "You don't think he speaks of that?"

"Yes…I destroyed Garand Tome," Kryven said, looking Garrack squarely in the eyes. "I broke open that cesspit of corruption you people pathetically called a city and killed ever last dvergr I could find. Though it cost me many fine men, I cleansed that rat hole for the good of the world."

Stiger glanced over at Braddock, who seemed deeply stunned by what he had just heard. The dwarf took a half step backward and stumbled, almost falling to his knees. Stiger caught the dwarf by the arm and steadied him. Braddock was heavier than he appeared. Garrack seemed just as affected by the general's words.

"I had kin in Garand Tome…" Braddock said, going deathly white in the face.

"No longer," Kryven hissed with a savage smile. "I will do to you as I did to them."

"Why?" Braddock asked in a near whisper.

The general cast one last scathing look at Stiger, whirled and started back to his lines. In the general's haste, he had left his helmet resting on the table.

"My sword has drunk much dvergrish blood," said Ithax, with a smile aimed at the two dwarves. "I particularly enjoyed killing your womenfolk and children."

Braddock roared in rage and shook Stiger off, easily knocking the captain aside. The thane drew his sword and charged, moving surprisingly fast for his size. Ithax stumbled backward, attempting to draw his own weapon, but it was too late.

Braddock was on the man and with a powerful thrust, his blade punched right through Ithax's armor, cutting deeply into his bowels and picking him up off the ground. Ithax gave a heavy grunt as his feet left the ground and the sword exploded from his back. Dark blood gushed out, coating the thane's arm and chest. Braddock snarled, leaned forward, and released the hilt. Mortally wounded, Ithax fell heavily on his back, to the ground, blade digging into the earth and pinning him firmly in place.

The other officer, Kevern, managed to draw his sword and was raising it to strike. Braddock stepped forward before the sword could be brought down and struck him with a blow from his fist, square on the jaw. So violent was the strike that the man's head snapped back with an audible crack and he crumpled to the ground, neck hanging at an unnatural angle.

General Kryven turned, having only gone several feet. He saw what had been done and his eyes widened in surprise and fear. Braddock looked over at Ithax, who writhed on the ground, unable to free himself. The thane stepped up to him and casually set a boot on his chest and gripped the sword. He gave it a powerful twist and jerk, severing the enemy officer's spine with a solid crack. Ithax moved no more.

It had all happened so fast that Blake, Eli and Stiger stood stunned, watching the thane vent his rage. The captain had not even had time to draw his sword.

"I am Braddock Uth'Kal'Thol," Braddock roared in heavily accented common for all to hear. He directed himself toward the enemy's position, a little over one hundred and fifty yards distant. The men there were just realizing that something had gone horribly wrong with the parley. "Thane of the Mountains, Ruler of the Clans of the Dvergr and Guardian of the Gate. I, who will call forth the clans, swear blood oath this day. I swear by my god and all others I will see the Cyphan Confederacy destroyed. Nothing shall be saved! All who come beneath my blade shall be put to the sword, your cities torn down, your people scattered, reduced to nothing but homeless vagabonds. I will salt your fields so that nothing will grow for an age! I will piss on the grave that was once your nation. When I am finished, your people shall be but a memory. No dvergr will rest until this truth has come to pass. We will avenge our kin of Garand Tome. You will know our vengeance, for we are coming."

Braddock turned his eyes to General Kryven, who had been rooted to his spot. The general seeming to realize his peril, turned and ran. Leaving the sword in Ithax's body, Braddock calmly pulled out a finely made dagger. Not seeming to be rushed or hurried, he took his time and threw it with deadly accuracy. It struck Kryven in the back of the neck with a meaty thwack, severing the artery, as evidenced by a massive gush of blood. The man went down like a ragdoll.

Braddock tipped his head back and let loose a roar of pure primal rage. He took several deep breaths and then, with a sucking sound, he calmly pulled the sword from Ithax's body and stumped up to the fallen General Kryven, bloodied sword in hand. He looked down on Kryven for a moment, then calmly retrieved his dagger and cleaned it on Kryven's cloak before returning it to its sheath. Braddock then raised his sword and with a single powerful blow, he separated General Kryven's head. There was a collective groan from the enemy lines. Braddock ignored them as he picked up the general's severed head by the hair and stomped back to Garrack.

"His skull will make a fine drinking stein," Braddock said as he threw it to Garrack. "Keep it safe, will you?"

"Aye, my Thane," Garrack said, deftly catching the head.

Stiger understood he had to gain control of the situation. For better or worse, he had tied himself to his new allies. He glanced at the enemy, who were now shouting, working themselves up into a proper rage at the murder of their leader. Stiger came to the conclusion that a fight would be inevitable.

"I think it might be wise to head back," he suggested. He turned and started walking, with Eli and Blake following behind.

"I like how they negotiate." Eli grinned at Stiger. "You could almost say Braddock made his point."

Stiger rolled his eyes at Eli, then hesitated and glanced back. The dwarves had not moved. Garrack, holding the grisly trophy, glanced over at the captain. Stiger nodded meaningfully toward Braddock, who stood with his back to the captain and gazed upon his newfound enemy.

"My Thane," Garrack said, coming up and placing a hand upon Braddock's shoulder. "It is time to go. Our time will come."

Braddock nodded, wiped his sword clean upon his leg and slid it back into the scabbard. He turned his back on the enemy and followed Stiger, Eli and Blake off the field.

They walked across the planking, behind the humans. The legionaries manning the fortifications watched the two dwarves in stunned silence as they entered the gate.

Garrack held up General Kryven's head, high as he could, for all to see. He barked out a triumphant shout. The legionaries roared back with approval.

"My kind of people," Garrack commented to Braddock as the legionaries continued to roar away. Ogg, standing next to Father Thomas, abruptly giggled uncontrollably at the sight.

"Close the gate," Stiger ordered to Blake and Ikely. "Get all of the men back to the wall. I expect that Kryven's second in command will want blood for blood. The enemy will attack us shortly."

"Yes, sir," Blake said and started shouting orders, recalling everyone to the wall, which was soon taken up by the corporals.

"Thane Braddock," Stiger addressed him. "What are your intentions?"

"I freely join your war against *these* people. Circumstances now dictate that this goes beyond the boundaries of the Compact. We will fight at your side and annihilate them entirely."

The thane held out a large, calloused hand to the captain. Stiger hesitated a moment before he took it, the dwarf's large and powerful hand swallowing his own. Behind them, Ogg began to laugh maniacally.

"In two days," Braddock said, ignoring the wizard, "I can have three thousand warriors at Grata'Kor, what you call Castle Vrell and another fifteen thousand over the next three weeks."

"We will stand with you in defense of valley," Garrack added. "As Legate Delvaris once stood with us."

Stiger felt overwhelming relief. He also felt pride in his ancestor, something he never thought to feel.

"Legate," Braddock added with an intense look. "You can safely fall back on Grata'Kor. Snow or no, we will hold the fortress together and once my army is assembled, we will take the fight to the enemy."

"It will be an honor to fight by your side in the defeat of our mutual enemies," Stiger said.

He looked up at the position of the sun. A massed roar sounded from the enemy's direction as they shouted their rage at the defenders of the line for the killing of their general. A fight today was almost guaranteed, of that Stiger was sure. The enemy would want revenge and any fighting was likely to be hot and heavy. If he had to pull off the line, it would be safer to do it after night fell, when the day's fighting petered out. Should he pull out immediately, he would be giving up an extremely defensible position and risk a potentially dangerous fighting withdrawal, essentially a running battle, back to the next defensive line through the torn-up road during daylight.

The more he thought on it, the more it made sense to hold until nightfall. With the day more than well-half-gone, Stiger had no doubt he could do it. Once the fighting for the day ended, he would be able to withdraw under the cover of darkness.

"I fear I may be compelled to hold this line at least until nightfall, when we can safely withdraw."

"Do what you must," Braddock said, "but take no more risk, as there is little point in doing so. Get your men safely behind the walls of Grata'Kor. Have no fear, Legate. Together we will annihilate that vile army out there."

"My Thane," Ogg said. "It is time we return."

"Can't you stay and help us?" Stiger asked of the wizard. "Rain death and fire upon the enemy, as their wizard did to us?"

"Unfortunately, no," Ogg said, turning his gaze upon Stiger. "I cannot stay. There are important things I must attend to. Besides, Braddock has work to do as well."

"I do," Braddock said. "I must get my army moving as soon as possible."

"What if they have another wizard?" Stiger asked, still hoping to convince the wizard to stay and lend a hand.

"You handled the first one so well," Ogg said with a giggle. He then appeared to struggle with himself, fighting down another giggle. He became serious. "Legate Stiger, you need not worry about the enemy having another wizard, at least for the present. The gods permit this plane six alone. I know them all. Yes, even the fool your elf here brought low. There is only one other, The Master of the Green Tower, who might be tempted to take up common cause with our mutual enemy. Should she decide to become involved, she will come for me first. Neither she nor I know the outcome of such an encounter, which is the reason she has not yet made her move. It is why I must conserve and store all the energy I am able. Holding onto so much of the gods' energy is slowly driving me mad. Though I wish to stay and assist you, I cannot afford to squander the energy I have stored, nor can I afford the little time left to me. I trust you will understand."

Stiger blinked at Ogg's explanation. Before Stiger could say more, Ogg lifted his staff and brought it down hard on the ground. The oddly-shaped crystal flared brightly, causing Stiger to shield his eyes. There was a sound of sucking of wind, followed by a clap of thunder. When Stiger looked, the three dwarves were gone.

Chapter Twenty

L IEUTENANT IKELY WAS standing on the top of the earthen rampart. He had his hands on top of the rough barricade, which came chest high, as he leaned forward to get a better view.

"Here they come!" Sergeant Blake shouted, looking out over the top of the wooden barricade. The sergeant was pointing toward the edge of the field, beyond the fortification. Just outside of the tree line, the enemy had massed a line of three infantry companies on the edge of the field. Gaps were opening in the enemy line of battle and men were pouring through onto the field in small groups.

It appeared they were carrying what looked like large rafts, made up of small tree trunks that had been lashed together. Ikely instantly understood these were bridges meant to cross the trench. He counted six teams. They were holding the bridges over their heads. A quick count revealed ten men to a bridge. Two-man teams emerged next, lugging large bundles of sticks bound together. These, the lieutenant figured, were aimed at filling the trench, though Ikely did not see how they could hope to fill it. Behind came serval more teams with scaling ladders. The ladder teams did not start across the field like the bridge crews and those carrying the bundled sticks, but instead set the ladders down on the ground, just to the front of the line of battle, which was waiting for the order to move forward.

Clearly, Ikely thought, *they were not idle during the negotiations.*

It wasn't the bridges, bundles of sticks or the ladders that worried Ikely the most. It was the infantry. They were uniformly armed and equipped, which suggested a professional, disciplined organization. They looked much more competent than the near rabble that had been faced previously.

A snowflake drifted lazily by, followed by a handful more. Ikely scratched at his stubbled jaw as he considered the enemy infantry. He turned to Sergeant Ranl, helmet in hand as he adjusted the felt padding inside for comfort before putting the heavy thing on and securing the straps. "Sergeant, bring the archers up."

A legionary waited off to the side with Ikely's shield. The lieutenant beckoned to him, who handed it over. Ikely thanked the man, who then returned to his post along the barricade.

"Archers, move up!" Ranl snapped to the thirty men who were waiting behind them at the base of the earthen rampart by about ten yards. The archers, mostly composed of dismounted cavalry troopers who had been run through a hasty archery course, rushed up to the top and to the edge of the wooden barricade.

"Target the center bridge," Ikely shouted to the archers. They had previously spotted and marked the ground across the field to the front for both the archers and artillery. Ikely realized, with the bridge carriers holding their bridges above their heads, they would make difficult targets. He considered ordering the archers to target the teams with the bundles of sticks and then immediately dismissed that idea. The bridges were the more immediate threat.

"Archers at the ready," Ranl roared. The archers nocked and raised their bows to the correct angle, aimed and drew back. Ikely held his hand up in the air.

"Loose," Ikely shouted and dropped his arm. Thirty arrows arced up into the air and fell amidst those carrying the middle bridge. The majority of the missiles impaled themselves in the top of the bridge. One of the carriers screamed, an arrow lodged in his leg. Staggering, he was knocked down by the man behind to be trampled by others on his team, who kept moving forward without interruption. Ikely pursed his lips at the poor result.

"Fire at will...bring that middle bridge down," Ikely shouted and the archers began picking individual targets. Thirty more arrows arced up, this time in a ragged volley, and came down with better results, hitting three men, two of whom immediately collapsed. The third was struck in the chest. He staggered on for several more steps before also collapsing to the side, hands grasped around the arrow shaft as he writhed in agony. The heavy bridge continued on for a few feet before abruptly tilting to the side. It crashed to the ground, crushing two of the men at the front. Their screams carried across the field.

"Continue to focus on the bridges," Ikely shouted and the archers set to work, each picking his own target.

"Sir," Ranl spoke up, palm of his hand resting on the top of his sword hilt while his fingers rapped it. With his other hand, he gestured across the field. "How about we hammer that line there with some artillery fire?"

The enemy would have most of the bridges in place shortly and that meant the infantry would soon begin their assault. Ikely decided the sergeant was right. It was time to begin softening up the infantry. "Yes, let's show them what they are in for. Have the catapults made ready for one hundred eighty."

"Yes, sir," Ranl replied and passed along the orders, shouting back to Corporal Durggen. The sergeant pulled out a small blue flag from underneath his armor, where he had tucked it in and held it ready.

Ikely turned back to the action. Another bridge went down. It crashed to the ground, where the force of the impact snapped the lashings and it came apart. The rest of the bridges would make it, he realized. There were just not enough archers to make a real difference. Once the bridges were laid, the enemy infantry would advance. Then the real fighting would begin.

The archers continued their deadly barrage, firing missile after missile at the bridge crews. The men carrying the bundles of sticks had dropped the bundles in the trench and begun to work at the oversized sharpened stakes, ripping them up so that the bridge crews could get through.

Shortly thereafter, with deep, hollow thuds, the first of bridges fell into place across the trench. This was almost immediately followed by a massed cry from the enemy line, arrayed in ranks across the far side of the battlefield. The order had been given to advance and the three infantry companies began their slow march across the field. Standards and pennants fluttering and snapping in the breeze, the enemy infantry line was quite a sight. They looked smart and well-turned-out. For a moment, only a fleeting moment, Ikely admired their courage and discipline. Then the feeling passed. These men meant to kill him and he aimed to do the same.

The lieutenant turned to look down the reverse side of the earthen rampart. There, at the base, the legionaries waited for the inevitable order to move up to the wooden barricade to prepare to repel the enemy. Standing in three ranks, they looked grim and expectant. Corporals and sergeants paced the lines, speaking to their men, working to calm nerves and fears by cracking jokes.

Ikely glanced off to his left, looking for the captain. He located Captain Stiger around thirty yards off, making his way back toward the center of the line, where Ikely was positioned atop the wall. The captain, still wearing General Delvaris's armor, complete with helm and blue general's cape, looked cool and confident as ever. He strode forth with a purpose that seemed infectious.

Ikely held a deep respect for his commanding officer. There seemed nothing that the captain was incapable of doing. He had taken an undisciplined and demoralized company and given the men their respect back while turning them into a well-oiled machine of first-rate killers. The captain had done the same for the garrison of Vrell.

Captain Stiger had been moving up and down the line, having a word with the men, passing out encouragement as he went. There was an impulsive cheer from a group he had just said something to, which was taken up by the entire line. The captain paused and punched his fist into the air. The cheer grew louder.

The lieutenant shook his head in admiration. The captain seemed to be born for this kind of thing, born to inspire and born to accomplish the impossible. The captain had taught Ikely a lot about leadership and for that the lieutenant was grateful.

On the march to Vrell, he and the captain had spent many nights talking quietly around the campfire. Most of it had been designed by the captain as instruction for his executive officer. They had spent hours talking, using sticks to sketch in the dirt, discussing strategy and tactics. They had discussed everything from formations to equipment to the ground and what made some officers great and others failures. They had also spent time talking through the battles the captain had fought in. Ikely had done his very best to take it all to heart and was doing his utmost to be worthy of his captain's trust. The captain had put his trust in his executive officer and for that Ikely felt deeply honored. He was determined not to let Captain Stiger down.

"Disperse the archers," Ikely ordered. Ranl passed the order along and the archers set off at a run for their preplanned positions along the barricade and top of the wall. There would be no more massed fire. Their job would now be that of identifying and picking off enemy sergeants and officers or simply targets of opportunity.

Ikely, from his spot, could look back and down toward the catapults, which the enemy could not see and had no idea existed. Ikely had only seen such artillery at practice, never in action. He was curious to see how they performed, though, to be honest, he was more interested to learn how the enemy would react. He hoped it would to be a shocking surprise.

"Sir," Ranl said, drawing the lieutenant's attention back to the field. The enemy were nearing the marked line that the catapults were sighted for. "I think we should let them have it."

"Give the order to commence firing," Ikely ordered, remembering to show only the calm and collected facade of an officer in control. On the inside, though, he was a bucket of nerves, but it would never do to show his anxiety.

Ranl gave the order, waving the small blue flag for Corporal Durggen. A rope was pulled and with a deep creaking groan and a loud crack, the first catapult released and fired, followed within seconds by the second machine.

The stones whistled ominously overhead, traveling in the direction of the enemy. Ikely followed the shot. The first stone tore a hole through the enemy's close-packed ranks, kicking up dust and clods of dirt, appearing to kill several outright. The second took off the head of a man in the front rank and slammed the man immediately behind to the ground.

The enemy seemed to hesitate in shock and then, with officers and sergeants shouting, continued forward with a roar, closing ranks. Ikely looked back at the catapults. Durggen and his men were working hard to reload the machines and at the same time adjust the range. It would be at least another two minutes before they could fire again.

"Sergeant Ranl, time to see to your duties," Ikely called. "Designate a man to spot and mark the range. The catapults are to fire at will."

Ranl saluted and turned to Corporal Smith, who had been waiting for that very purpose. He handed the corporal the blue flag and imparted some final instructions to which Ikely did not pay attention. The lieutenant was more concerned about the enemy steadily crossing the field and drawing closer by the second. His stomach did a nervous flip and he gripped his shield tighter. He wanted to be anywhere but here at the wall. Family, duty, honor and courage kept him from running. He ground his teeth. He was resolved to do his duty and see this through.

The snow had picked up and was coming down heavily. It seemed to be sticking, coating the ground in a light layer of white. Ikely glanced up at the sky. The snow appeared to only be a passing squall. He could see clear sky beyond. Turning back to the field, the enemy line was getting closer with each step. Beyond them, at the edge of the field, another fresh company was marching up, brilliant blue standard snapping in the cold wind. There was another thunderous cheer from the legionaries behind him and Ikely turned.

Captain Stiger had given the order to climb the rampart and man the barricade. Nearly six hundred men rushed to the top, with at least two men from each file carrying a large forked stick for the purpose of pushing ladders back and off the wall. Ikely stepped back to allow the legionaries by as they brushed passed him to take their positions at the barricade.

"Javelins at the ready!" Stiger called in a voice of steel. He had climbed the wall and stood just ten yards away. Dressed in General Delvaris's kit, he looked like the gallant general of song, tale and legend. He was looking at the approaching enemy line. The front rank readied their javelins. There was a slight hesitation, then… "Release!"

Grunting with the effort of their toss, the legionaries heaved their deadly missiles into the air. The javelins looked to Ikely like a wave crashing onto the beach, as they rose up and then slammed down in the middle of the close-packed ranks of the enemy. Unprepared for the barrage, the enemy shivered as scores fell, but continued to come on, a tribute to their discipline, training and courage.

"Second volley at the ready!" Captain Stiger called and the men behind passed up their javelins. This time, the enemy was ready. They raised their rounded shields above their heads. "Release!"

Again the wave climbed into the air and then crashed down. The small, round shields that the enemy carried did not provide full body protection. Men screamed and cried out as the javelins found soft flesh. A number of shields were hit and pierced by the iron javelin heads, long, skinny shafts passing cleanly through, ripping into hands, arms, faces and necks that had been sheltering behind. Those that penetrated a shield but did not wound immediately rendered the shield useless, for the long shanks of the heavily weighted javelins were made of soft iron so that they bent upon impact and made it impossible to remove rapidly. The soldiers cast their ruined shields aside and continued the advance with less protection than they had moments before.

The enemy infantry reached the trench and began to crowd around the bridges. Priority was given to the ladder-bearers, who crossed first. The archers leaned over the top of the barricade and loosed their deadly missiles down into the mass of men below. So tight were the concentrations that it was difficult to miss and screams penetrated the wintry air.

Ladders went up and the enemy began to climb. Large stones were thrown over the top, crushing heads, shoulders, and knocking men from the ladders. Those who made it to the top were met with shield and short sword. The noise generated by the fighting was loud. Men shouted and screamed. Swords clashed, clattered and battered against shields and armor. Ladders were pushed back and off. Some men clinging to the ladders screamed as they fell; others lost their grip and dropped off and into the trench. A scaling ladder packed full of men crashed down onto a bridge. Those waiting their turn were knocked down and crushed. Several were thrown over the side of the bridge and into the trench. Those not lucky enough to land on a bundle of sticks were impaled by the sharpened stakes below. Ikely watched the action intently, looking for trouble spots where he would need to intervene.

A creaking groan, followed by another crack, saw a ballista ball sailing over Ikely's head. It landed in middle of the fresh company that was marching onto the field. The ball tore through several men before coming to a rest in the dirt. The second catapult released and another stone ball went flying across the field. It hammered into the ground right before the lines of the men, showering them in a spray of dirt. The men near it shrank back but continued on.

Ikely wondered what it would look like to see an entire legion's artillery at work, instead of just two machines. He had difficulty understanding how one would stand up to such a barrage? How could an enemy army withstand such power?

"Lieutenant," Stiger greeted him gruffly, having come up along with Eli. He took a moment to survey the entire line from this vantage point, first looking to the right and then to the left. After a moment, he nodded. "I will take over here. Brent has the right. Sergeant Boral currently has the left. I want you to assume command there," Stiger ordered curtly. "If you need help, send a runner."

"Yes, sir," Ikely replied with a salute and set out for the left flank, determined to do his duty.

CHAPTER TWENTY-ONE

"CORPORAL! I WANT you there yesterday!" Stiger shouted to corporal Beni, pointing exactly where he expected Beni to lead his reserve file. The enemy had managed to get several men over the top of the barricade and his legionaries in that position were fighting desperately as more rebels clambered over. If allowed to continue, the situation could deteriorate.

"Follow me!" Beni shouted and his file rushed forward, scrambling up the rampart and slamming into the rebels, bashing with their shields as they pushed forward. One of the enemy was hit so hard that he'd been knocked right over the barricade and into the trench below. Short swords jabbed out viciously as the legionaries went to work. Within seconds, Beni's reserve file had overwhelmed those who had made it over the top. The last remaining enemy, still on his feet, threw himself over the barricade and down into the trench, rather than be cut down like his fellows.

A bow twanged right behind the captain. Eli fired at a target who had made it up and over the wall in a different spot. This was followed by a shrill scream that was abruptly cut off. Stiger paid it no mind. He was busy studying his line, looking for problems to develop.

A short distance to the right, a legionary over-extended himself and stabbed a man on the top rung of a ladder.

Letting go of the ladder, the wounded enemy grabbed the legionary's arm as he fell, dragging the legionary over, both disappearing from sight. The next man on the ladder pulled himself over the side and punched his sword at the nearest legionary, who was caught off guard and stepped back. On his feet, the enemy soldier began swinging his sword in wide arcs to keep the legionaries back, just long enough for more of the enemy to clamber up the ladder. Before Stiger could issue any orders, Lieutenant Brent rushed forward with a reserve file and sealed the breach.

"Lieutenant," Stiger called as Brent stepped back, breathing heavily. Blood was spattered across the lieutenant's armor and face.

"Sir," Brent turned and walked over. His sword was dripping with the blood of a man he had just killed. A few scraps of flesh hung from it.

"Lieutenant," Stiger said as a ballista ball whistled overhead, followed shortly by a dull crump. "With Lieutenant Banister's death, I am short on officers and cannot afford to lose you. Please be kind enough to not go forward again. You have nothing to prove. Do you understand me, sir?"

"I understand, sir," Brent said and then nodded. "I will not take any unnecessary risks."

"Very good." Stiger patted the lieutenant on the shoulder. "Carry on."

Stiger took a moment to look around and study the action along the barricade. His men seemed to be holding up quite well, battling back the enemy attempts to force the wall.

"I don't think there were ever finer men," Stiger said quietly to himself as he watched the action a few moments. He moved over to where Ikely had stationed himself. Ikely, in firm control of his side of the line, nodded in greeting, not taking his eyes off of the action. There was another deep creaking groan, followed by a sharp crack, which announced the launching of a stone. It whistled overheard. Stiger followed the missile, which impacted amongst the masses of the enemy forming on the other side of the battlefield.

The enemy had brought up two fresh companies. It was only a matter of time before they formed a battle line and moved forward. Stiger studied them. If these units were anything like those that were assaulting his line, they were well-disciplined and motivated. The Cyphan Confederacy was renowned for the quality of their army. It seemed that reputation was well-earned.

The pressure on the wall seemed to ease, and Stiger looked down upon the enemy beyond the barricade. They were pulling back. Sergeants where blowing harshly on whistles to get the attention of those who had not begun to start moving.

"Javelins! Javelins at the ready!" Stiger shouted up and down the line. "Javelins at the ready!"

"Sir," Ikely said in protest. "They are withdrawing!"

"The more I take out now, the fewer we will have to deal with later," Stiger replied harshly, not having the time for a debate. The enemy would soon be out of range. Stiger saw there was no time for the men to ready for a massed volley.

"Release at will!" Stiger shouted and the men who had them ready threw, grunting with the effort. At first a few arced up, followed rapidly by more. The first javelins landed with a clatter and clash. As more javelins landed, the enemy began to fall in increasing numbers, screaming and crying out in pain. The great mass of the enemy looked up and back on the plunging javelins. They turned and ran full out for the safety of the other side of the battlefield.

Stiger watched with deep satisfaction as the enemy pulled back and out of range. That last javelin toss had hurt. They began reforming behind the fresh companies that had been brought up. As this was happening, another fresh company arrived from up the road and began to march onto battlefield.

Wounded were crawling or stumbling back toward their line in ones and twos. Those unable to move lay where they had fallen and cried out for help or simply screamed their torment to the world. The dead in their many numbers lay were they had fallen. Stiger glanced over the edge of the barricade and down into the trench. Wherever a bridge was located, there were piles men. He estimated that at least a couple hundred lay beneath the earthen rampart and in the trench. Among the heaps of enemy dead and wounded, the occasional scarlet cloak from one of his legionaries could be seen.

"This is a cold business," Stiger said quietly to his executive officer, turning to face him. "While you are able, never hesitate to inflict hurt upon the enemy. There is no fairness in war."

"Yes, sir," Ikely said.

Stiger turned to look across his line. On this side of the wall, there seemed few wounded, which was to be expected. The enemy had brought no artillery or missile fire. Those few who had been injured were being tended to and carried rearward on stretchers. Stiger felt pained seeing his men in such a state. At the same time, he also felt relief. They were headed toward the aid station where Father Thomas waited with the medics, to the rear at the next defensive line. When they arrived, they would be well-cared-for. Stiger bowed his head and offered a brief prayer, begging the High Father to spare as many of his men as possible.

The sky was beginning to darken. Looking back upon the enemy, Stiger figured there were at least a thousand to fifteen hundred upon the battlefield. There would be time enough for the enemy to have one more go at it, perhaps even two, before it became too dark for them to conduct an effective assault. When that happened, Stiger would withdraw.

"The men are giving a good accounting," Blake said. The sergeant had been checking the men along the wall. He had been in the thick of the fighting, rushing from trouble spot to trouble spot and was covered in blood, dirt and grime. Men such as the sergeant were selected from the toughest of the tough, who had proven themselves repeatedly and did not shirk from a good fight.

"They are good boys," Stiger said, looking over at the sergeant with a nod of agreement and approval.

"That they are, sir," Blake concurred with a broad grin. "Turned out to be one right fine day!"

"The day is not over yet," Stiger said as a legionary rushed up and drew his attention away from Blake. The legionary hastily saluted, breathing hard.

"Sir, Lieutenant Brent begs to report our scouts have encountered enemy skirmishers probing around and behind the right flank. He believes the enemy might be attempting a turning movement, but he sees no sign of it yet."

"Tell Lieutenant Brent I am sending help." Stiger said, accepting the report.

The legionary saluted once more and started back the way he came.

"Eli." Stiger turned toward his friend. "Take two of the reserve files and push those skirmishers back. Find out if they are trying to flank us."

"Watch yourself," Eli said quietly, stepping close. Then he nodded and set off.

"You too," Stiger said quietly to Eli's back. He scratched at the stubble on his chin, watching Eli take two of the reserve files with him. As disciplined and motivated as they had proven to be, if the enemy managed a turning movement on his flank, despite the rugged and broken ground, things would get sticky fast. He turned toward Ikely. "Get word to the sergeants and corporals. I want them reminded that if I give word to pull back, they are to do so in order. I will tolerate no panic."

"Yes, sir," Ikely said. He hesitated a moment, looking his captain square on. Stiger wondered for a moment if Ikely could read his concern. The lieutenant gave a brief nod and left to carry out his orders.

"Sir!" Blake called. "Here they come!"

Stiger turned and saw that the three fresh companies were marching steadily across the field. Behind them came a contingent of archers, maybe forty strong. The archers wore only light leathers, but they were uniformly equipped and Stiger took them for a professional auxiliary formation. *Now things will become more difficult*, Stiger thought.

"What was that about this being a right fine day?" Stiger asked of his sergeant.

"Why, sir, we have the enemy exactly where we want 'em," Blake said with a cheerful grin. "They are quite obliging and keep comin'. Could you ask for more?"

"Sergeant," Stiger said, returning Blake's grin and pointing. "Concentrate our archers. I want them focusing on those archers. Hurry now…there is not much time."

"Yes, sir." Blake set about bringing the archers up and concentrating them to oppose the enemy formation.

"Javelins at the ready!" Stiger called. Javelins were handed up to the men at the front. Looking back down the reverse slope of the rampart at his supply, Stiger estimated that he had enough left for three more good throws, at best. The enemy came across the field, arrayed for battle and silent. The only thing that could be heard was the steady tread of their boots. The silence in and of itself was a little disconcerting, which was its intended purpose.

The legionaries stood and waited for the enemy to come nearer. With a deep creaking groan, followed by a crack, another stone ball whistled overhead. It smashed into the center of the enemy line, causing an immediate gap four deep and eliciting a hearty cheer from Stiger's men. There was nothing more motivational than friendly artillery at work, Stiger thought.

The enemy continued on, stepping around and over the bodies, rapidly closing the gap that had been created in their line of battle. Stiger was impressed. The men they were facing were clearly well-trained and for a moment Stiger felt regret that he must inflict hurt and death upon them.

"Release!" Stiger roared when he judged they had moved into effective range. With grunts across the line, the men threw their weighted javelins up into the air and at the enemy. Rounded shields came up and with a loud clatter and crash, intermixed with screams, the javelins crashed down into the advancing line. Dozens fell. Many were forced to discard their shields.

"Second volley!" Stiger called harshly. Javelins were passed forward. The enemy was so close it would be hard to miss their mark. "Release!"

The wave of the deadly missiles crashed down into the enemy battle line with another deafening clatter and crash as the triangular-shaped heads punched through both shield and armor. Dozens more fell under the barrage, including many who had just lost their shields. Stiger saw the archer formation halt and raise their bows, pointing them skyward.

"Raise shields!" Stiger called up and down the line. "Raise shields! Prepare to receive arrow shot!"

The legionaries took shelter, squatting down and raising their shields above their bodies for protection. Those who could crouched behind the barricade for shelter. Stiger waited until the last moment to make sure his orders were being followed and then also crouched down behind the barricade. He raised his own shield over his head and body. There was a series of thunks as arrows struck nearby shields, with many harmlessly bouncing and clattering off. An arrow buried itself in the dirt nearly two feet from Stiger's foot. He pulled his foot in closer to his body. A man screamed a few feet away as an arrow penetrated his shield and pierced his hand, pinning it to his shield.

Looking up, Stiger spared the wounded man a brief glance before he peeked over the top of the barricade. The enemy were at the bridges and working their way across. The ladders would be going up again soon. Stiger estimated the enemy archers had time for maybe one or two volleys before they risked hitting their own. At that point, the massed arrow barrages would cease and the enemy would have to contend with isolated, independent fire. Stiger looked around and saw his own archers braving the arrow storm to return fire. Blake was there, shield held to the front, encouraging them on with shouts and curses.

"Javelins at will," Stiger roared.

The last of the javelins were passed forward. Legionaries rapidly stood, using their shields as protection against missile shot, and hurled the javelins down on the enemy, who were crossing the bridges, before ducking back under cover of their shields and the barricade. One man was not quick enough. An arrow took him in the neck and he toppled over the side of the barricade and into the trench below without making a sound.

"Draw swords!" Stiger ordered and up and down the line the swords came out. Stiger felt the familiar tingle as he drew his. The sword seemed to sing as it came free from the scabbard.

The top of a ladder thunked into place directly to the front of Stiger. He stuck his sword in the dirt, flipped over his shield and, using the end pushed, with all of his might. The men below, holding the base of the ladder, strained against him, throwing their weight into it, attempting to keep the ladder steady and in place as others began to climb.

"Help me!" Stiger yelled to the legionary next to him, who was still huddled behind his shield. One of the large forked sticks lay at his feet. Stiger jerked his head at it. The legionary looked up, saw what was happening, dropped his shield and grabbed the stick. Putting the forked end onto the top rung of the ladder, he pushed for all he was worth. Together they heaved the ladder away from the wall. In open space, the ladder teetered for a moment, threatening to swing back onto the barricade, before the men below lost control. The scaling ladder, with several men halfway up and clinging tightly to it, crashed backwards into the trench.

"Take that, you bastards," the legionary yelled at the men below. With an earsplitting crack, an arrow struck the legionary in the chest, bouncing harmlessly off his armor.

"That was close," the legionary said with a relieved grin directed at his captain. A second arrow struck him in the cheek, driving up into his brain and knocking his head back with the force of the impact. He fell backward and crumpled without uttering a sound, slowly rolling down the reverse side of the rampart. Stiger immediately ducked back down behind the barricade, watching the man roll until he came to a stop, an unmoving tangle of arms and legs. He had only been a foot from the man when he had been shot! Stiger shook himself and was reminded that, in war, death was frequently random. It came to the experienced and inexperienced alike.

"Don't forget the stones!" Stiger roared at the nearby legionaries who were still sheltering from the arrows. Several looked up at him. "Drop them on their heads!"

The legionaries jumped into action and in moments, heavy stones, which had been piled up every few feet, were heaved over the other side with grunts. They were almost immediately rewarded for their efforts with shouts, screams and curses from below.

Stiger glanced around to see how his line was doing. Very few of the enemy had made it to the top of the wall, with many of the scaling ladders being forced back and over into the trench. When the enemy managed to make it over the top, the legionaries stood, presented their shields in a wall and pushed into them, short swords jabbing out. Stiger's line was holding and the enemy was paying a heavy price for their foolish, yet determined, attempt on his line.

Studying the situation, Stiger decided the problem for the enemy was that they did not have enough bridges and ladders to make their assault more of a success. They were just throwing lives away, which Stiger was fine with, though he had trouble understanding why they were doing it. He wondered idly, had General Kryven lived, would the man have sacrificed his men in such a way? Stiger suspected not.

The attempt at storming the line went on for a few more minutes before it became a half-hearted effort. Shortly thereafter, the enemy began pulling back under the harassing fire of Stiger's archers, who had plenty of ammunition.

Unfortunately, Stiger sighed, he was out of javelins and was unable to inflict more pain upon his enemy. The enemy archers also pulled back.

The three companies who had made the original assault had been reformed, though they now stood just inside the tree line, outside catapult range. Seeing this, Stiger wished he had some good bolt throwers, which had better range. He took a few moments to study the situation and then sent runners for Ikely and Brent. He wanted a direct report from his officers.

"Do you think they will come again, sir?" Brent asked, looking up at the darkening sky. Brent had a light flesh wound on his neck and was touching it gingerly.

Stiger glanced at the setting sun, which had sunk just beneath the tops of the trees, casting long shadows over the body-strewn battlefield. He then turned his attention to the enemy.

"Perhaps," Stiger said, feeling that it was likely the enemy would strike one more time. "How are your men holding up?"

"Tolerable sir," Brent said, running a hand through his sweat-matted hair. He carried his helmet under his left arm. "My boys are tired, but they will endure. By the gods, they will endure, sir."

"What happened with those skirmishers probing around your flank?" Stiger asked of Brent. He was still concerned about an unexpected turning movement. Despite the caltrops and other obstacles laid out in the forest, Stiger felt that the enemy had had more than enough time to begin one. With luck, they had only thought of it after the first assaults and were still blundering and struggling through the forest. Off into the trees, the terrain was broken and rugged.

"Eli and the reserve files pushed them back, sir," Brent said. "Once they did, we had no more trouble. Eli took a couple of his scouts and went looking farther beyond the edge of our line. If they are intent on a flanking movement, Eli will find them, sir."

Stiger nodded and was silent a moment. He glanced back up at the sky once more. He judged it was perhaps less than an hour until complete sunset. He wanted nothing more than to pull back out of this position and was now feeling apprehensive about having made the decision to remain despite the risk. Perhaps the wiser course might have been to withdraw the moment he had returned from the failed parley.

He considered giving the order now and then discarded the idea. If he did so now, the next assault might well catch him with one boot off and the consequences of that could be quite serious. Then again, if the enemy managed to pull off a turning movement before dark, things would get complicated. Stiger glanced over to the right, wondering how Eli was faring and if he had found anything.

"Lieutenant?" Stiger asked of Ikely, looking for his report.

"We can easily hold," Ikely responded calmly. "Spirits are high. I hope they come again, sir."

"Gentlemen," Stiger said, "as soon as it is dark and the enemy ceases their activity, I intend to withdraw. We will do so in order and with speed. We will leave behind a handful of skirmishers to convince the enemy we still man this line. Once we reach the next defensive line, we shall give the men a few hours rest before turning to march hard for Vrell. With our new allies, I no longer see any compelling reason to attempt to further delay the enemy."

"With what we did to that road," Brent said with a sudden grin, "it should take them some time to overcome."

"Where is the captain?" a voice shouted urgently. "The captain! Where is he?" Stiger's head snapped around to look in the direction of the shout. Scout Corporal Marcus was running up the line. "The captain? Where is he?"

Several legionaries pointed and Stiger stepped forward, raising an arm, a feeling of dread washing over him.

"Sir," Marcus said, breathing heavily. He hastily saluted. "The enemy has a large force pushing through the forest on the right! They should hit the edge of our line in just a matter of minutes."

"Shit," Stiger said, feeling a cold sensation in the pit of his stomach. As if on cue, a horn blasted from the woods on the right. Another horn, from the enemy massing to his front, answered. He looked over at the right flank and then across the field. The enemy was preparing for another direct assault.

Why had there been no warning from Eli? Stiger asked himself worried. *What could have happened to him?*

Where was he?

Stiger's shoulders sagged as he realized what an idiot he had been. The enemy had intentionally fixed his attention with assaults that had no hope of succeeding, blinding him to the real threat, a flanking movement, which must have gotten underway the moment they first attacked, perhaps even before. They must have thoroughly scouted out his position and known the lay of the land. Instead of the broken and rugged ground hindering the turning movement, it had likely helped to conceal it. Stiger's position was now completely untenable. He felt a feeling of despair. He was looking at a disaster.

His thoughts churned. His officers were looking to him for direction, but he wasn't sure what to do. Then he remembered General Treim, his mentor, giving sage advice a long time ago.

"Sometimes," Treim had lectured Stiger, "even a bad decision is better than no decision."

Something snapped in the captain. He ground his teeth as anger and rage boiled his blood. If he did not do something fast, the enemy would be able to inflict serious harm on his small force, perhaps even destroy it.

Glancing around, Stiger knew his men. They were legionaries, accustomed to a difficult life, trained and disciplined to a high standard. Even the garrison companies had proved they were tough. His men would do as he asked, of that he was sure. Stiger's mind began working out what he needed to do to effectively withdraw.

"Gentlemen," Stiger said, turning to his two officers, resolved, "we will withdraw immediately. Brent, get back to the right, take Marcus with you and prepare to receive the enemy. You must hold long enough for me to begin pulling back the main body. Understand me? You must hold at all costs."

"I will buy you that time, sir," Brent said. He offered a smart salute and started off at a run for the right, with Marcus at his side.

"Ikely," Stiger growled, turning to his executive officer, a man he knew he could rely upon. "Begin organizing the men and start them withdrawing down the road and into the defensive corridor. I will handle the rearguard as the rest pull back. We must withdraw in order. Any panic could be the undoing of us."

"I understand, sir," Ikely said gravely. "You can count on me."

Stiger nodded, then added, "Make sure you get to the next line and prepare it for a defense. The enemy might just follow us right back to it before they give up for the night."

"Yes, sir," Ikely said, saluting, then offered the captain his hand. "I will see you there, sir."

Stiger shook his hand hard. "Yes, I will see you later tonight."

There was a cheering from across the field. Stiger and Ikely turned to look. The enemy was coming for another try at the wall. This time they were bringing many more bridges and a lot of additional ladders.

"I believe it is about to get interesting," Stiger said and drew his sword.

CHAPTER TWENTY-TWO

THE SUN HAD completely set and night was coming on. The moon was up, occasionally peeking out between the clouds, bathing the land and the struggle below with her pale, ethereal light.

Stiger had given up the left flank. He had formed a shield line near the center, facing what had been his left. The enemy had managed to get several dozen men over the wall on the left, but nothing too serious yet. They were slowly forming up. As they absorbed additional men who made it over the wall, they gave the appearance of not being prepared to push forward and join the fight.

The men in the center, still holding the wall, battled furiously and so far had managed to keep the enemy at bay. On the right flank, the situation was more serious. The enemy pushed out of the forest in company strength and slammed into the end of Stiger's line.

Lieutenant Brent had only just managed to organize a shield wall to hold them off. Stiger had been obliged to send reinforcements to bolster that line by stripping his already thin center. Brent's formation was now five deep. Giving ground grudgingly, he was slowly pulling back toward the center. As they moved backward, the wall paralleling the formation was abandoned. Those men coming off the wall were absorbed into Brent's ranks. The pressure on the lieutenant was intense, but at the same time, with each backward step, he was inflicting hurt upon the enemy.

Stiger stood atop the wall in the center, watching it all, or really what he could see of the action. In the field, the enemy had clearly pushed forward nearly everything they could manage. Stiger was not worried about his center or right. It was his left that was the problem. Once they got up enough men, he would be in real trouble.

There was a deep creaking groan, followed by a crack. Another ballista ball whistled by unseen in the dark. A few moments later, following this launch, there was a flash, followed by a large gout of flame, which lit up the night. The wagon had been set afire. A torch-bearer who had lit it walked over to the catapults. He touched the flame to first one and then the other catapult. Doused in dragon's breath, both machines immediately caught fire, burning furiously, flames reaching up toward the heavens.

Stiger shielded his eyes to protect his night vision as he looked in the direction of the road toward Vrell. Several hundred yards away and obscured by the dark, the open road was blocked by fallen trees. A path, wide enough only for one man to pass, had been left. This path ended at the next defensive line. The path had become a funnel and chokepoint as the bulk of his men escaped. It also made a successful withdrawal much more difficult. As long as his men did not panic and maintained discipline, things should work out. This was a perfect example of why the legions trained hard and often.

"Corporal Durggen," Stiger called into the night as loud as he could, making his way toward the burning catapults. The nearer he got, the more intense the heat became. "Corporal Durggen!"

"Here, sir!" The corporal ran over, looking exhausted.

"Set up a defensive line a little ways behind the catapults," Stiger ordered. "Start with your file. I will send you additional men. You will become the rearguard once we pull back."

"Yes, sir," Durggen replied, saluting fist to chest.

"Good man. I am relying upon you. You and your men must hold."

"We will hold, sir," Durggen said.

Stiger hesitated for a moment, wanting to say more. Durggen was young, and if it had not been for the condition of the company prior to Stiger's arrival, he would still be a ranker. He had no doubt about the corporal's ability or intention to hold, but his lack of experience and the responsibility Stiger was heaping on him was perhaps too much.

"Good man," Stiger said again, clapping the young corporal on the shoulder. "I will send Sergeant Ranl to take charge just as soon as I can."

The relief in the corporal's eyes confirmed Stiger's suspicions. It did not mean that the corporal was incapable of doing the job, only that he needed a little more seasoning.

"All right, you sorry lot," Durggen shouted at his file. "You thought you earned yourselves a rest? Well, you thought wrong. Time for some real soldiering. Fall in, you lazy bastards."

Stiger left the corporal and moved over to the left, where Sergeants Boral and Blake stood fast. They had arranged their defensive formation four deep and twenty across. This force represented half of the files that had been manning the left. Stiger had already sent the rest down the road toward Vrell. Those remaining represented his blocking force, keeping the enemy on his left in check.

The men rested their shields on the ground and waited tensely, watching the enemy to their front. It was only a matter of time until the enemy got organized and came at them.

"Sergeant." Stiger approached Blake.

"A lovely evening for a fight, sir," Blake greeted him enthusiastically. "Though the enemy here does not seem terribly obliging as those bastards assaulting the wall."

"They don't, do they…" Stiger said, trying to get a sense of the enemy before him in the darkness. What he could make out was around a hundred or so men milling about. It looked as if a sergeant was attempting to create some order. Once they became ordered, it was extremely likely they would advance.

"I believe they will be coming before long," Boral said. "Things will get interesting soon enough."

Stiger agreed with that assessment. Allowing the enemy time to become organized was a dangerous proposition. He could not allow that to happen.

"Prepare to advance," Stiger snapped.

Both Boral and Blake looked crosswise at the captain, as if to make sure they had heard right.

"We are going to push them," Stiger explained in an irritated tone. He hated having to explain himself but knew, in this instance, the more his sergeants understood his reasoning, the more helpful they would be, especially if they had to make decisions on their own. "We are going to push them before they can become organized and push us. I only want them shoved back a little to buy us some time. Once we accomplish that, then we fall back on the double to this spot."

"Shields," Blake roared. The men instantly pulled their shields up. "Close up the ranks! Prepare to advance!"

The men closed up, with the front rank bringing their shields to the front.

"Advance," Stiger ordered harshly, his voice beginning to crack from the strain of continual shouting. The men started forward. The distance closed rapidly as the shield line pushed forward. At first, in the darkness, the enemy did not seem to notice the legionaries advancing upon them. Someone pointed, saying something excitedly and another shouted. Less than ten yards away, several of the enemy took a nervous step backward. The enemy sergeant roared what Stiger took to be a string of invectives at his men. The enemy settled down and those who were in formation brought their shields up and swords out.

"First," Stiger shouted to his men, providing what encouragement he could, "we're going to show them our shields! Then we're gonna give them no less than two inches of sharpened steel!"

"HAAAAH!" the men roared, momentarily overriding the din of battle behind them. "HAAAAH!"

The sergeant on the other side intensified his efforts, shouting and shoving men into position. Stiger was impressed with the discipline of the enemy as they rapidly fell into a thin line.

"Draw swords!" the captain roared, pulling out his own. With a hiss, the legionaries drew their short swords. Seconds later the two lines met in a resounding crash of shield on shield. There was a momentary struggle as Stiger's men pushed hard at the enemy as each side attempted to achieve dominance over the other. Shields locked, the enemy could only batter against the legionaries' larger shields, which became more difficult as Stiger's men pushed bodily into them. Shields parted ever so slightly and the deadly short swords darted out, striking armor, shield and flesh. It only took two inches of penetration for a legionary short sword to mortally wound and every legionary knew it.

For a moment the enemy held firm and then grudgingly began to give ground as more and more of their number fell. The legionaries continued to push forward, the front rank stepping over the dead and wounded. The second rank stabbed down and into the bodies of the fallen, intent on ensuring they did not rise again. Killing the wounded was harsh, but no one wanted to take the chance of receiving a sword in the back as the line continued forward.

"Close up that gap!" Stiger shouted after a legionary tripped and fell over a body. The man in the second rank stepped over him and right into place. Sergeant Boral helped the fallen legionary to his feet and shoved him back into line at the rear of the formation.

"Stabbing!" Blake roared, enraged. "Legionary Pallo, in the legions, real men stab and jab! Fucking slash like that again and I will put you on report! The next man that slashes will be up to his neck in the latrines, shoveling shit for the next ten days! Proper sword work, boys! Come on! Make me proud!"

The enemy sergeant, who was screaming encouragements at his men, took the position of a fallen man in the front rank as the fighting became more desperate. He was a large man, and appeared to be a scarred, hard-bitten veteran. Stiger would have recognized the man as a sergeant anywhere. He was the glue holding the enemy formation together.

"I want that man taken down!" Stiger shouted, pointing. "That man needs to go!"

Swords jabbed out, again and again, in an effort to take the big sergeant down. A legionary opened himself up to strike at the sergeant, which turned out to be a mistake. A sword snapped out and caught him under the armpit. Mortally wounded, the legionary fell like a stone. Without hesitation, the man in the rank behind stepped forward to take his fallen comrade's place.

The enemy sergeant continued to shout encouragements to his men as he fought. A legionary slammed his shield boss with all of his might into the sergeant's round shield, surprising the man and knocking him off balance. Another legionary to the left saw an opening and jabbed his sword into the sergeant's leg, punching through, exploding out the back side. The sergeant screamed as the blade was yanked back out and fell to a knee, dropping his shield. The next sword took him in the throat, abruptly cutting off the scream. With their sergeant's death, the enemy, still maintaining their line, began to backpedal much faster.

"Halt!" Stiger called, having seen the sergeant brutally cut down. His legionaries staggered to a stop and dressed their line under Blake's shouting. The enemy continued to backpedal, opening the distance between the legionary formation and their own. "Second rank to the front!"

The second rank stepped forward to become the first. The men of the first rank, chests heaving from the exertion, stepped back to the rear of the line and took their places. A few grabbed their canteens and took a gulp of water.

"Sir," Sergeant Boral said, drawing Stiger's attention to the right. Stiger's push had taken them about thirty yards from their original position and the enemy had gotten men up onto the undefended wall to their right. Stiger knew he could go no further. If he continued, the enemy would get behind them and eventually another officer or sergeant would arrive to organize them.

"About face!" Stiger shouted and the formation immediately turned about. "On the double! Move out!"

Armor jingling, the men swiftly withdrew, double-timing it in formation as if they were simply executing another practice maneuver on parade.

"Halt," he called as soon as the panting legionaries reached their original position. "About face!"

The formation turned about and faced the direction they had just come from. The enemy they had just pushed back seemed confused by the sudden maneuver. Without their sergeant, they did not appear overly eager to press forward. This is what Stiger had wanted to achieve.

"Sergeant Blake," Stiger ordered. "Hold here."

"Yes, sir," Blake acknowledged. "We will hold this here position."

Stiger nodded and climbed back up the wall to the center of his line, where his men were struggling to hold back the enemy. With the lack of officers, Sergeant Ranl was busy directing the defense.

Stiger was headed for his sergeant when he saw a legionary stagger back from the wall, wounded. An enemy pulled himself up over the top, followed quickly by another, cutting down the wounded legionary. A third dragged himself over the barricade. Stiger's men at that spot abruptly found themselves struggling against not only those attempting to scale the wall, but those who had made it over. Stiger looked for a reserve file, prepared to give them the order to go in, when he realized with no little amount of alarm that there were no more reserves. This breach could prove the undoing of his center. He had to do something and fast.

Stiger felt his blood boil with rage as a second legionary went down.

Some things you just have to do yourself, he thought grimly.

Stiger dragged out his sword and advanced. He felt the familiar electric tingle he always felt, but this time it somehow seemed stronger, almost as if the sword was feeding upon his rage. It was not until he was on the enemy, shield presented forward and sword held ready, that he realized the blade was emitting a pale blue light. Before he could react, Stiger was on the enemy.

He slammed his shield into the first man, knocking him violently back before punching out with his sword. The sword struck armor, scraping across a chest plate. A sword hit his shield in reply, blow communicated painfully to his arm behind the shield. Stiger hammered his shield into the man again, this time knocking him bodily down. A quick thrust at his exposed neck ended the struggle.

Stiger was almost immediately pressed roughly backward as an enemy struck at him with shield and sword from the side. Caught off balance from the unexpected attack, he was forced to backpedal almost to the inner edge of the rampart's slope until he was able to firmly plant his feet and shove back. At the same time, he struck out with his sword at where he thought the enemy's unprotected sword arm would be and was rewarded with a yelp of pain.

The pressure against his shield lessened. Stiger advanced, attacking with both sword and shield as he moved forward. The man tripped and fell over the body of the first man Stiger had cut down and tumbled to the ground. Without hesitation, the captain stabbed downward, efficiently silencing him.

The final enemy that had made it up over the wall fell to the dirt, a legionary standing over the body, breathing heavily from the exertion of the fight.

Stiger turned to the wall where a fourth man was about to climb over. The captain struck out with his shield, slamming it into the enemy's face. There was a sickening crunch and scream as the soldier fell from the ladder he had been climbing.

Recovering, Stiger leaned over the edge of the barricade and stabbed downward at the next man clambering up, who, seeing the strike coming, jumped from ladder and into the trench below. Knocked off balance by the jump, the ladder slid along the outer side of barricade before crashing down, taking another man with it into the trench.

Stiger stepped back, breathing deeply and grinned at the legionary who had downed the last man over the barricade. The legionary nodded his thanks to his captain. Stiger glanced down at his sword. It was no longer glowing.

Did I imagine that?

Wiping the blade clean on the body of a fallen enemy, Stiger sheathed his weapon and, despite the darkness, tried to get a sense for the battle as a whole. He looked over on his right. Brent's men had pulled back almost to the center of the line.

The lieutenant was under heavy pressure. A second company had emerged from the tree line, adding strength to the first. To make matters worse, the enemy had managed to get more men over the parts of the wall on the right that had been abandoned. Those men had been added to the two companies pressuring Brent, who had been forced to extend his line and thin its depth to keep from being flanked. This meant that the rotation of ranks came quicker, allowing the men less time to rest and recover before they were back at it.

Stiger glanced along his center. It was clear his men in this position could not hold much longer. As it stood, there were just too few left holding the line. The breach he had just stopped was evidence of that.

"Sergeant Ranl," Stiger said, stepping up to the man. "It is time to pull these men off. Send half up the road. The other half are to fall in with Corporal Durggen. He has formed a defensive line beyond the catapults. Take command there. When the blocking forces on the left and right pull back, you will be the rearguard. Understand?"

"Yes, sir," Ranl said. "Send half my boys up the road, the other half to fall in with Durggen's boys and then we are to act as rearguard when the left and right pull back. Correct?"

"Yes," Stiger said. "Send a man to inform Lieutenant Brent and Sergeant Blake before you begin your withdrawal."

"Corporals on me!" Sergeant Ranl called to his corporals after having sent a runner to Brent and Blake. The corporals hustled over and gathered round. "Rax, Cauis, Nomas, Marcellas, pull your files off the line and withdraw. The rest will hold while they pull back in order! Once they are out, we will step back and join the rearguard behind the catapults. Understand?"

There were nods all around.

"Let's get to it, then," Ranl said.

The four files pulled back and down off the wall. Once behind, they formed up and marched briskly toward the path and Vrell. Stiger watched them for a moment as they passed the burning siege engines.

"Time to go," Ranl said, coming up to Stiger. The remainder of the sergeant's men were starting to back down the rampart, presenting shields toward the enemy, who had already gotten over the top of the barricade, where moments before the legionaries had held them in check. "I would not want to leave you behind, sir."

Stiger nodded and fell back with the legionaries. His anxiety had begun to grow. This would be the most dangerous part of the withdrawal.

Brent had increased the pace of his backward movement. One of the corporals was calling a steady cadence so that the men were in step as they pulled backward under the heavy pressure that appeared to be mounting by the moment.

"One, two, three, four... One two, three, four..." Brent had a whistle in his mouth and every few minutes blew on it hard, signifying the changing out the front rank to give those men a brief breather before they were thrown back into the thick of it.

"Lieutenant, how is it going?" Stiger asked, having come up behind the lieutenant.

"My boys are holding in there, sir," Brent said. "Though we are withdrawing, we've really stuck them good."

"Sergeant Ranl has a rearguard formed just beyond the catapults," Stiger explained. "Once you reach his position, pass through and get your men on down the path as soon as you can."

"I understand, sir," Brent said.

"Good."

Stiger hurried over to Blake's position. The enemy to their front did not look at all interested in pressing the issue and appeared content to simply watch the legionaries who had just handled them so roughly.

"Sergeant," Stiger said to Blake. "Get your men moving... Sergeant Ranl has the rearguard and is positioned right behind the catapults."

Sergeant Blake immediately began reforming the men to march. In seconds they were formed up into a marching column.

"On the double! Move out!" Sergeant Blake called and the column jogged off toward the catapults, armor and equipment jingling as they went.

Stiger jogged with them. They passed the burning catapults. Fully engulfed, the heat was almost enough to singe. Stiger found Sergeant Ranl with the rearguard.

Sergeant Blake's men quickly moved through. A dense group of closely-packed men could be seen farther along, waiting their turn to make it onto the path that led to safety.

Stiger saw that Boral had elected to remain with the rearguard. The captain was briefly reminded of the incident concerning Lieutenant Peal that was yet to be resolved. Stiger put that from his mind and turned to watch Brent. The lieutenant was skillfully fighting his men, moving closer, pulling back one slow step at a time. There was no point in hurrying him along. Stiger needed to buy all the time he could get to evacuate his men down the path and off the battlefield.

The minutes passed slowly as Brent's force gave ground, fighting doggedly as they inched backward.

"Let's make this count," Stiger shouted to the rearguard as Brent's men came within ten feet, then five.

"Time to earn your pay, boys," Ranl shouted. "Make room for them to pass through then close up ranks quick-like."

Brent's weary defenders began to pass into and through Ranl's formation. A good number were lightly wounded and a few seriously so, but they remained in line, a credit to their toughness and discipline. Stiger wondered how many men he had lost. Once through, the front rank closed up and the enemy, who hesitated a moment in the face of a fresh force, pressed in with savagery, screaming as they came.

"Nice work," Stiger shouted to Brent. The noise of the fighting was deafening. "You delayed them long enough for nearly all of our men to escape. Get your boys moving down the path. Hurry now!"

Brent nodded and began passing orders to his sergeant. About to join Ranl behind the rearguard, a thought suddenly occurred to Stiger.

"Have you seen Eli?" Stiger asked, grabbing Brent's arm and pulling the lieutenant close so that he could hear the reply.

"I thought you knew, sir." Brent blanched. "I am sorry, sir...the lieutenant fell to the enemy."

"What?" Stiger asked in a near whisper, completely shocked by the news. It was as if he had been punched in the gut. "Eli's dead?"

"I am sorry, sir," Brent said again. "One of the scouts reported he was struck down. He is gone."

Stiger released Brent's arm and stumbled backwards into Ranl, who turned to look at who had hit him from behind before returning to the action. Brent turned away to get his men moving for the path.

"Gone," Stiger whispered to himself, a hollow feeling in his heart. "No..."

"Sir?" Ranl asked. Under pressure, the rearguard had begun to fall back one step at a time and the captain was in the way. "Are you okay?"

The captain looked at the sergeant blankly.

"Are you wounded, sir?" Grabbing the captain's arm, Ranl pulled him along while at the same time quickly looking Stiger over for injury. He turned to Boral. "Take the captain down the path."

"No," Stiger shouted, a rage boiling up in his breast. It was a terrible, desperate burning desire to kill every last one of the enemy, to make them pay. "I will fight. I am going to kill them all!"

Ranl blinked in surprise as the captain drew his sword and threw himself forward toward the front rank, pushing between the legionaries and punching his sword forward. It scraped across the armored chest of an enemy. Stiger's rage grew at not being able to bleed the man before him.

His sword flared with a bluish light that illuminated those nearest. He jabbed again. This time, his sword easily slid through the man's breastplate as if it were made of simple cloth and the enemy before him dropped like a stone. His next jab found the flesh of an enemy's arm, tearing and cutting through tendon right to the bone. The enemy soldier dropped his sword, screaming, and was immediately swallowed up by his formation as the next man stepped forward to take his place.

Stiger's rage mounted and with it the sword burned brighter as he struck another man down. Those nearest flinched back as Stiger jabbed and stabbed, but the press from behind pushed them onward. A sword punched Stiger in the chest, point blocked by his armor but knocking him back slightly. The powerful blow momentarily stunned him, and with it, the sword's fire dimmed.

Sergeant Ranl waded into the press and grabbed Stiger in a vicelike grip, wrapping him in a bear hug, pulling him off his feet and backward, just as a sword punched out into the space where the captain had been. The ranks closed back up.

"Let me go," Stiger cried in a maddened rage, his sword flaring with brilliance, almost as if ignited by his rage. "I will kill them all for Eli!"

"No, sir," Ranl said, struggling with his captain. "You won't."

Boral joined in and helped to hold Stiger back.

"Sir," Ranl said forcefully once they were a few feet away. "You need to get a grip! These boys here are counting on you!"

Stiger struggled for a moment more before the words struck home. He blinked then forcibly brought himself under control and with it the sword's brilliant glow died away. The sergeant was right. He had a deeper duty and responsibility. This was no time for selfishness. It was no time for revenge.

"We need you here, sir," Ranl stated firmly, giving the captain a physical shake and shooting a nervous glance at the captain's sword. "*I* need you."

"I am here," Stiger said, breathing heavily. "You are right. Sergeant, return to your post."

"Yes, sir," Ranl said, looking relieved. He released hold of the captain and turned back to the fighting. A sharp glance from Ranl told Boral to stick with the captain. Boral nodded in reply. Stiger did not miss the exchange and mentally reprimanded himself for losing control.

The fighting was intense as the rearguard held their ground for a few minutes at a time before retreating a few paces to once again stand their ground. This allowed those last few waiting their turn time to start down the path to escape. Each minute allowed more men through, and in less than ten minutes, only the rearguard remained inching closer toward escape.

Sergeant Ranl brought the rear ranks up to the path, called for a rotation of the first rank and sent those men through. Rank by rank, men started down the path. All the while, the fighting to the front was ugly and hard. Corporal Durggen, nursing a wound to his right forearm, was pushed out of the line by Ranl and told to go. Clearly relieved, the corporal went, stepping by the captain and onto the path.

The enemy finally realized that the legionaries were escaping and pressed in harder, yelling in their own language at the legionaries as they came on. The fighting became even more intense as the enemy threw themselves forward. Still, the legionaries fought doggedly on, using sword and shield to hold the enemy back.

"Sir," Ranl said when all that remained was the first rank, "it is time for you to go."

"No, sergeant," Stiger said firmly. "You first. I will be along shortly."

Sergeant Ranl reluctantly turned and left Stiger commanding the last of the men. The captain stood to the side of the path, trees and brush piled around them. Thankfully, the opening to the path only allowed access to a few of the enemy at a time. The closer they got to the path, the more it narrowed, allowing one man at a time to step back and run to safety. In the close confines of the piled-up trees and brush, there was barely enough moonlight to see and much of the sword and shield play now was guesswork.

The men kept backing up, with Stiger at their back, tapping one man at a time and telling him to go, until there were only two left.

"Go," Stiger snapped to the next man, who immediately took a big step back, turned and ran for all he was worth. The captain brought his shield up to cover the last man. He was about to tell him to go when the man's shield was ripped away. Exposed, he was cut down under a flurry of sword strokes.

Stiger turned and ran for the passage, finding Sergeant Boral waiting for him. The enemy saw them run and a cry went up. The chase was on as they rushed down the path, the enemy close behind.

CHAPTER TWENTY-THREE

STIGER SAT BEFORE his campfire, staring despondently into its depths. A cold wind made its way through the forest, rattling the leafless limbs above with its passing. Almost two weeks had passed since Eli's passing and the loss still weighed heavily on his heart. It had been upon his orders that his closest friend had been sent to his death. Eli's would be yet another shade that haunted his lonely nights, made more so by their closeness.

Like all his men, he was tired, sore and weary. During the days that followed the big fight before the entrance to his defensive corridor, the enemy had changed tactics and pushed deeply into the forest along both sides of the road with light units while the main body worked to clear the road and advance.

Because of the loss of most of his trained scouts, Stiger's small force had been closely dogged for the last week and a half as the enemy pursued him. Falling back had proven more difficult since Stiger could not use the road, which he had destroyed. He and his men had been forced out, away from the defensive corridor into the forest paralleling the road. His pace had been slower than he would have liked, owing to his decision to bring all his wounded with him as he fell back. He knew other officers would have abandoned the wounded without a second thought, but Stiger could not bring himself to do that. Many were carried on litters, which slowed their march considerably. Whenever the enemy got too close, there had been a handful of small, vicious skirmishes. In these instances, Stiger had felt compelled to turn and strike savagely at the forces dogging him.

With each counterpunch, Stiger had managed to inflict heavy casualties and then disengage, falling farther back. In the last skirmish, he had even managed to completely annihilate an entire company before turning his tired and weary men back in the direction of Vrell. It had allowed him to finally put some space between his beleaguered force and those pursuing.

The noise of the camp surrounded him as the men settled in for the night. They had stopped at the last defensive line that had been built. It lay along the road and just before Castle Vrell, which was less than ten miles distant. Stiger would have pushed straight onward, marching through the night, but his men were exhausted and needed rest, even if it was only for a few sparse hours. In the morning, well before sunrise, they would break camp and push onward to Vrell and the safety of her immense walls.

Stiger threw a stick into the fire, which flared up, burning brightly. A long time ago, Eli had returned not only Stiger's life, but his self-respect. Bitterly, he knew now he would never be able to repay his friend for that kindness.

He rubbed at his tired eyes. He needed sleep more than anything else but knew if he tried, it would not come. Marcus's latest report, delivered less than an hour before, was that two light infantry companies were camped no less than fifteen miles distant. Farther back, the enemy was working to clear the road one mile at a time and making good progress. It was a monumental task and one Stiger would have very much liked to impede. Unfortunately, with the loss of Eli and without a sufficient number of trained scouts, there was little he could do. Through sheer numbers alone, the enemy had the scouting advantage and with it came the initiative. Only three of Eli's original force remained and they had been worked to exhaustion. Stiger feared if he turned to attack, he would potentially give the enemy a chance to visit destruction upon his weary force. He had done all he could to impede the enemy. It was time to return to Castle Vrell.

Wishing he had never heard of Vrell, he pulled out his pipe, tapped it clean and filled it with the last of the captured tobacco. He tried to enjoy the taste, but found he could not. Instead, he continued to stare into the depths of his fire and think on the future, the dwarves and the coming spring.

"The gods as my witness," Stiger whispered to himself, "I will make them pay."

"Tea, sir?" Ikely asked. He was carrying a mug of tea that the cook had prepared.

Stiger nodded gratefully and the lieutenant set the steaming mug down next him. Not making a move for it, the captain continued to stare into the fire. The lieutenant looked as if he wanted to say something, but instead turned away and went to his own campfire a few feet distant.

A snowflake, illuminated by the orange glow of the fire, blew past Stiger's nose, quickly followed by another. Obscured by heavy cloud cover, there was no moon. Beyond the firelight of the camp, it was pitch black, as if a veil had dropped across the land. Watching the flakes continue to fall, Stiger wondered briefly if this might herald the first significant snowfall of the winter. He hoped it would. Anything that made the enemy's life more difficult appealed to him.

He tossed another stick into the fire. Then he picked up the tea, which had cooled and took a sip. Though the enemy had paid dearly, Stiger's casualties had also been heavy, numbering over two hundred and fifty, including...Eli. Yes, his men needed a prolonged period of rest to recover, at least one lasting for several weeks. Once back at Vrell and behind the castle's walls, they would get it.

Lieutenant Lan had reported that large numbers of dwarven warriors had arrived at the castle, with more showing up daily. It had taken some convincing for the lieutenant to accept the fact that the dwarves were now allies. Stiger had traded no less than four dispatches with Lan, until he had tired and simply ordered the lieutenant to allow the dwarves into the castle and to cooperate with them.

The lieutenant had also reported that the dwarves had brought along a number of gnomes. According to Lan's dispatches, the little creatures were half the size of a dwarf and malicious. The dwarves had advised him to simply let the gnomes alone. Both the dwarves and gnomes were working tirelessly to help strengthen the castle's defenses.

Looking back on his campaign to slow and delay the enemy, Stiger felt like he had failed. Losing Eli was a failure in and of itself. Yet he knew deep down that he had not failed. The enemy was always going to get to Vrell regardless of his actions. The only thing Stiger had changed was their timing. So in the end, he had succeeded in what he had set out to do. Not only had the enemy been sufficiently delayed, he had secured a powerful ally to boot. With the dwarves' help, it was a certainty that he could hold the castle and the valley for the empire.

Stiger suspected that Braddock and he were of a like mind when it came to dealing with the enemy. Still, he could not see anything happening until spring, for soon the pass would be snowed in. The winter months would be devoted to rest, recovery and training. He took another pull on his pipe and then nearly froze with alarm.

Though he was surrounded by campfires, with his men settling in for the night, Stiger sensed something was wrong. A presence lurked behind him, no more than a few feet away. Stiger's eyes narrowed suspiciously. Another assassination attempt? His sword lay next to him, leaning against the stump he was sitting on. Casually, he tapped out his pipe, sprinkling the ashes onto the cold ground, before setting it next to him. He leaned back, as if stretching and prepared to reach for his blade.

"You know, one might rashly conclude you perhaps made an error in judgement when turning down a comfortable life at court," a familiar voice said. Stiger was dumbstruck and then he leapt to his feet. A heavy and dark weight lifted from his heart as Eli stepped by him and up to the fire. The elf was grinning as he drew in the warmth from the blaze, holding out his hands to warm them. "We both know Miranda would have loved to keep you, ah, shall we say… close. The word is close, yes?"

"A life at court is not for me," Stiger said, a slight catch in his throat. He cracked a smile, the first one in days. *Eli's alive!* "Besides, the only woman for me is Tehver'Na."

Eli chuckled softly at the jest. He selected a log a few feet away and sat down, looking over at his friend. "Her father would see you dead first, of that I am sure."

"Perhaps." Stiger was grinning too. "We wouldn't really know until I asked for her hand."

"Yes," Eli said with mock seriousness. "I am confident he would end your days for even the mere suggestion of such a union."

They looked at each other. "You're really all right?" Stiger asked, his voice hoarse.

"Better than you, methinks. You look like shit...that is the right saying?"

"Yes, that is the correct saying," Stiger chuckled and wiped at his eyes. He could hardly believe it. "And I feel like shit too...though not so bad now."

Ikely, at his own fire, heard his captain's chuckle and looked up. Jumping up with an excited shout, he rushed over.

"Eli," Ikely said, clapping the elf on the shoulder. "We thought you were dead! However did you manage to survive?"

"I fear I almost did not." Brushing aside his hair, Eli showed the side of his head, which was badly bruised. "I was hit by something sufficiently blunt to put me down. When I came around, I found I had been pulled aside by my new friends."

"New friends?" Ikely asked. "What are you talking about?"

Eli nodded behind the captain, in the direction of Stiger's tent. They turned to look. Standing beside the captain's tent was a redheaded elven woman, along with two other male elves. All three were dressed in soft leathers of woodland green and brown, the kind that elven rangers preferred. They carried bows slung across their backs and short swords at their sides. The female elf stepped forward while the other two remained where they were. Her intense eyes were fixed upon the captain.

"Captain Stiger and Lieutenant Ikely," Eli said formally, standing. "May I present Taha'Leeth, daughter to Lord Taha'Efan of the Lorica."

Stiger stood and formally bowed, as did Ikely. The captain had lived for a time with elves and found her name interesting. Elves were organized into what could be described loosely as tribes, or perhaps even extended families, with each one being headed by a Lord. This effectively meant that Taha'Leeth was the equivalent of a princess. More interesting to the captain, Stiger had never heard of the Taha. Only one who had lived among elves for an extended period of time would have picked up on it. Stiger looked questioningly at Eli.

"She is not of my people," Eli explained, understanding the captain's unspoken question. "She and her people come from across the Narrow Sea far to the South."

Stiger studied Taha'Leeth and her two companions. Like all elves, they looked capable and confident.

"The elven nations have an accord with the Empire. What were they doing working for the enemy?" Stiger asked, returning Taha'Leeth's gaze. She betrayed no emotion, but continued to look at him with unblinking eyes. Stiger felt his heart flutter. Her eyes seemed so deep they were bottomless. Stiger shook himself slightly and glanced over at Eli when his friend did not answer. "Well?"

"They are a subjugated people," Eli explained sadly and with some hesitation as if carefully picking his words. "The equivalents of slaves, forced to fight for the Cyphan Confederacy. Thinking themselves the last of their people, they had no idea that other elves live free."

"How does that change things?" Stiger asked, eying the new elves critically.

"We would like the honor to fight alongside our brother," Taha'Leeth said in broken common, nodding in a nonhuman sort of way toward Eli. Stiger found her accent appealing.

"You are rebelling? Against the Cyphan? Is that it?" Ikely asked, eyebrows raised.

"Yes," she replied, her eyes flashing as she gave the lieutenant a sharp glance. "We will no longer fight for the overlords, not while we can live free like our brother."

"I see," Ikely said.

"Your empire recognizes my brother's people?" Taha'Leeth asked turning back to Stiger.

"We do."

"My brother's people live free?" she pressed, eyeing the captain carefully.

Stiger nodded in confirmation.

"Won't your people at home suffer?" Stiger was wondering if this was somehow a trick of the enemy. Eli seemed to believe her and she appeared sincere enough that he understood this was in all actuality no lie, blind or charade.

"They will bring their people north," Eli explained, as if it were as simple as that. "I could say no more before now for fear that word would reach the enemy. I hope you understand."

Stiger blinked in surprise at the explanation, realizing that Eli had considered this information so vital he could not even trust it with him.

Then it hit Stiger. Eli was talking about moving an entire people north to elven lands. A move across half of the world! Looking at Taha'Leeth, the captain wondered how numerous her people were and how difficult a task that would be.

"Can they do it?" Stiger asked, recovering from his astonishment.

"We are the High Born," Taha'Leeth said confidently.

Stiger almost smiled at her. If anyone could accomplish something impossible, it would be an elf.

"At the moment, her people offer us their assistance in the fight against our enemy. Currently, it is just her and two other rangers," Eli explained. "The rest have gone home. Once they see to their people, they will send more to join our cause."

"I see," Stiger said, studying Taha'Leeth, wondering about her age. Like every other elven woman he had ever met, she had that ageless look that made her appear no older than her early twenties. Despite her youthful looks, he knew she could be twice Eli's age.

Her eyes were captivatingly deep. As if being drawn in, he began to lose himself to her beauty, which tugged heavily at his heart. He found himself irrationally desiring nothing more than to please her, to grant her every wish, to protect her and her people from harm.

POWER, a voice roared in Stiger's head and with it came a feeling as if he had been plunged abruptly into an icy bath. The pull and depth of Taha'Leeth's beauty lessened, then faded enough so that Stiger shook his head in confusion and was able to break eye contact. He felt a slight headache and rubbed at his tired eyes. When he looked back up, he saw what he took for surprise in her eyes. Then it hit him and he shot a glance over at his sword, which was still sheathed in its scabbard! It was resting where he had left it, leaning against the stump he had been sitting on. The sword had spoken again.

This one has power. Old power...old...power...

Stiger abruptly grinned, despite the shock that the sword had spoken. He realized that she had tried to put a glamour on him and the sword had somehow broken the charm. When Stiger had lived with the elves, some of the girls had played similar tricks upon him, twisting his heart cruelly for their own amusement. He had been helpless to their torments. They had continued to do so until Eli had discovered their game and put a stop to it.

"Enough of that nonsense," he said lightly. Eli had brought them here and had, in a way, vouched for them. "If I accept you and your people, you will not play such games with me and my men. If you do, I will know you for an enemy and I will kill you myself."

One of the elves with Taha'Leeth stepped forward, hand going for his sword, until she sent him back to his place with a simple look. She turned back to the captain and considered him for a moment with unfathomable eyes, tilting her head as she did so, reddish hair cascading past her shoulders.

"It was a mistake to try to win you over in such a way," she said quietly, looking down to the ground. Stiger recognized it as a rare apology from an elf to one who was considered an inferior being. It was all he was likely to get. "We will attempt no such guile with you or your men. I swear that upon my house."

Stiger was silent a moment. He knew that swearing against one's house was rarely done. He glanced over at Eli, who had an inscrutable look. Stiger realized that Eli was obviously wondering how he had broken the glamour. Stiger shrugged as if to say *guess how*. It was about time he dealt Eli a surprise or two.

"I would recommend accepting their offer," Eli said after a moment. "You could do worse for allies. That is, if you wish my opinion on the matter."

"Seetha'sha da sotha lo," Stiger said, in what he knew was poor elven... *I would be honored to have your people at my side.*

Taha'Leeth's flat countenance gave way to a dazzling closed-mouthed smile and Stiger realized she had feared he would reject her offer. So genuine was her smile that he could not help grinning back.

"Sir!" A legionary approached at a trot, armor jingling. He stopped cold when he saw the three strange elves. The legionary's hand went for his blade and then he saw Eli and hesitated.

"It's all right," Stiger reassured the man. "They are friends."

"Yes, sir," he said, relieved, then remembered himself, braced to attention and offered a salute. "Sir, Lieutenant Brent requests your immediate presence."

"Please advise the lieutenant I will be there shortly," Stiger said.

"Sir." The legionary hesitated nervously. "He said to bring you straight away, sir. Urgent, sir."

"All right," Stiger said, a sinking feeling in his stomach. It could only mean one thing. The enemy was closer than he thought. He grabbed his sword and once again felt that strange tingle that came and went so fast he was not sure it had occurred. He glanced down at the sword and considered it for a fraction of a second before he secured it in place. As Braddock had said, it was a powerful artifact.

What else is it capable of?

He turned to the others. "I will be back shortly. Ikely, please remain here so that no one else is unduly alarmed by the presence of our new allies. Eli, with me."

Stiger then followed the legionary across the camp to the fortified line, on which several sentries patrolled. He found Brent near the road directly to the center of the fortification, where the gate was located, allowing access to the road away from Vrell. The reserve file had been called out. Several members held torches, which guttered under a cold breeze. They were standing guard around three figures.

"We have visitors," Brent announced, striding over to them. "One of them is that dwarf Garrack." The lieutenant recognized Eli and broke out into a large smile. "Eli! You are alive!"

"It would seem so," Eli grinned back. Stiger suspected his friend was enjoying the experience of miraculously returning from the dead.

"What about them?" Stiger asked with a nod, drawing Brent's attention back to the group.

"Ah, yes, sir," Brent said, grinning momentarily at Eli before becoming serious again. "The other two are human, wearing old style legionary officers' kit. They asked to speak to the Legate, sir. Ah, specifically you, sir...well..." Brent's words trailed off.

"Well what?" Stiger asked. He had already had far too many surprises for one evening and was in no mood for any more.

"One of them is speaking the old tongue, sir," Brent said.

Stiger looked at the lieutenant. For the masses, the old tongue was rarely spoken, as it had mostly died out in favor of common. Only the nobles, clinging to tradition, still bothered with the old tongue. The language was primarily spoken while the senate was in session and exclusively at court. Beyond that, it was rarely, if ever, used or taught to anyone of lower birth.

"Sir, he is speaking Lingua Romano," Brent said, keeping his voice down. They were several feet away.

"The Roman tongue?" Stiger asked in surprise. There were several variations of the old tongue, Lingua Romano being the oldest and most pure. It dated back to a time of legend, before even the founding of the empire.

"He claims he is Titus Pontius Sabinus, Primus Pilus, First Cohort of the 13th Legion! The other says he is Severus

279

Ash Vargus, Centurion, Second Cohort of the 13th and Councilman of the Valley."

"What?" Stiger asked sharply. The 13th existed in name only. Not only that, the old cohort system had been abolished over two hundred years prior during Emperor Midiuses's reforms of the legions. "Are you serious?"

"They are, at any rate," Brent breathed, glancing back toward Sabinus, Vargus and Garrack, who were still surrounded by the watchful eye of the reserve file.

"Best speak with them then," the captain said after a moment. He stepped around Brent and approached. Sergeant Ranl was there too. He gave the captain a wary look as the men stepped aside for their captain.

Sabinus and Vargus both had the bearing of hard-bitten, battle-scarred veterans. Though their kit was archaic, like General Delvaris's, the two wore their outfits like a second skin. Stiger had no doubt the men before him, no matter how fantastical their claim, were somehow genuine.

Sabinus and Vargus snapped to attention and offered a crisp salute. The eyes of the two centurions ran over him. It felt like he was being evaluated and measured. Stiger met their querying expressions with a countenance of steel.

"What do you want?"

"Legate Stiger," Sabinus said stiffly and formally in the old tongue. "Centurion Titus Pontius Sabinus and Severus Ash Vargus reporting for duty."

Stiger glanced with a questioning look over at the dwarf.

"Legate," Garrack greeted gruffly in heavily accented common and handed Stiger two scrolls he had been holding. "I have a letter from your emperor, well, a previous emperor and another from your blood relation, Legate Delvaris."

Stiger looked down at the two scrolls, at a loss for words. Both were sealed, one with the Delvaris family crest and the other with the imperial seal. The scrolls had the feeling of great age to them.

"I have dun me duty and unsealed vault of the 13th as foretold by Oracle and pledged by my family," Garrack said solemnly in his broken common. "I expect 'dem scrolls should answer many of your questions."

Stiger carefully broke open the seal on the imperial scroll first and tilted it toward the torchlight. He could not see clearly enough, so he jerked his head at one of the legionaries with a torch. The man quickly stepped forward and offered his light. Stiger began to read. As he read, he eyes grew wide at the contents and his hands began to shake slightly. He glanced over at Garrack, Sabinus and Vargus briefly with a questioning look that rapidly grew to one of shock and awe as he read further.

"I apologize for our late arrival sir," Sabinus said. "We got here just as soon as we could. Unfortunately, Third Cohort is still forming, but they should be ready in a week."

"You knew of this?" Stiger, looking from Sabinus over to Garrack, handed the scroll to Eli, who began reading. The captain's voice was a near whisper. He was almost afraid to open the second scroll. The surprise at finding Eli alive and well was nothing compared to the contents of the scroll he had just read.

If it was to be believed, he had been appointed to command the 13th Legion. The scroll, signed and sealed by Emperor Atticus, stated the conditions required for such an appointment. The man destined to command the 13th had to be a serving legionary officer, and the descendent of Delvaris who freed the 13th's Eagle. Only that nameless individual could be appointed commander of the 13th. Stiger had met those conditions, which meant the late Emperor Atticus's decree made over three hundred years ago promoted him to Legate, a position which no longer existed amongst the modern legions. Surely the current emperor would countermand such an appointment, yet the scroll added that the current emperor would be aware of the pending appointment and would be bound to honor it until such a time came that the prophecy was fulfilled.

How could this be? What prophecy? Stiger asked himself in dismay, struggling to maintain a stony-faced exterior. He looked over at Garrack with a questioning look. He had so many questions but did not know where to start.

"Yes...is true...you now Legate," Garrack affirmed, a broad smile blossoming on his brutish features. He pointed a finger at Stiger and wagged it. "With small force, you fight like tiger. Just wait. Together we kill many enemies. We grow our legend. Cyphan Confederacy no more when we done."

Stiger glanced at Eli, who had finished reading the scroll. The elf, whom nothing ever appeared to surprise, looked astonished.

"Part of the 13th still serves?" Eli asked of Stiger. "With two additional cohorts maintained by the valley. How is that possible?"

Stiger shook his head and then took the scroll back. He reread it once again to be certain he had not misunderstood its contents. He looked up at Sabinus. He was not even sure what to say. He was about to break the seal on the second scroll when his attention was drawn away.

"We," Sabinus said and jerked his thumb behind him into the darkness and beyond the fortification, "await your orders, Legate."

Stiger looked and saw nothing. Then, gradually he began to hear it, at first softly and then louder. The sound grew as it neared. Stiger had heard it many times before. It was the steady tread of many sandaled feet.

"I believe the term is 'gods blessed,'" Eli said with a grin directed at Stiger. "The gods have plans for you. There is no denying it now."

As the sound of marching drew nearer, a legionary horn blared, shattering the night and then Stiger's eyes went wide at the sight of what emerged from out of the darkness.

EPILOGUE

GENERAL TREIM STEPPED out onto the grand balcony of the king's palace. The balcony provided an impressive view. He could easily see the greatest city in the North laid out before him. It had been burning for three days, ever since its fall. His eyes watered from the smoke as he moved to the marble railing and looked down. The stench of smoke and death caused him to wrinkle his nose, but he did not shy away. The view represented suffering, anguish and despair beyond measure. But it also represented victory and triumph. Victory or despair and suffering, it all depended upon your viewpoint.

The palace was perched on a large hill, affording the general an excellent view of his recent and final conquest. The looting, rape and pillaging had been stopped after the first twelve hours and still the city burned. Lines of newly-made slaves could be seen snaking their way out of the city and into a life of captivity and servitude. Most of the males would be sent to the mines, with a handful selected for gladiator school. The more educated ones would be sold as tutors, accountants and into other such skilled professions. The women would end up in service-oriented work or the pleasure houses. Children would be separated from their parents and taught a trade. All would spend the remainder of their lives toiling in one manner or another for the glory and greater good of the empire.

The general's aides had estimated that they had taken nearly two hundred thousand slaves. Though he was already wealthy, his cut of the spoils would make him one of the wealthiest and most powerful men in the empire. The thought did not elate or excite him. To Treim, it was only a fact, nothing more. He had done his duty and as such, it was his due.

It had taken six legions and an allied army more than ten years of heavy fighting, but it had finally been done. The Rivan were no more. The former kingdom was now destined to become an imperial province. The land would be parceled out by the emperor to deserving nobles, who in turn would sell it to settlers, speculators and investors. A portion would also be set aside for legionary retirement colonies. In short, the fall of the Kingdom of the Rivan would enrich the empire greatly, both in plunder and land.

The general placed his hands upon his hips. He was satisfied. His time commanding armies was finally at an end. He had served the empire well and now looked forward to a long, quiet retirement. He would be able to afford to spend his time alternating between the senate and his peaceful estate on the outskirts of Mal'Zeel. He had already written to the emperor expressing his desire to retire.

General Treim expected he would enjoy looking after his lands while occasionally helping to shape future imperial policy in the senate. More than anything, he looked forward to spending the days with his wife and three children, all of whom he had not seen in more than two years. He was also looking forward to the Ovation that was now his due.

"Sir." Colonel Aetius hurried out onto the balcony. The colonel's face was covered in ash and he appeared distraught. He had been placed in charge of extinguishing the fires and had been hard at it. All available hands, save for the newly-minted slaves, had been put to the task. This was not being done to preserve the city, but to save the loot that would be taken back to the empire. It included any and all precious metals, jewels and jewelry, art, furniture, tools…anything and everything that could be sold or had a value. Only after everything was salvaged would the final destruction of the city begin. The emperor had decreed that nothing would be permitted to stand, not a building or a wall. Everything was to be razed. A sad ending to a city that had rivaled Mal'Zeel in wealth and power for more than a thousand years.

The general was surprised to see alarm on his old friend's face. Something was wrong. The colonel held out a dispatch that had already been opened.

"General Treim, this just in from command," Aetius said, handing it over. Aetius was a veteran and the general wondered with dread what could have shaken him so. He immediately began reading. After a moment, he looked up at the colonel and then continued reading. He could not believe the contents.

"Defeated?" Treim asked aghast, looking up at Aetius for confirmation.

"Hard to believe," the colonel nodded gravely. "Impossible to fathom."

Treim turned away from the colonel. The realization that his dreams of retirement were once again only dreams crashed home. Crumpling the dispatch in his fist, he held it for a moment before dropping it. The discarded missive landed among the ashes at his feet. Treim was silent for a time as he looked out across the ruined city. Julia, his wife, not to mention his children, would have to wait. So would his Ovation and triumphant return to Mal'Zeel.

He turned back to the colonel, face hardened with resolve.

"Prepare the 2nd, 3rd, 8th and 14th legions to march," General Treim ordered. It was late afternoon, too late in the day to begin a route march. The men would need a good night's rest. "We will begin moving at first light. The 31st and 32nd along with our allies, will remain to clean up and to follow when practical. Send for my senior officers. I expect their attendance in three hours' time."

"Yes, sir," the colonel said, saluted and left to carry out his orders.

Treim turned back to look out at the once grand and now ruined city, destined to become a footnote in the histories. A light snow had begun to fall and mix with the smoke. He had broken the Rivan army in the fall. To keep them from recovering over the winter, he had gone against the recommendation of his officers and advisors and conducted a rare winter offensive. The drive had been difficult and costly, but it had all paid off handsomely.

His men were looking forward to spending their back pay and bonuses. They deserved a long rest. However, due to the incompetence of General Kromen, they would be denied their just reward. In a few hours' time, nearly seventeen thousand men from four crack legions would be highly pissed off with him at having to march, in the dead of winter, without an opportunity to savor the fruits of their hard-fought victory. But there was simply no other choice. No time could be lost. The empire was in deep peril and would soon need every sword available to battle the might of the Cyphan Confederacy.

For a moment he thought on Captain Stiger, the young officer he had taken under his wing when no one else would. Stiger's father and he had served together as lieutenants and become close friends. In later years, they had faced each other on the field of battle and yet when the dust had settled, their friendship still ran deep.

To the disgust of many, when Marcus Stiger had begged a favor, Treim had granted it. The general was not sorry he had taken the young Stiger on, as Ben had rapidly become one of his finest junior officers. Having come to view Ben as his protégé, he now regretted having sent him south. It had been a mistake. It was not the first he had ever made and surely would not be his last.

Treim bent down and retrieved the dispatch amidst the ashes. He opened the crumpled paper and once again reread it. It would be a long, hard march south. He wondered if Ben Stiger had managed to survive the calamity that had befallen the southern legions. Or were his bones rotting on some distant battlefield?

Shaking his head, he turned away from the view and walked into the palace, his mind now fixed on the campaign to come.

End of Book Two

ABOUT THE AUTHOR

Marc Edelheit was born in New York State. After graduating from college with a Masters in Education as a Reading and Writing Specialist, Marc became a teacher and ultimately a middle school administrator. He is currently an executive in the healthcare industry, staying up late at night to work on his novels. Marc is also the host of a successful (free) history podcast 2CentHistory.

A NOTE FROM THE AUTHOR

I hope you enjoyed *The Tiger* and continue to read my books.

A <u>positive review</u> would be awesome and greatly appreciated, as it affords me the opportunity to focus more time and energy on my writing and helps to persuade others to read my work. I read each and every review.

Grammar suggestions and any spelling corrections are most welcome. Please contact me through email or amazon.

Don't forget to sign up to my newsletter on my website to get the latest news.

Thank you …

Marc Alan Edelheit

Coming Soon

Chronicles of an Imperial Legionary Officer

Book 3
The Tiger's Curse

Care to be notified when the next book
is released and receive updates from the
author? Join the Newsletter mailing list!

http://www.MAEnovels.com

Facebook: Marc Edelheit Author
Twitter: Marc Edelheit

Also:
Listen to the Author's Free History Podcast at

http://www.2centhistory.com/